W9-AJR-907

THE DARK FRONTIER

By Eric Ambler

Novels

The Dark Frontier
Background to Danger
Epitaph for a Spy
Cause for Alarm
A Coffin for Dimitrios
Journey into Fear
Judgement on Deltchev
The Schirmer Inheritance
State of Siege
Passage of Arms
The Light of Day (Topkapi)
A Kind of Anger
To Catch a Spy (Ed.)
Dirty Story
The Intercom Conspiracy
The Levanter
Doctor Frigo
The Siege of the Villa Lipp
The Care of Time

Essays

The Ability to Kill

Screenplays

The Way Ahead (with Peter Ustinov)
The October Man
The Passionate Friends (from the novel by H. G. Wells)
Highly Dangerous
The Magic Box (from a biography of W. Friese-Greene)
Gigolo and Gigolette (from a short story by W. Somerset Maugham)
The Card (from the novel by Arnold Bennett)
Rough Shoot (from the novel by Geoffrey Household)
The Cruel Sea (from the novel by Nicholas Monsarrat)
Lease of Life (from a story by Patrick Jenkins)
The Purple Plant (from the novel by H. E. Bates)
Yangtse Incident
A Night to Remember (from the book by Walter Lord)
The Eye of Truth
The Wreck of the Mary Deare (from the novel by Hammond Innes)
Love Hate Love

Autobiography

Here Lies

ERIC

AMBLER

THE DARK FRONTIER

THE MYSTERIOUS PRESS

New York • London
Tokyo • Sweden • Milan

The characters in this book are entirely imaginary and have no relation to any living persons.

First Published 1936

The Mysterious Press, 129 West 56th Street, New York, N.Y. 10019

Printed in the United States of America

First Printing: March 1990

10 9 8 7 6 5 4 3 2 1

Library of Congress Cataloging-in-Publication Data

Ambler, Eric, 1909–
The dark frontier / Eric Ambler.—Rev. ed., with a new introd. by the author.
p. cm.
ISBN 0-89296-413-8
I. Title.
PR6001.M48D37 1990
823′.912—dc20 89-13117
CIP

To
Betty Dyson

CONTENTS

THE DARK FRONTIER

INTRODUCTION

The aging thriller writer who makes prefatorial apologies for the shortcomings of his early work also makes a fool of himself. The fact that, although once young and inexperienced, he has learned much about his craft over the years is of no interest to new readers. They are looking for entertainment, not excuses.

They may, however, be entitled to explanations, especially of what may appear to be gross anachronisms. *The Dark Frontier* was my first published novel and I wrote it in 1935. What then, it may be asked, was I doing in those far-off days using the term "atomic bomb" so familiarly and describing the effects of an atomic explosion as if the hideous thing already existed?

I lay no claim to special prescience. Having had a scientific education and through it gained access to academic journals, I had read about the early work of Rutherford, Cockcroft and Chadwick in the field, and understood some of its implications. How superficial that understanding was will be apparent now to any high school senior. The atomic bomb that I deduced was the work of a small team directed by one exceptional man of talent with a chip on his shoulder and grudges to bear. The difficulties of producing substances like enriched uranium, and the enormous resources, economic and industrial, that would be needed to overcome them, were factors I was able to ignore because I was only dimly aware of their existence.

My estimate of the critical mass likely to bring the bomb-maker to the threshold of a fission chain reaction was more cagily vague. "A little larger than a Mills grenade" was my 1935 guess and I allowed its explosive force to shift a thousand tons of rock. In 1935 I knew, theoretically, that E probably equalled Mc^2, but could not quite accept the numerically awesome consequences of the equation. I mean, c^2 was such a huge and weird multiplier. And in some ways I was handicapped by my own experience of explosives. I knew what it felt like to throw a Mills grenade thirty yards and the way the burst clouted your ears if you threw short or were slow getting your head down. I knew because while a college student I had served in the Territorial Army, a British volunteer outfit rather like a State National Guard. Multiplying the violence of an infantry weapon out of all proportion to its size and normal destructive power seemed a dramatically acceptable device. With TNT I felt that I was on even surer ground. One evening in January 1917, when I was nearly eight and living in London not far from Greenwich, there had been an accident at a munitions plant two miles away across the river. They were processing TNT there; something went wrong and over fifty tons of the stuff blew up. Not even on the Western Front had there been such an explosion. It killed and wounded hundreds and flattened an entire factory area. The blast wave hit our street with great force and broke a lot of windows. I remembered the feel and sound of it. The idea of using a kiloton of TNT as a measure of explosive violence, even for a fictional nightmare bomb, seemed farfetched and possibly absurd. In the welter of impulses, literary, political and commercial, that drove me to start writing *The Dark Frontier*, the wish to parody was, at first, central. I intended to make fun of the old secret service adventure thriller as written by E. Phillips Oppenheim, John Buchan, Dornford Yates and their cruder imitators; and I meant to do it by placing some of their antique fantasies in the context of a contemporary reality. For plot purposes, the reality I thought I needed was one of those unexpected threats to world peace, one of those dark conspiracies of evil men, that will succeed unless our hero can brave all dangers and arrive in the nick of time to foil the wicked in their devilish moment of near triumph. The development of an atomic bomb in a small Balkan state ruled by a corrupt Fascist-style oligarchy was likely, I thought, to yield an interesting crop of villains. The real, though maybe not immediately present, danger of the atomic bomb was surely a most convincing threat to world peace. After all, it had convinced me. Quite so. But this was parody. Were there not unities to be observed? Don Quixote should not be expected to tilt at windmills defended by machine guns. I should have threatened the world with something more obviously farfetched—a secret army of robots, say, or a polar submarine base sited over a volcanic thermal spring. Or, if I were going to fool with matters that should be taken seriously, perhaps I should think again and discard the idea of parody. But I was halfway through the book by then and reluctant to admit to myself the size of the mistake I was making. Besides, I felt committed to my folly. For the young, for new writers, parody can seem like a safety precaution, a form of insurance against adverse criticism.

It brings with it other handicaps and illusions. The matter of size and scale must be understood. Max Beerbohm, perhaps the century's master parodist, was always brief. With Max's help Henry James, G. K. Chesterton and Rudyard Kipling are each brought to judgement and petrified, temporarily at least, in a few short pages. Max's four acts of "Savonarola" Brown's great poetic tragedy may be read aloud with stage directions, and to hilarious effect if well read, in less than thirty minutes. But Max was wise not to find the missing fifth act himself. The joke is over at the end of the fourth. Satire can be sustained by a single comedic idea and the wit to pursue it. Parody requires an established root system of critical insight and the constant nourishment of humour. Max could not have written *The Battle of the Books* and Jonathan Swift could not have trifled so engagingly with Joseph Conrad's heart of darkness. Parody can be the expression of literary dandyism.

Why then, it may be asked, if I were so alive to the difficulties of parody, especially those of sustaining it at length, did I take the risk? It is a fair question, so I will skip the nonsense about youth being a time for risk-taking, rule-breaking and experiment. Instead, I will try to give what I believe to be the answer.

When the English novelist Mary Webb died in 1927 not much notice was taken of the event. Her five or six novels, though of the earthy primitive, regional romantic school then in vogue, had not been popular. The circulating library public, while not averse to purple prose, tended to prefer the less fervid tone of others working in the genre, of healthier ladies like Sheila Kaye-Smith. The *Oxford Companion*'s summing up of Webb as "passionate, involved and frequently naive" still holds good. Perhaps she had been too close to the rustic quiddities and bucolic squalor about which she wrote. She was a country schoolteacher who married another teacher, worked in the country as a market gardener and died wretchedly, after a long struggle with exophthalmic goitre, at the age of forty-five. A year later she was made famous and two of her novels, *Precious Bane* and *Gone to Earth*, hastily retrieved from oblivion, had become best sellers. It could have happened only in England, but even there it was remarkable. British politicians have often declared their love of literature and even quoted the Latin poets in their speeches, but few have been prepared to praise the work of a particular novelist. One sees the difficulty, of course; the kind of fiction a politician enjoys, or pretends to enjoy, will tell the voters more about the man's true disposition than may be good for his political health. Prime Minister Disraeli, himself a novelist, had a short, impudent answer for those who sought to probe his literary taste buds—"When I want to read a novel I write one." In 1928 Prime Minister Stanley Baldwin, the trusty, pipe-smoking, true blue Tory statesman who had seen England safely through the General Strike and whose safe hands were later to accept the abdication of King Edward VIII, threw caution to the winds. He praised a novelist publicly. True, she was a woman and dead; there would be no political mileage in it for anyone except her publishers; but the event was still extraordinary. The occasion Baldwin chose for the delivery of his eulogy was the annual dinner of the Royal Literary Fund, an old and honourable charity. He praised her lyrical intensity and evocation of the Shropshire landscape. The speech was widely reported in the better newspapers and the Mary Webb bandwagon began to roll. Mr. Baldwin gave it a final shove by writing an introduction for a new edition of *Precious Bane* and the other novels soon began to appear in a collected edition. As Britain sank deeper into the Great Depression, Mary Webb's purple prose, "blending human passion with the fields and skies," according to Baldwin, penetrated the circulating libraries and lingered about the shelves like the after-smell of a cheap air freshener. This was true artistry. Mr. Baldwin had said so.

At the time my literary tastes were those of any other guilt-ridden young man who had rejected all orthodox religious texts in favour of the teachings of C. G. Jung, G.I. Gurdjieff and Oswald Spengler. The novels of Dostoyevski and the plays of Ibsen were my bedside books. I wallowed in the nether worlds of George Gissing and Knut Hamsun and mooned with George Moore over the fate of *Esther Waters*. For me in those days misery and madness were the stuff of dreams, even when the dreamer was as troubled as Strindberg or as haunted as Kafka. Why, then, did I find *Precious Bane* so insufferable?

Mainly, I think, because of its pretentious breast-beating. All that blending of human passion with the fields and skies that Mr. Baldwin so admired was for me no more than an untimely and artless revival of the Victorian poets' pathetic fallacy by an author writing beyond her means. The incidence of psychoneuroses and violent crime among Shropshire yokels may have been exceptional at the time, but the attempt to render it as high tragedy was a mistake. Mrs. Webb's adolescent insights stimulated by overdoses of schoolroom Wordsworth could produce nothing more tragic than high-sounding gush. I hated it, and in doing so failed to appreciate the rich splendour of its absurdity.

INTRODUCTION

Cold Comfort Farm was published in 1932 and was an immediate success. The author, Stella Gibbons, was thirty at the time, and although she had published a book of poetry and worked as a magazine journalist, this was her first novel. As parody it was and remains unique. Who could resist her brisk way of explaining primal scene trauma as "saw something nasty in the wood shed" or the aura of dignity with which she invested Big Business, the bull, and the herd of wayward cows he served so faithfully? Their very names—Graceless, Pointless, Feckless, Aimless—brought a gust of fresh air to the milking shed. *Cold Comfort Farm* followed the narrative pattern of the genre it was to destroy by describing in rather too much detail the history of a family. Mary Webb's harelipped heroine had been Prudence Sarn. The Cold Comfort family are Seth, Elfine and Aunt Ada Doom. But the book has long ceased to depend on its elements of parody. In 1933 France took the unusual step of awarding Stella Gibbons, an Englishwoman, the important Femina Vie Heureuse Prize for literature. *Cold Comfort Farm* is a wittily conceived and beautifully written comic novel. The French were recognizing it as a work of art.

Stella Gibbons seems never to have quite recovered from this early success. None of the good novels she wrote later was nearly as good as the first, and her only sequels to it were short stories. She has always thought of herself as a poet, and more interested in the nature of God than in human beings. Well, it must be an eerie moment when one finds oneself in one's eighties and still the only novel-length parodist to be published in the twentieth century. Mine cannot have been the only prentice hand to have been tempted by the brilliance of her achievement.

A revised edition, then, presents the failed parodist with

a chance to tidy up. What came out of the defective parody was a thriller with a difference. True, it invited some suspension of disbelief, but it did not expect the reader to swallow nonsense or to tolerate really bad writing. However, one of the hidden dangers of parody is that one may find oneself actually enjoying the process of writing "in the manner of" some excruciatingly awful stylists. I recall, in particular, E. Phillips Oppenheim. The Prince of Storytellers his publishers used to call him. He made a fortune which ran to a yacht on the French Riviera. Some of his novels had such good stories to tell that for his teenage readers, of whom I was one, the rococo style seemed part of the entertainment. I was a teenage smoker too. These bad juvenile habits catch up with the sinner later in life. Thirty years or more after *The Dark Frontier* was published, a respected and, at that time, greatly feared literary critic named Clive James made my work the subject of an essay in the *London Review.* He had his reputation as a killer to sustain, of course, but I escaped with only a few bruises and one bad cut. He was laying off the booze at the time and I introduced him to V8 juice. He drank it without audible complaint and went on his way, but I may have been fooling myself. The cut was deep. In his piece he used a sentence from my first novel to demonstrate that I had improved slightly as a writer over the years. The middle-aged Ambler, he assured us with a smirk, would never think of describing a well-dressed woman as "exquisitely gowned." The young Ambler hadn't even hesitated.

I was appalled. How was I to explain that it had been the young Ambler parodying the euphuistic Oppenheim who was to blame? He was supposed to be a critic. Why hadn't he seen that the phrase "exquisitely gowned" was pure Oppenheim? It ought not to have been there, of course. The fault was mine. Back in those days young authors, and old, were expected, rightly in my opinion, to be their own editors. There were house styles in punctuation and in euphemism for the coarse or blasphemous—"beggar" for "bugger," "crikey" for "Christ" and so on—which one accepted uncomplainingly because one was told that irritating or giving offense to book-buying librarians and straight-laced readers was not the best way to sell books. In those days readers were more touchy and often wrote pedantic letters of complaint to publishing houses or, worse, to the big book wholesalers who could refuse to stock a book and distribute it. They had copy editors who read books in proof for them. That was to protect themselves against the absurd libel laws of England, as well as to report on dirty words. None of them would have bothered with "exquisitely gowned." That was left to me, and I missed it. I worked on those revisions at night. I must have nodded.

Well, the blot has gone at last. However, there are, I find, limits to what may legitimately be done by way of revision. For instance, quite early in the story our amnesiac hero finds himself in Paris and committed to a dangerous Balkan adventure. Feeling that he may be called upon to defend himself, he goes into a gunsmith's in the boulevard St. Michel and buys a Browning automatic and ammunition for it.

When I first re-read this I laughed aloud. A gunsmith in the old Boule' Miche'? I ask you. As every old Paris hand will recall, the lower end runs through the heart of the Latin Quarter and along one side of the Sorbonne. In the early thirties it was the cheap and noisy section of an arrondissement which included the Luxembourg Gardens, the boulevard Saint Germain, much of the

University of Paris and most of the attractions of what was then understood by the phrase Left Bank. The river end of the Boule' Miche', however, had big, impersonal cafés and their patrons did not include Sartre and Picasso. Their customers were mostly office workers who lived in the suburbs and students, students of all ages and levels of poverty. The goods in the stores were shoddy and those who sold them spry. There was a ready-to-wear men's tailor who exploited the fad for jackets without lapels—"*très chic, très sport, presque cad" Prix CHOC 280ff.*—and a milliner who pirated scarf designs from the Right Bank couturiers and sold reproductions printed on art silk with dyes that ran. In the narrow side streets there were dismal apartment buildings, *prix-fixe* restaurants and small hotels where, on at least one floor, bedrooms were available by the hour. It was a quarter in which one might find a place to pawn a revolver but would not expect to buy one.

In my time as a writer I have committed a few solecisms and made some silly mistakes, but I have not, on the whole, been careless. When unsure of facts and unable to verify guesses, I have gone warily. I was especially careful with what used to be called "local colour." I could not really believe that I would have placed a gunsmith in the boulevard St. Michel unless I had known for certain that there was one there. Memory had to be assisted. I thought myself back into one of those small hotels behind the Sorbonne—in the rue Victor Cousin, since we are recalling the irrelevant—where one could live so cheaply when the French franc was eighty to the pound sterling. How did one get there? One walked from the Métro station, Luxembourg. Ah, yes. That was it.

In the early thirties it became a habit with me to go as often as I could to France. I had to travel cheaply: never first class and second only when there was no third available. This was usually on international trains or on fast night services between cities. My fellow travellers on these second-class journeys were mostly French of the middle bourgeoisie of small business, travelling salesmen and the like. Unaccompanied women would most likely have sleeping car reservations. The characters I studied most attentively were the travelling salesmen. I knew something of the ways of their English counterparts, and the mere fact of one of these prosperous knights of the road denying himself the comfort of a *couchette* in a sleeping car meant to me that he was almost certainly fiddling his expense account. Of course, those were the golden days before credit card billing made false expenses less easy to claim.

Preparations for dozing the night away tended to have a ritual quality. First, there would be the stroll along the corridor to check that the sample cases were safe in the baggage racks, then a visit to the WC. Outside in the corridor again a cigarette would be smoked. Back in the compartment there would be the loosening of the collar stud, the unlacing, or unbuttoning, of ankle boots and, finally, the application of scent. This was eau de cologne or a similar lavender water, and it was sprinkled liberally on a handkerchief which was then used to wipe the face and hands. The whole compartment benefited, of course. Ventilation was poor and we were a smelly lot in those days. Middle-class townsmen might change their underwear twice a week if they were single or if they had married money, but for most once a week was customary. A daily change was for the rich or the depraved. A sprinkling of cologne was evidence of a respectable upbringing, as was the possession of a clean white handkerchief. For those allergic to lavender, the alternative defense against the smells of confined humanity was tobacco, and there were always plenty of compartments for smokers on the trains. Nights spent in them, however, invariably seemed much longer. In the small hours there would be noisy disputes about window-opening and *courants d'air*. The *non-fumeurs* were more restful.

And probably still are. The intention behind this thick slice of European social history was not to encourage non-smokers or to sell deodorants but to explain how I came to know that in France in those days a great many travelling men used to carry guns. They carried them in their overnight bags along with the bottle of cologne, the flask of rum or brandy and yesterday's newspaper. The bag was of the satchel, briefcase type—the French called it a *serviette*—and when it was open, the contents were clearly visible. Not that there was ever any attempt at concealing them. The first time I saw one of these guns was when its owner put it on the seat beside him while he rummaged in the bag for a box of toothpicks. It was a .25 single-action revolver, made in Belgium and, I found later, popular because cheap.

How cheap I never discovered. The French friends whose views I sought thought strongly about guns. The husband said that in town only jewellers needed guns. The wife said that women of a certain age should have pistols to protect their honour or to take their revenge on faithless men. I asked if it were true about *crimes passionelles* going unpunished in France. "The little guns women keep in their purses never do much harm," she said with a shrug. "If the man is unlucky the law is reasonable."

But that was in the towns. What about the country? Ah, said the man, there one needed a heavier weapon. Every peasant and all his kids had shotguns and would mistake a man for a rabbit if given half a chance. In the Dordogne and parts of Provence it was still bandit country, as bad as Corsica. Here in France those at greatest risk were the *automobilistes.* In bandit country the possession of a private car was sufficient evidence of personal wealth, and highway robbery was all too easy. All drivers with any sense went armed. When driving, he kept his gun, an excellent Czech automatic, wrapped in grease-proof paper, in the door cavity pocket on the driver's side. At other times he kept it locked in the toolbox with the spare inner tube and first aid kit. It was no trouble; border police and customs men expected drivers to be armed; the *gendarmerie* in some parts of the country counted on it.

I could not quite believe all this; I did not want to believe it. That French travelling salesmen should find it necessary to carry guns I was prepared to accept. French thieves went armed—*Paris Soir* said so—and it wasn't only jewellers who carried valuable samples. In the movies nervous householders kept revolvers in the drawers of bedside tables. Perhaps some French householders did so too. But in car-door pockets? Surely not. Door pockets were for maps and driving gauntlets and slim boxes of Balkan Sobranie cigarettes.

The girl with whom I had been sharing a bed had left me and gone off with rich Greek friends to Cannes. The following day I had to go back to London and my job in advertising. The idea of moping in a café did not appeal to me so I went in search of a puppet theatre I had heard about. It was in the Luxembourg Gardens. That was how I came to know that there was a gunsmith's in the boulevard St. Michel. It was at the upper end near the Luxembourg, away from the Latin Quarter I now loathed, and was located in the ground-floor arcade of an office block. The display window was *très sport*—shotguns in blued steel and walnut, decoy birds and suede ammunition waistcoats—but in the showcases at the back of the store there were plenty of handguns.

I had decided to put the whole subject out of my mind; but on the cross-Channel steamer from Dieppe to Newhaven I got talking to a Frenchman in the bar. He was going to London for the first time and asked the barman how to get from Victoria to Belsize Park. The barman, a Brighton man, did not know for sure. I did. The Frenchman was going to work in an Oxford Street language school for six months to see if he liked the work. My guess was that he would not, but instead of saying so I asked if he drove a car. He did; at home he drove his father's. When he drove did he carry a revolver?

The gun, he explained somewhat sheepishly, was his father's. Old-fashioned men, men of a certain age, liked to carry a gun when they were driving.

This was Freudian country. I preferred to read Jung. Again I put the subject out of my mind, until, a couple of years later, I needed an approximate location for a gunsmith in Paris. I see no reason to revise it. Nowadays, I read neither Freud nor Jung.

I rest my case. However, for the ill-natured who like to poke at old scar tissue to see if wounds have really healed, the sentence, "She was exquisitely gowned," was part of a descriptive paragraph placed just before the electric power failure in the Zovgorod Opera House—the very page before.

Eric Ambler,
London 1989

STATEMENT OF PROFESSOR H.J. BARSTOW, F.R.S., Physicist, of Imperial College, University of London

The events in this book comprise, I am told, an account of my life during the period April 17th to May 26th of last year.

This I am unable either to confirm or to deny. I have been shown a photograph, taken by a press photographer and forwarded by the British Consul in Ixania,* in which a person resembling myself can be seen alighting from a large car at the steps of the Chamber of Deputies in Zovgorod.* Unfortunately, a portion of the face is obscured by the body of a soldier who had moved forward across the lens of the camera. In any case, my features are cast in a mould too commonplace for me to accept the photograph as proof of my presence in that picturesque city. The fact that there are machine-guns and barbed wire visible in the background of the picture seems to me to

*These names are, of course, fictitious. The reader will appreciate the reason for this irritating discretion when he knows the facts. In any case, it is possible that inclusion of the names might be regarded as a contravention of the Official Secrets Acts (1911 and 1921).

render it even more unlikely. I am nervous of firearms and detest the noise they make.

More considerable evidence of the probability of this amazing story is contained in the narrative of Mr. William L. Casey, of the New York *Tribune*, who was in Zovgorod during the period in question. Mr. Casey's account of the affair has, I feel, a ring of truth about it; but I would warn the reader, as I warned myself, that journalists are inclined to let imagination run to self-deception. Mr. Casey will, I am sure, forgive my scepticism. If what he writes is true then he has suffered worse things at my hands. Besides, he can always turn on me and say: "Well, what *did* you do during those five weeks?" I shall not be able to tell him. He will refer me to the waiter, George Rispoli, to the Hotel Royal in Paris and to the rest of the evidence so carefully woven into a logical pattern by my other biographer, and I shall admit once again in words that, in my own heart, I have never doubted: that this story is true.

Here, however, are the few indisputable facts.

Forty years of age and a bachelor, I am, by profession, a physicist and, during the four months preceding April 17th, my services had been retained by a British government defence research department to make a feasability study of a set of proposals for a new weapon system employing an ultra-high explosive. The matter was highly secret and my task of the utmost urgency. I worked day and night for many weeks. The strain soon began to affect my health. On April 10th I called in to see my medical adviser, Dr. Rowe.

His report was not encouraging. I received what practically amounted to an ultimatum. I must either take an immediate and long holiday or else the consequences—a breakdown.

STATEMENT OF PROFESSOR H.J. BARSTOW

I compromised by finishing my work and setting out a day or two later alone in my car for Truro in Cornwall, with the idea of spending a week or two there and then, perhaps, crossing the Channel to Brittany. I left London at 6.30 A.M. on April 17th. I had no adieux to make. A note to my mother who lives in Kensington, a postcard to my sister in Norwich and an instruction to my housekeeper about forwarding letters had completed my domestic arrangements. I had fifty pounds in cash and a small suitcase. By 1.30 P.M. that day I was in Launceston, and stopped there for luncheon at the Royal Crown Hotel.

At this point my memory becomes disjointed. I remember entering the hotel; I do not remember leaving it. I remember raising a glass of sherry to my lips; but I have no recollection of the meal that followed it. Of the sinister Mr. Groom, I know nothing. I remember vaguely feeling unwell and going into the hotel lounge to rest. There, I know, I looked at a book on the jacket of which was an illustration of a man holding a pistol. I think I was waiting for the rain to stop. I must have grown impatient for I recollect next that I switched off the windscreen wiper as I started to climb the road across the moor. I clearly remember running along it for about five miles; then I think I felt sleepy. The next memory that remains in my consciousness is finding myself in the Bâle-Paris express between Mulheim and Belfort, with the *chef-de-train* forcing cognac between my teeth. That was on the 26th of May, over five weeks later. Of what passed during the interim, I have no personal knowledge. My possessions on the 26th of May consisted of the clothes I stood up in, my wallet and my passport. My mind is hazy on the point, but I feel sure that a woman's photograph (which I did not recognise) was in my wallet when I examined it on the train. I subsequently failed to find either the photograph or my passport.*

Much has happened since that 26th of May. For some months afterwards I was seriously ill. It was towards the end of my convalescence at Brighton that they first brought me this story to read. It affected me in a remarkable way. To read one's own biography must always be a peculiar experience. Yet, in my case, self-appreciation was supplanted by a curious feeling of sympathy for this strange debonair Henry Barstow with his enthusiasms, his vanity, his sentimentality, his melodramatic daring. The trees outside my bedroom window were leafless, the nights were long and my mind dwelt in the twilight land of convalescence. At that time he and his incredible story permeated my thoughts. I used to spend the nights thinking of him and of his Countess. But with the return of health these dreams have faded. Perhaps he still wanders, lonely like a ghost, along the back streets of my mind. Who knows? For me he has become a shadow, featureless—like a man behind a light.

Henry Barstow

January, 193–.

*I was subsequently informed that they had been "lost." The British Embassy in Paris issued the necessary papers for my return to England.

PART ONE

THE MAN WHO CHANGED HIS MIND

1

APRIL 17th

By half-past twelve, Professor Barstow was feeling tired. He had already driven one hundred and eighty miles that day. It was with a sigh of relief that, some three-quarters of an hour later, he turned his car into the courtyard of the Royal Crown Hotel at Launceston.

He alighted, stretched himself and, with methodical care, locked the doors. Then he checked each one.

Professor Barstow did everything methodically, whether it was applying the laws of electrodynamics to a case of electronic aberration or combing his Blue Persian cat. His very appearance spelt order. His lean, sallow face, his firm lips pursed judicially and his neat dark grey suit expressed with quiet eloquence the precision of his habits. His lectures before the Royal Society were noted and respected for their dispassionate reviews of fact and their cautious admissions of theory. "Barstow," an eminent biologist once declared, "would be a genius if he wasn't so afraid of his own thoughts." Which remark, following closely, as it did, upon the publication of Barstow's critical study of the Lorentz transformations, was, to say the least of it, surprising. The truth of the matter is, perhaps, that he distrusted his imagination because it told him things he did not wish to believe.

At that moment, he was distrusting it with more than ordinary force for it was telling him something he did not want to believe; namely, that he was a sick man who should be dozing peacefully on the verandah of a spa hotel, not careering up and down precipitous hills at the wheel of his car.

He dismissed this notion firmly, went into the hotel and ordered a well-done steak. While it was being grilled he sipped at a glass of sherry.

It was, he reflected, a long time since he had had a holiday. And then, for no apparent reason, he suddenly found himself thinking of long-forgotten Cambridge days and of another spring when he had almost decided to abandon his brilliant promise as a physicist and try for "the diplomatic."

Queer, now he came to think of it. He'd been feeling very much the same then as he did now. That was the year he'd read so hard for the math tripos. Fifteen hours a day he'd been putting in; far too much for a youngster. No wonder he'd nearly cracked up; no wonder the diplomatic had looked so attractive all of a sudden. But then he'd always had a fancy for it. His day-dreaming had always been of statesmanship behind the scenes with himself as the presiding genius, of secret treaties and *rapprochements*, of curtain intrigue conducted to the strains of Mozart, Gluck and Strauss, with Talleyrand and Metternich hovering in the background. Queer, too, how dreams of that sort stayed with you. One half of your brain became an inspired reasoning machine, while the other wandered over dark frontiers into strange countries where adventure, romance and sudden death lay in wait for the traveller.

Not that there would have been much adventure or sudden death in a diplomatic career—he knew that well enough now—while it had been romance, disguised as the middle-aged wife of his father's junior partner, that had sent him back to work nursing an undeclared and hopeless passion. It had endured, he remembered now, for less than a week. He sighed.

He was still considering the pallor of his youthful follies when he took his seat in the dining-room. He ate his steak slowly. The room was empty with the exception of himself and a plump white-haired man whom he did not notice particularly until, glancing up from his plate, he was surprised to find himself the object of a fixed stare.

"A lovely day, sir," remarked the white-haired man as their eyes met.

"Yes," said Professor Barstow, and then, not wishing to appear brusque, "Yes, very."

He always felt a little ill at ease when addressed by strangers and made no attempt to continue the conversation. But the white-haired man was persistent.

"Are you staying in Launceston, sir?"

Professor Barstow shook his head.

"I'm going on to Truro," he said. "You are staying in the hotel?" he countered politely.

The white-haired man nodded absently. Then, with a sudden air of decision, he moved his chair nearer to Professor Barstow's table and leant forward earnestly.

"Six months ago I was in China. Before that I was in South America. Before that, I was in Turkey. For six years I've been out of England. For six years I've been looking forward to the time when I could come home and settle down. Now I *am* home, and what do I find?"

Professor Barstow, his interest only faintly aroused, shook his head gravely. He had decided that the man must be a travelling salesman of some sort. They were notoriously talkative.

The white-haired man sipped at his coffee dramatically.

"Nothing," he said, "absolutely nothing! I've been home a month now. For the first three days the sight of green fields and clipped hedges excited me. Now it bores me. All I find is a particularly venomous species of Egyptian mosquito and a landscape of petrol pumps."

"Surely you exaggerate a little?"

"Perhaps I do," answered the other gloomily, "but when you have been nourishing your soul on expectation, reality is apt to be disappointing."

Dismayed by the emotional trend of the conversation, the Professor hastened to divert it.

"You have retired?"

The white-haired man looked at him for a moment before replying. The Professor was an unimpressionable man, but it occurred to him that his first estimate of his companion was certainly wrong. His plump geniality had deserted him. A pair of cold, calculating eyes stared unblinkingly from below the bushy white eyebrows. Their owner ignored the question.

"Tell me, sir," he said thoughtfully. "I feel sure that I have seen your face before somewhere."

The Professor felt rather than saw the cold eyes fixed upon him as he answered.

"About a year ago," he said, "I became, for the space of two days, what the newspapers are pleased to call 'news.'

My photograph was blazoned about the press in the most embarrassing fashion."

The white-haired man recovered his lost geniality like magic.

"I knew it! I knew it!" He slapped his knee triumphantly. "I never forget a face, but the name sometimes eludes me. Just a minute, just a minute, don't tell me," he went on as the Professor opened his mouth to speak, "the name, let me see . . . the name is . . . Barstow . . . Professor Barstow."

"You have an amazingly good memory, sir."

"Cultivated, Professor, cultivated," chuckled the white-haired man. He regarded the Professor with renewed interest.

"If I remember rightly," he said, "you caused quite a commotion by announcing that atomic energy would shortly be harnessed for the uses and abuses of mankind, or words to that effect."

"I did nothing of the kind," protested the Professor irritably. "The statement I made before the British Association has been grossly misrepresented. All I said was that important developments in the hitherto unexplored field of applied atomic energy might prove to be mixed blessings; a mild speculation on my part upon which the most sensational constructions have been placed."

His companion, who had drawn his chair right up to the Professor's table, was following him with close attention.

"An amazing coincidence, amazing," he murmured with apparent irrelevance; then, "Professor, I should be honoured if you would take a liqueur with me."

The Professor accepted without hesitation. His experience with the newspapers still rankled and he was glad of this opportunity to explain himself to such a sympathetic audience.

For a time their conversation became general. The white-haired man's name, the Professor discovered, was Simon Groom. He talked fluently and incessantly. His knowledge of foreign affairs was remarkable. The Professor, an assiduous reader of the *Times* foreign page, heard for the first time of a major crisis just past. The facts were stated with an easy familiarity that left no room for doubt. He found himself speculating on the nature of Simon Groom's mysterious profession. The problem was soon to be solved. Groom steered the conversation once more to the subject of the Professor's work.

"You know, Professor," he began, cutting the end of his cigar carefully, "you know, I can't help thinking that when you made that reference in your lecture to the fact that atomic energy in harness might prove a mixed blessing, the sensational aspect of the point was not entirely absent from your mind."

He leant back and regarded the Professor quizzically.

The Professor was silent. The first thought that came to his mind was that this Groom was yet another of those confounded reporters trying to trap him into an admission. For the hundredth time he cursed the impulse of a year ago which had led him from the firm paths of facts to the slippery slopes of prediction.

"Mr. Groom," he said stiffly, "I am not prepared to add anything to my original remarks. The whole thing is regrettable and most distasteful to me."

His companion was unabashed. He smiled and withdrew his cigar from his mouth.

"Professor, I apologise. I should have stated the reason

for my question. Chance has brought me into contact with the one man whose help I need. Let me explain."

Without waiting for the Professor to speak, he continued:

"Have you ever heard of the firm of Cator & Bliss? I see that you have. Cator & Bliss, Professor, is, as you probably know, one of the largest armament manufacturing organisations in the world. We and our subsidiaries supply quite a large proportion of the world's armaments. The French Schneider Creusot Company, our own Vickers-Armstrong group, Skoda, the Bethlehem Steel Corporation, the Du Pont Company and a number of small concerns supply the remainder."

He paused for a moment.

"Professor," he went on, "I should be grateful for your assurance that what I am about to tell you will be treated in the strictest confidence."

It is doubtful whether anything could have induced the Professor at that moment to withhold the pledge required of him. He nodded gravely.

"You may rely upon me."

Simon Groom drew at his cigar slowly before continuing.

"It is a curious commentary on human ideals and aspirations," he said, "that never does man's knowledge advance so rapidly as when he is creating a weapon of destruction. In England our subconscious realisation of this fact expresses itself in a mistrust of 'new-fangled' things. The French are more definite. They say '*Le mieux est l'ennemi du bon.*' There are hosts of cases in point. The aeroplane, for instance: greater strides were made in its development during 1915 than during the whole of the previous ten years. The knowledge gained by commercial chemists in the search for more destructive explosives and more virulent poison gases doubled the size of the chemistry books. Why, even the science of healing advanced considerably. That is, of course, as soon as the conservation of manpower became necessary rather than merely desirable," he added with a faint smile.

The Professor raised his eyebrows.

"The point I am trying to make, Professor," Groom went on, "is this. War, with its demands on mankind for offensive and defensive instruments, rocks the cradle of most constructive endeavours today. The warships of yesterday produced the liners of today. The ferro-concrete fortifications of the battle area produced that wonderful new building they are putting up in North London. Bearing those facts in mind, Professor, what, I ask you, is the logical field for the development of a new and incalculable force such as that of applied atomic energy?"

"The ideals of science are constructive, not destructive," answered the Professor stiffly. "Science in the past has been shamefully exploited. But it has learnt to protect itself."

Simon Groom shook his head.

"No, Professor, you are wrong. While scientists are men, science cannot protect itself. The desire for supremacy which is in the hearts of all men prevents it. Even as I talk to you now, events are proving you wrong. The first atomic bomb has been made!"

Of the multitude of sensations which chased through the Professor's mind on hearing this, the first was one of frightened suspicion. Was he sitting there talking to a madman? It seemed the only possible explanation. But, meeting the cold, level gaze of the man facing him, he began to think. Then suspicion faded and fear gripped him. Supposing it were true? Finally, he laughed.

"You have a somewhat grim sense of humour, sir."

"I thought you would laugh," said the other calmly; "but suspend your judgment for a moment, Professor, and let me put a question to you. Of all the laboratories in the world, from which would such a development be most likely to come? I speak, of course, in terms of facilities, not in terms of morals."

The Professor considered for a moment.

"Well," he said finally, "the developments which I had in mind last year, when I spoke then, could come ultimately from one or two sources. It is difficult to assign definite superiority to any one institution. There are to my knowledge laboratories possessing advanced equipment capable of carrying out experiments along those lines in London, Chicago, Schenectady, Paris and Berlin. You may take your choice."

Simon Groom looked perplexed.

"Alas, Professor, I was hoping that you would be able to help me. This thing was done in none of those places. Have you ever heard of Zovgorod? No? Zovgorod is the capital of Ixania, and it was in that city that the work of which I am speaking has been carried out."

The Professor chuckled.

"Mr. Groom," he said, "you are an excellent actor, but your imagination betrays you. Why, the cost of even the pilot plants to do such work would be more than Ixania's entire budget."

A look of annoyance appeared for a moment on Simon Groom's face.

"I am not joking, Professor," he replied firmly; "to you my story may sound melodramatic and rather absurd. It *is* melodramatic—reality is often disconcertingly so—but it is not absurd. These are the facts."

He paused impressively and glanced at his cigar.

"Ixania," he said, "is a state with national aspirations. You may question the right of so insignificant a strip of unproductive country to attempt to give rein to such ambitions. It depends upon your philosophy. A disciple of Rousseau would say 'yes' with all the fervour of his sentimental creed. For myself, I incline more towards the Nietzschean view. Be that as it may, Ixania has for years looked towards the heights with all the gnawing envy of the weak for the strong. Now, as if in answer to her prayers, she has produced a man of genius. Her peasants are wretched, her bourgeoisie is corrupt and her government is ineffectual; yet by a freak of biology or destiny, or both, this thing has happened."

Simon Groom looked thoughtful for a moment. His cigar seemed to fascinate him. The Professor's air of disbelief had departed. He leant forward.

"Who is he?"

Groom puffed smoke from his mouth.

"Little is known about him," he said; "his antecedents are obscure, probably with reason. He was educated at Zürich and at Bonn University, no one quite seems to know how. At Bonn he was brilliant. The subject he chose for his thesis involved a question which had perplexed his own professor of physics. He propounded a theory which was subsequently proved sound and then, very impertinently, demanded the chair of physics on the strength of it. From Bonn he went to Chicago and worked under Professor Thomson for about six years. About three years ago he left Chicago—there was, I believe, some sort of scandal—and returned to Zovgorod. His name is Kassen."

The Professor uttered an exclamation.

"Kassen," he repeated eagerly. "I've heard of him."

"I thought you might have done so," Groom assented. "He made quite an impression at the McTurk Institute."

"But what has Kassen to do with atomic bombs? I read a paper of his once in the *Proceedings of the Physical Research Society*. It was, I remember, a most restrained and unsensational piece of work."

"Quite so, but, as I have pointed out, your scientist is also a man. Kassen has been twice humiliated, at Bonn and at Chicago; and, rightly or wrongly, he nurses a grudge against the world. Knowing the sullen temperament of the average Ixanian, I am not surprised. At any rate, grudge or no grudge, the bomb has been made. The trials were carried out over three weeks ago. A representative of Cator & Bliss was present, needless to say in an—er—unofficial capacity. The trials were made in the mountains about a hundred miles north of Zovgorod. The occasion was reported in Bucharest, some hundreds of miles away, as a minor seismic disturbance. Actually, a small Kassen bomb just a little larger, I am told, than a Mills grenade, shifted over one thousand tons of rock."

"But that is horrible," gasped the Professor, and then, as reason overcame his unconscious acceptance of the statement, "—and incredible."

"Horrible, certainly," agreed Groom, "but incredible, no. You are no doubt aware that ordinary high explosive depends for its action on a sudden and enormous expansion in volume. Trinitrotoluol, for instance, when detonated with fulminate of mercury, expands by something like 500,000 volumes in a fraction of a second. The Kassen bomb, so far as I can gather, is an extension of the principle. Under the influence of the bomb, ordinary silicon rock or earth in its vicinity undergoes an atomic change on detonation, producing huge volumes of some inactive gas such as nitrogen, argon or helium. In other words you are using the earth as your high explosive. The Kassen bomb is merely a special kind of detonator."

The Professor was silent. He gazed out of the window on to the garden in front of the hotel. Some daffodils were waving their heads gently to the breeze. There was a green and peaceful air about that spring afternoon. The Professor had a momentary feeling that he had just woken from a nightmare and that the fading horror of it still clung to him. As he forced himself to meet Groom's eyes again, he found that he was trembling.

"Why do you tell me this?"

The other leant forward.

"About a fortnight ago, a representative of the Ixanian Government arrived in England stating that he wished to purchase plant for the manufacture of confectionery. One of the firms he approached happens to be controlled by Cator & Bliss, and as the inquiry called for machinery of a non-standard type it was passed to head office. There is nothing unusual in that. What is unusual is that the specifications laid down are either the work of a man completely ignorant of confectionery manufacture or of a man who wants to adapt confectionery plant to another use. Certain persons took an interest in the matter, and orders have been given to secure the contract at any price. This will enable us to delay, at any rate for the time being, any attempt to manufacture Kassen bombs on a large scale."

The Professor fidgeted.

"Mr. Groom, I cannot help feeling that these confidences are a trifle—well—indiscreet. I am, after all, a perfect stranger to you and . . ."

Groom raised his hand.

"Professor," he said, "I have learnt to put my trust in two things only—the Fates and my own intuition. They tell me that this is an important opportunity. I accept their advice gladly. It is absolutely essential that we gain possession of complete information relating to the manufacture of the Kassen bomb. My object in revealing these facts to you is not as indiscreet as you imagine. I wish to put a proposition before you. But first I should, perhaps, explain my position a little more clearly. I am the foreign representative of Cator & Bliss and a director of the company. Any proposals I may put before you can be confirmed in writing within two hours if necessary. My colleagues on the Board have complete faith in my judgment in these matters. We understand one another?"

The Professor nodded slowly.

Groom became very businesslike.

"Briefly, my proposition is this. I am, at the moment, awaiting news; news of the departure of the Ixanian representative for Zovgorod. He is expected to leave almost immediately. I shall follow. My agents in Ixania will keep track of him and find out the precise source of his instructions. My knowledge of Ixanian officialdom tells me that it will not then be difficult to get the information we require. Now, Professor, it is almost certain that attempts will be made to palm off worthless information on me. I need a technical adviser. The technical resources of Cator & Bliss are, of course, unrivalled in their sphere, but this is work of a more specialised nature. There is only one man in the world who knows more about the possibilities of applied atomic energy than you, and his name is Kassen. That balance can be redressed. Professor Barstow, I want you to come with me to Zovgorod. I offer you the post of technical adviser to Cator & Bliss."

2

APRIL 17th AND 18th

It was some moments before Professor Barstow could grasp the other's meaning.

"I see," he said at last.

"Naturally," continued Groom smoothly, "your position in relation to Cator & Bliss would remain confidential. With regard to the financial aspect of the matter, I think I may safely say that you can, within reason, name your own figure. The only stipulation we should feel compelled to make is that the results of work shall remain the sole property of Cator & Bliss."

The Professor took a firm grip of himself.

"And if I should refuse your offer?"

"In that unlikely contingency, you will, of course, remember your word that what I have told you should be treated as strictly confidential. I would suggest to you also that, as a responsible citizen, you would hesitate to precipitate an international crisis that would certainly result in war—that is, always supposing that you could persuade anyone to accept the rather fantastic truth.

"However," he continued, "I hope there'll be no question of your refusing, Professor. There is too much at stake.

Imagine the consequences to Europe if this third-rate state were permitted through a freak of chance to secure absolute power. Power is for the powerful. Let power fall into the hands of the weak and the rest is tyranny. Here, Professor, is a chance to serve not only science but civilisation too. You will find the rewards not unworthy of your efforts."

The Professor stood up with an air of decision. He spoke very distinctly.

"Mr. Groom," he said, "earlier on in our conversation I said that science can no longer be exploited. I meant that. You ask for my co-operation in an undertaking which, you say, will serve both science and civilisation. Allow me to correct you. It is an undertaking that will serve only one section of the people—the shareholders of Messrs. Cator & Bliss. If what you tell me is true, if this man Kassen has so far lost his reason as to direct his abilities in the path of destructive effort rather than creative, it is an affair with which mankind as a whole should deal. My answer to your proposition is 'no.'"

Groom laughed.

"Am I to assume, Professor," he asked, "that you propose to inform the League of Nations of our conversation?"

"As you were good enough to remind me a moment ago," replied the Professor, "I gave you my word that I would respect your confidence; though, to be sure, few would believe me if I did not keep my word. Besides, candidly, I am hoping that this is all a very unpleasant dream and that I shall soon wake up."

Groom sighed.

"Ah, Professor," he murmured, "if only we could all mingle facts and fancies so successfully. Personally I believe questions of ethics are never anything but questions of points of view. I am still hoping that you will come round to my point of view in this matter."

For once, Professor Barstow let himself go.

"Not a chance in Hell, Mr. Groom," he said firmly.

Groom rose to his feet slowly. His lips had stretched into a thin smile, but his eyes, boring mercilessly into the Professor's weary brain, had narrowed to pinpoints of cold fury. His voice seemed to be coming from a great distance.

"All the same, Professor, I shall not accept your refusal. For the next few days I expect to be at the Ritz Hotel in Paris. I am travelling by air today. Should you change your mind . . ."

But the Professor heard no more. As he stood there, a terrible numbness enveloped his brain, a numbness that shut out everything but the thudding of his heart. With an effort he pulled himself together; but when at last he raised his eyes, Groom had gone.

He sank into his chair, reached for his coffee, found it cold and, resting his head on his hand, gazed out of the window.

The sky had become overcast and there was a fine drizzle of rain falling. Amid the confusion of his thoughts there rose an intense desire to postpone his departure for Truro. Again there swept over him the feeling that he was waking from a nightmare. The blood hammered in his head as he arose and left the dining-room. "*Should you change your mind* . . ." Groom's parting words fitted themselves to the rhythm of his beating heart. The Professor shook himself. He was losing control. Hardly knowing what he was doing, he blundered across the hall to the deserted lounge.

A large wood fire crackled in the hearth and he settled

himself in a comfortable armchair adjacent to it. He was comfortable, he was warm, he had just had a good lunch, he was tired. The circumstances beckoned sleep. But to the Professor's overwrought mind sleep was slow to come. A horrible scene haunted his mind with recurring persistence.

He was lying on a hillside. Below him there was a flower-strewn valley. Children were playing there. He could hear their voices, thin and shrill, on the wind. Then he noticed that the children were not alone. Near them, concealed by a fold in the ground, were men, men in uniform. They seemed to be talking earnestly together over something too small for him to see. The next moment they scattered and ran. They seemed to be swarming all over the hillside. Then they stopped and turned to watch the field of flowers and the children playing. Everything was quiet except for the sound of the children's voices on the breeze. Suddenly, there was a quick rumble beneath his feet. Before his eyes the field rocked. With a tearing, splitting roar a huge crack appeared in it, widening to emit a fountain of blackened earth which rose and hung in the air like a curtain. Then the curtain fell, slowly, as if it were wind borne, to unveil the scene behind it. With a cry of horror the Professor awoke.

A log had fallen from the grate on to the hearth and was flickering fitfully where it lay. For a moment he remained staring at it, the memory of that last dreadful picture still imprinted upon his mind.

As he replaced the log on the grate, he endeavoured to collect his thoughts. What, he asked himself, could he be thinking of? He, an intelligent and respected man of science, to allow himself to be carried away by the wretched delusions of a hotel crank? It was absurd! Yet, try as he would, he could not quite picture Simon Groom as a harmless eccentric. That cold, level, calculating gaze, that calm, assured, authoritative manner; they, at any rate, were not the usual trappings of dottiness. He tried to dismiss the whole business from his mind.

"But supposing it were true?"

The question gnawed away in spite of his efforts. Just supposing! As Groom had pointed out, no one would believe his story and even if he could get someone to take his word, the consequences might prove disastrous. Perhaps, after all, it was better that Cator & Bliss and Company should handle the matter in their own way and for the edification of their own shareholders. At any rate, such power was better in their hands than in the hands of the Government of Ixania. Cator & Bliss would at least distribute their newly won power—to those who could pay for it. The Government of Ixania, on the other hand, would almost certainly use it to impose their territorial ambitions on their unfortunate neighbours.

"The Balance of Power," murmured the Professor to himself, "must be preserved."

But hadn't people been saying that for hundreds of years? Hadn't Cardinal Wolsey prescribed it as the foreign policy of Henry the Eighth? Hadn't every European statesman since that time striven for it? Weren't they still striving for it with their pacts and treaties and alliances? And yet there had been wars; and it looked too as if there always would be wars. What else could you expect while war was still regarded as a feasible means of settling international disputes? What else could you expect while peoples wanting peace still believed that "national safety" lay in preparedness for war? What else could you expect from a balance of power adjusted in terms of land, of arms, of man-power and of materials; in terms, in other words, of money? The actual outbreaks of wars might be heralded by exchanges of ultimatums, expressions of hatred and defensive mobilisations, but the real wars were made by those who had the power to upset the balance, to tamper with international money and money's worth; those who, in satisfying their private ends, created the economic and social conditions that bred war. The largest item in national budgets today was for past and future wars. It seemed almost as if war were the greatest and most important activity of government.

What was the solution? Obviously, the system was at fault; the money structure that made such tampering possible. That would have to be altered certainly; but meanwhile, while the peoples of the world were learning how to do so, the old structure might collapse and crush them. This invention of Kassen's, for instance: science did not wait for the social conditions that would make it an unmixed blessing. In a different, better world order, the invention would have had a constructive purpose—the provision of power. As it was, the genius of Kassen, perverted and contaminated by the archaic savagery of unbridled nationalism, had produced an infernal machine. That such a situation had been inevitable no one realised better than the Professor. Science had taken the ordinary man unawares. Too late now to talk of new world orders. His destruction was imminent. He still drove his Ford, or his Citroën, or his Opel, or his Morris-Cowley; his wife still washed his children and darned his socks; but in a laboratory in a tiny Eastern European state, in the board-room of Messrs. Cator & Bliss, and in this very hotel, other men were busy knocking the props away.

How could they be stopped? And, even supposing they

could be stopped, who was to do the stopping? Even supposing that the ordinary man could be warned of his danger and organised for action, how would he proceed? The very existence of his organisation would probably precipitate the Armageddon it was designed to avert. No, the only chance for the ordinary man lay in the appearance of some extraordinary man to champion him; some man with superhuman qualities and superhuman abilities capable of frustrating the combined efforts of Kassen, the Ixanian Government and Messrs. Cator & Bliss and of doing his work both unobtrusively and effectually.

Where was such a man to be found? It was in a fit of desperation that he picked up the book.

It had been left by its owner on the sofa next to the Professor's chair. It lay open, face downward, displaying the full expanse of a bright yellow jacket. One half of this was devoted to a list of the publisher's other offerings while, on the front cover, above a three-colour reproduction of a lantern-jawed man with a blue jowl and an automatic pistol, was the title, in blood-red letters.

CONWAY CARRUTHERS, DEPT. Y.

The Professor's first instinct was to put the book down again. It was someone else's property. Then a paragraph on the open page caught his eye. He began to read.

Carruthers stiffened (ran the paragraph), *then, with the agility of a panther, leaped and caught hold of the cornice with both hands. Below him he could see Krask climbing doggedly up the fire escape, an automatic gleaming in his hand. There was no time to be lost. With a sudden heave of his powerful muscles, Carruthers drew himself into the shelter of the window parapet.*

For the moment he was safe. But Krask had seen him and Carruthers heard him slip the safety catch of the Mauser. For once in his life Carruthers was in a quandary. To return to the inside of the building spelt certain destruction—Schwartz would see to that. Krask unarmed he could deal with easily; but there was the Mauser to be reckoned with, for Krask had the reputation of being a deadly shot. Then, that amazing resourcefulness which had made the name of Carruthers feared and hated by the criminals of four continents came to the rescue. Rapidly, yet calmly, Carruthers unwound from about his waist a long length of thin silken cord. It had been made for him by a Japanese fisherman whose life he had saved. Thin though it was, it could support the weight of a full-grown man and had helped him out of many a tight corner. Now, with practised ease he tied a running noose in the cord and coiled it lasso-wise in his hand. He edged his way cautiously to the lip of the cornice. Krask was now about twenty feet below, puffing and blowing, his coarse face streaming with sweat, but his automatic held ready for instant use. Carruthers made a final adjustment to his noose. An Arizona cowboy whom he had befriended had taught him all the secrets of the lasso. With a hiss the cord snaked out. Krask heard it. The next thing he knew was that the Mauser had been snatched from his hand. He paused, baffled. Then panic seized him. He turned to run. He did not get far.

"One more step," said Carruthers pleasantly but with a steely ring to his voice, "and you're a dead man!"

Professor Barstow sighed. It was years since he had read anything like that. Barstow the mathematician had no use for Barstow the romantic. Yet, in some men the romantic vision never fades. Pure reason may distort it; everyday life may leave it uncultivated; yet it remains—to trap men in their weaker moments, and sometimes trick them into strength. Reason had worn the Professor to the verge of collapse. Romance, in the highly coloured person of "Conway Carruthers," beckoned. It was, therefore, understandable that the Professor should turn to the beginning of the book and start to read in earnest.

Your true adventure and mystery story lover demands but one thing from heroes—competence. Be he detective or be he master criminal he must be a paragon. If he is at a loss it must be only momentarily; his vast armoury of experience must be ready at a moment's notice to supply a weapon equal to any desperate occasion or a train of thought leading ultimately, if circuitously, to the correct goal.

Professor Barstow was no exception among such readers.

Conway Carruthers more than satisfied his requirements.

Nothing was beyond the powers of this remarkable man. His age, judging by his relations with other characters in the book, might have been in the neighbourhood of forty. Against this estimate, however, must be set the evidence of his physical prowess which would have done credit to an Olympian athlete of twenty-five. On the other hand, he had somehow found time during his adult lifetime to save the lives of, or otherwise befriend, natives of a remarkable number of countries. The gratitude of these fortunates contributed largely to his success. Certain death might stare him in the face and he would extricate himself from his predicament by means of a trick learnt from a Patagonian Indian or a Bessarabian moujik. The outcome of a humanitarian encounter with a Chinese juggler or a Batavian stevedore would retrieve an apparently hopeless situation from disaster. Yet this curious erudition would have been useless without his amazing insight into human character and motives. Indeed, his ability to perceive enemies was only equalled by his talent for creating them. Let him but get near enough to a man to observe that his eyes were set too close together and Carruthers could read the evil there like an open book. Under Carruthers' steely regard, moreover, apparently innocent occurrences were shown in their true and sinister colours. From the glint of the murderer's knife descending behind him (and perceived in the nick of time) to the slight scratch by the keyhole of the old escritoire, nothing escaped him. Withal he was the very soul of discretion. Kings, queens, cabinet ministers, ambassadors, eastern potentates—all poured their confidences into his ears. Behind that high, clear-cut forehead reposed state secrets of awe-inspiring portent. Yet the lips of Conway Carruthers were sealed irrevocably. Free from the fears and the vanities, the blunderings and the short-comings of ordinary men, he was of that illustrious company which numbers Sherlock Holmes, Raffles, Arsène Lupin, Bulldog Drummond and Sexton Blake among its members.

Groom and his business momentarily forgotten, the Professor followed Conway Carruthers on the trail of his prey. In London he saw an attempt on Carruthers' life foiled; in Paris he saw the *Chef de la Sûreté* welcome Carruthers as an old friend; in a suburb of Berlin he saw Carruthers fight his way out of a den of international crooks. The ever-competent Carruthers, a grim smile on his thin lips, a steely glint in his eye, pursued his quarry with the Professor at his elbow and a smiling fate to guide him for forty-three pages before reality intervened.

It is interesting, if unprofitable, to speculate on the part played in world history by the owner of the book. We can only record, however, that he chose to enter and claim it just as the Professor turned to page 44.

He was a short man in large plus-fours.

"I left a book on the sofa there," he began.

The Professor started guiltily and apologising profusely handed Conway Carruthers over.

"You're welcome, you're welcome," the other assured him. "I know what it is myself. Once I start these darn things I can't put them down for long until I've finished them. That's what I like; a rattling good yarn that takes your mind off things. My wife likes a bit of real life in her reading, but who wants to read about real life? I don't. Give me Carruthers. There's nothing real about him."

The Professor returned his farewell nod absently, but as he sat watching the rain trickling jerkily down the windows, the other's parting words still drifted through his brain. "*There's nothing real about him.*"

If only Conway Carruthers *were* real. In the resource, the competence of that fantastic character, there was something curiously satisfying. Carruthers would have dealt with Kassen and his bomb. Carruthers would have handled Groom. Above all, Carruthers would have known what he should do now. If only he were sitting in that chair, his steel-grey eyes alert and ready, his long, lean, sensitive fingers manipulating his tobacco pouch calmly and precisely. In the Professor's tired brain the phantasy became vivid to the point of reality.

"And so," murmured Carruthers, "we are to save civilisation." For an instant, the hard line of his mouth softened. Then the mask reasserted itself. "The first thing," he snapped, "is to forestall Cator & Bliss. I leave for Zovgorod tonight."

To his surprise, the Professor realised that he himself had spoken the last sentence aloud. With a start he pulled himself together. In Heaven's name what was the matter with him? The chair opposite was empty and he had been talking to himself. Feeling strangely frightened, he rose and walked to the window. He had a sudden desire to get out of the place, into the air, on to his holiday at Truro. Let Groom and Kassen and civilisation look after themselves, he was tired, tired, tired.

* * * * *

As it leaves Launceston the road rises steeply on to the moorlands which lie between there and Truro. There is not perhaps a more desolate stretch of country in England and most motorists take the main road across the moor sooner than risk a breakdown miles away from a garage. The Professor, however, preferred to avoid the beaten track and took a secondary road.

He hoped that the clean moorland wind would refresh him; but the drone of the engine and the roar of the wind served only to hasten the drowsiness that was stealing over him. His first realisation of it was a swerve that sent him perilously near the edge of the road. He had dropped off to sleep for a moment. There was a curious sensation of lightness in his head as he strove to collect his thoughts. A curious lightness and . . . something else. Normally he would have stopped the car and revived himself with a sharp walk; but now panic seized him and he put on speed. He must get on faster, faster, away from the jabbering of voices buzzing in his brain maddeningly. They rose to a frantic, clattering babel as the car accelerated. Suddenly, with a sharp *click*, they ceased and he could hear nothing but soft, scratching, scuttling noises which grew gradually, gradually nearer, getting louder and louder, almost reaching him and dying away again, leaving only the hum of the engine and the beating of his heart. Then they came again, only this time, amid the hellish maelstrom of sound that battered at his brain, he heard a voice, Groom's voice, speaking slowly as if from a great distance.

"Should you change your mind . . ."

With a sob he drove his foot down on the accelerator.

"Should you change your mind . . . should you change your mind . . . should you change your mind. . . ." The words had fastened on to the rhythm of the engine. He could not escape them, could not shake them off. *"Should you change your mind . . ."* His grip on the steering-wheel tightened until the knuckles were white. The sweat ran into his eyes. *"Should you change your mind . . ."* The repetition was maddening. Then, gradually at first, but with ever-gathering momentum, another sentence took up the rhythm.

But now it was the voice of Conway Carruthers, a stronger, more compelling voice that seemed to overwhelm the other.

"I leave for Zovgorod tonight. I leave for Zovgorod tonight. I leave for Zovgorod tonight."

With a cry, the Professor flung up his hands to his head.

The car hit the embankment at the side of the road with a grinding crash. The Professor, opening his eyes a fraction of a second later, saw the radiator rising and twisting in the air before him. Then he felt himself sinking, sinking.

* * * * *

It was dark and the moon had risen when the Professor opened his eyes.

He was lying on the side of the embankment. He sat up with an effort. He could see the outline of his car where it lay overturned by the side of the road. His head ached abominably. He put his hand to it. The hand came away black with blood in the moonlight. He rose to his feet unsteadily.

A stream ran by the foot of the embankment. He clambered down to it painfully and bathed his head. The water was ice cold and revived him a little. He crawled back to the car.

It lay almost completely upside-down and wedged between the slope of the embankment and the road. He knew that it was useless to attempt to right it. The rear end, however, was relatively undamaged and the Professor managed to retrieve his suitcase from the trunk. Then he returned to the road.

For a moment he paused undecided as to which way to go. To the left of the road the moor gleamed like silver before him. Suddenly he spoke. He seemed to be repeating a lesson learnt by heart.

"And so," he said slowly, "we are to save civilisation." He paused. When he went on, his voice was stronger. "The first thing is to forestall Cator & Bliss—I leave for Zovgorod tonight."

He buttoned up his coat collar, then, with a resolute step, he left the road and trudged off southward across the moor.

* * * * *

On the evening of the day following that on which Professor Barstow lunched at Launceston a man carrying a suitcase walked into the Imperial Hotel at Plymouth and asked for a room.

Two things about him impressed the reception clerk.

One was a dried trickle of blood on the man's temple. The other was the cold, unwavering stare of his steel-grey eyes.

"Number three-five-six, sir," said the reception clerk. "Do you mind signing the register?"

He handed him a pen.

The man took it and signed without hesitation.

The clerk gave the name no more than a passing glance.

He signalled to the hall porter.

"Send Mr. Carruthers' luggage up to three-five-six," he said.

3

APRIL 19th AND 20th

His scarf adjusted to conceal the lower half of his face, his hat pulled down well over his eyes, the man who called himself Conway Carruthers boarded the train for Paris at Havre.

There were few passengers that day and he had no difficulty in securing a compartment to himself. Concealment, he told himself, was important at that stage for it was possible that he might be recognised. Still, thanks to the faultless organisation of Department "Y," he had a convincing *alias*. As Professor Barstow, the eminent physicist, his presence would excite no suspicion, where the name of Conway Carruthers would arouse both suspicion and counter-productive fear.

He took out his passport and examined it.

Everything was in order. But for the name it might have been his own. He smiled grimly at the idea of the worthy Professor Barstow embarking on so hazardous an undertaking. It was almost as amusing as the picture of Groom confiding in Conway Carruthers of the Secret Service under the impression that he was a harmless scientist. Little did the arms-maker know what that mistake would cost him.

He rang for the waiter and ordered an *aperitif*.

He had already decided to profit by Groom's blunder by accepting the offer made to him on behalf of Cator & Bliss. The plan had many advantages. As Groom's ally, he would, for instance, have access to that gentleman's secret sources of information in Zovgorod. In any case, there was nothing to be gained by showing his hand at this stage. Up to a point, his programme coincided with Groom's. Both of them wanted Kassen's secret; both wished to prevent the manufacture of the Kassen atomic bomb in Ixania. What happened when those objectives were reached was another problem.

He wished now that he had had time to find out the name of the Ixanian representative before he left England. He had already made up his mind to ask his friend, André Durand, at the Paris *Sûreté* for information about Groom. Durand might also have been able to help him on the subject of the other.

Where a plan of campaign was concerned, Conway Carruthers always preferred the simple and positive to the ingenious and problematical. His adventures had taught him that where human motives were at work anticipation was a dangerous thing. True, the unexpected happened with almost monotonous regularity, but anticipation led to a game of "double-bluff" with chance in which the odds were all against the human player. Tortuous-minded enemies credited him with superhuman cunning. In reality, it was their own cunning that defeated them.

It would be too late when he arrived in Paris to do anything but find an hotel. In the morning he would see Durand at the *Sûreté* and afterwards, armed with information, pay his momentous visit to Groom at the Ritz. Until then, speculation was both unprofitable and dangerous. Having taken this decision he rose, finished his drink, and made his way to the restaurant car.

He chose a seat at the end of the car from which he could see the other diners and ordered a *Sole Meunière* with a light French white wine. Then he sat back and watched his fellow-passengers.

The train was now travelling fast. The heavy window curtains swung uncertainly in the shaded amber light of the tables. The jangle of cutlery and the tinkle of glass formed a background to the rhythmic thud of the wheels. The warm scent of cigar smoke hung in the air. Unreality brooded over the scene. It was theatrical. *Act One: the stage is empty when the curtain rises. There is a fire glowing in the hearth. A single lamp sheds a soft light on the scene. Heavy shadows lurk in the corners of the room. There is silence for a moment, then the voices of people approaching are heard.* Only *this* stage wasn't empty; the people were there, rows of them; but with the same remote quality in the murmur of their voices and their flickering movement.

Facing Carruthers on the opposite side of the gangway, a fat man was attempting with stolid lack of success to combat the motion of the train and transfer soup from his plate to his stomach. Beyond him, a wizened little fellow who looked like a chartered accountant was eating oysters and reading the *Times*. A man and a woman, their heads bent forward across their table, were talking rapidly in what sounded like Russian. An elderly Englishwoman was drinking tea. All different, yet with one common denominator—they were all eating and drinking. It robbed them of their individuality. In the shaded amber light, with the jangle of cutlery and the tinkle of glasses, they appeared a kindly, stupid set of people. The munching jaws of the wizened man, his earnest, preoccupied air, a large crumb of bread on his upper lip—these things gave him an almost childlike quality. Yet separate these people from this environment and there would be a different tale to tell. The fat man might prove to be an escaping murderer, the wizened one an international jewel thief, that man and woman talking in Russian, they might . . . At that moment the woman looked up. For the first time, Carruthers saw her face.

The story goes that Conway Carruthers of Department "Y" was quite impervious to ordinary human feelings. But this Conway Carruthers, the one who had walked into being out of the Cornish moorlands, leaving only an overturned car and the husk of a personality behind him, was more vulnerable. He experienced an overwhelming desire to know that particular woman.

You will find such features as hers in the paintings of the Umbrian schools; pale, delicate, oval features they are, the cheekbones gently modelled, the eyes dark and lustrous, the black hair drawn back sleekly from the high, white forehead. But it was her mouth that gave character to her face. It had a quality of inflexible resolution that seemed strangely to emphasise the intrinsic beauty of the rest.

She was dressed expensively and well in a dark-brown travelling suit which contrasted agreeably with her pale complexion. Her elbows resting on the table, her small, slender hands clasped easily together, she had an air of complete poise and self-possession as she idly surveyed her fellow-travellers.

For an instant her eyes met those of Carruthers watching her. Then she turned away and went on talking to her companion. Soon afterwards they rose and without a glance in Carruthers' direction left the restaurant car. It was with a curious sense of elation that he returned to his own compartment. Somewhere, somehow, their paths would cross again, of that he was certain.

When the train drew into the Gare du Nord an hour later he was asleep.

* * * * *

The following morning he left his hotel early to visit the *Sûreté*.[1]

It was a clear, sunny spring morning and, as he strolled along the Quai d'Orsay, Carruthers found himself wishing that his business were not quite so urgent, that he might stay awhile in Paris and enjoy the season. He arrived at the graceful building that houses the French Scotland Yard all too soon.

Entering, he approached the *agent de police* in the office by the door and asked crisply for Monsieur Durand.

"Monsieur Durand?" repeated the man, "but which one? There are here four of that name."

Carruthers was nonplussed. Four Durands? But he had never known that before; he had just asked for his friend Monsieur Durand and Durand had come, his eyes beaming with delighted recognition, his arms outstretched to greet him with an "Ah, the good Carruthers!" and a kiss for both cheeks. What had happened?

[1]Carruthers spent the night in Paris at a small hotel, the Royal, on the Left Bank. He gave his name as Barstow. He left the hotel at 10:30 in the morning, without his suitcase and intending apparently to return. He did not do so and his case was ultimately sold by the hotel management to pay his bill.

He tried again. He explained to the increasingly suspicious *agent* that it was his friend the great Durand that he sought, the Durand of a hundred daring exploits, the Durand whom France had rewarded with the red button of the Legion of Honour, the famous *Chef de la Sûreté*.

The *agent* permitted himself a smile. Only another lunatic after all! It might be amusing to humour him.

"Monsieur's name?" he asked gravely.

Carruthers told him.

The man lifted the telephone at his elbow.

"*Chef de la Sûreté*," he demanded, rolling the words round his tongue, and then, "Monsieur Convay Carruthers wishes to see you, Monsieur Durand."

Carruthers waited confidently.

The *agent* replaced the receiver and turned to him with an immense affectation of surprise.

"Monsieur Durand regrets he cannot see you," he said, shaking his head sadly.

"But—" began Carruthers.

"Monsieur cannot see you," reiterated the *agent* sharply. It was a good joke, but it had gone far enough.

Carruthers expostulated. It was absurd. His good friend Durand had always seen him. Had he been given the name correctly? It was inconceivable that he should not wish to see Conway Carruthers—Carruthers who had helped him out of so many desperate situations, Carruthers who had given him the credit for so many famous captures. It was incredible.

The man became angry. If Monsieur did not remove himself immediately, Monsieur would be removed and he himself would do the removing.

Carruthers turned away.

So it was true. Durand, his good friend Durand whom he had helped so often, would not see him.

As he walked back the way he had come he felt his knees trembling a little. A great bitterness filled his heart. Durand had betrayed him. Then he pulled himself together; his eyes held a steely glint, his mouth tightened. Very well, he would do without Durand's help. He had always played a lone hand before—he would play a lone hand again.

* * * * *

His first action was to buy an automatic and some ammunition at a gunsmith's in the boulevard St. Michel. It was a Browning, a deadly little weapon, and Carruthers spent ten minutes practising with it in the gunsmith's range before continuing on his way to see Groom at the Ritz. He did not anticipate having to use the Browning, but he felt it was well to be prepared. He hailed a taxi.

Gone was his pleasure in the spring morning. Sitting back in his taxi he marshalled his thoughts in preparation for his meeting with Groom. At all costs Groom must not expect that he was other than a peaceable scientist. Could he maintain the pose? Carruthers felt that he could. After all, was not his own knowledge of atomic physics fully equal to that of this Professor, this Barstow? Carruthers felt that it was. Once let him examine Kassen's work and the secret would be Kassen's no longer. Meanwhile, he must gain Groom's confidence. It should not be difficult. What happened when Groom discovered, as he must eventually discover, the sheep's clothing was of no importance at the moment.

When he stepped out of his taxi and entered the rococo portals of the Ritz he felt confident of success.

The information clerk was very polite.

Monsieur Groom? But certainly. If Monsieur would be so good as to wait one moment. A rapid conversation on the telephone followed. Then he turned apologetically, profound regret in every line of his features.

"Monsieur is most unfortunate," he said. "Monsieur Groom departed from the hotel ten minutes ago."

Carruthers' first impulse was to disbelieve the clerk. It was a ruse to put him off the scent. Then, remembering that it was as Barstow and not as himself that he was there, the absurdity of the notion struck him. The hotel clerk would have no reason to deceive him. He began to ask questions.

The clerk was most anxious to help. The hall porter was summoned. Yes, he remembered Monsieur Groom; he had been generous. He had left for the Gare de l'Est only ten minutes earlier.

Quickly, Carruthers asked for a railway time-table. One was produced. He soon found what he was looking for. Groom had undoubtedly left to catch the train for Bucharest, the junction for the branch line to Zovgorod.

"Is there a ticket office in the hotel?" he asked.

No, but there was a *Wagons-Lit* bureau round the corner. If Monsieur desired . . .

Pressing a ten-franc piece into the man's hand, Carruthers dashed out of the hotel and round to the *Wagons-Lit* bureau.

Here again fortune favoured him. The man there remembered Groom from Carruthers' description. He had bought a ticket to Zovgorod that very morning and had booked a compartment to himself in the Roumanian through-coach to Bucharest. The train left in a quarter of an hour. Monsieur might catch it if he hurried.

Carruthers fumed with impatience while the complicated ticket was being prepared. By the time it was ready he had a taxi waiting. Spurred with a fifty-franc note and the promise of another if he were in time for the train, the driver flung the Renault round the corners at racing speed.

They swept up the approach into the station yard with a minute to spare. Tossing the promised fifty francs into the driver's lap, Carruthers leapt out and raced into the station. The indicator told him that the train was on *Quai I*.

Whistles were blowing as Carruthers sprinted on to the platform. The train was already on the move when he leapt into the last coach.

He made his way along the corridor to the Roumanian through-coach. The first compartment in it appeared to be empty. He had pushed back the sliding door and entered before he noticed a large ticket marked *RÉSERVÉ*.

Suddenly a hand fell on his shoulder.

He spun round.

"So you changed your mind after all, Professor," said Simon Groom.

4

APRIL 20th

Carruthers did not lose his composure for an instant.

"Ah, Mr. Groom!" he said calmly; "the very person I am looking for. Yes, I changed my mind after all—it is, I believe, the scientist's privilege."

Groom gazed at him for a moment in silence; then, motioning him to a seat, he himself lounged back on the cushions opposite and lit a cigar. A faint and not too pleasant smile showed on his lips as he exhaled the blue smoke.

"Professor Barstow," he said at last, "you have surprised me."

Carruthers waited.

"Yes," went on Groom, leaning forward, "I am surprised and, to tell you the truth, a trifle put out."

Carruthers, filling his pipe, felt the other's beady eyes fixed upon him.

"You see," he continued, "I have always been inclined to pride myself on the accuracy of my judgments of men. That being so, I find this, shall we say, *volte-face* on your part almost incredible. True, I did suggest that you might on mature reflection feel more disposed to accept my offer, but frankly I did not for one moment suppose that you would actually do so. May I inquire what induced you to forsake your somewhat—er—impractical ideals?"

Carruthers had expected this.

"Mr. Groom," he said, "I will be equally frank with you. I have not forsaken my views on the subject. I still believe in them implicitly."

Groom raised his eyebrows.

"But," continued Carruthers thoughtfully, "there were, I decided, other factors to be considered. I am a poor man, Mr. Groom. I have, for some time now, been handicapped in my research work by lack of funds. I asked myself a question. Could I, in fairness to myself, afford to refuse your offer? I decided that I could not. After all, your failure to secure particulars of Kassen's secret eventually is in any case unlikely. Why should I not assist you to hasten the process?"

He had chosen the reason for his acceptance carefully as that most likely to be viewed sympathetically by a man of Groom's calibre. He had not been mistaken. A glance at Groom's face told him that his explanation had done much to lull the other's suspicions.

Groom nodded appreciatively.

"Professor," he said with a disarming smile, "I see that you are a man after my own heart. I salute the good fortune that prompted me to inform you of my movements."

Carruthers saw the trap immediately. Groom was trying to ascertain if his presence on the train was traceable to the activities of a third party.

He laughed.

"I could wish," he said, "that your information had been

a trifle more detailed than it was. It is more by luck than judgment that I am with you now. I missed you at the Ritz. The hall porter there was, however, able to help me."

This seemed to satisfy Groom.

"Well, Professor, I may be surprised and my self-esteem has certainly suffered, but I confess that I am glad to see you. Supposing we adjourn to the dining-car; we can perhaps discuss business better over luncheon."

"Mr. Groom," remarked Carruthers later, "we may disagree on points of ethics, but in the matter of food and wine my admiration for your judgment is profound."

Groom shrugged.

"One does one's best, but these trains . . . !" He raised despairing hands. "I trust the Bordeaux is not entirely undrinkable; the motion is enough to ruin any wine."

"An excellent choice."

"Then perhaps we can proceed to business. In the first place, Professor, I want to impress upon you again the necessity for absolute secrecy. It is possible, though not, I believe, probable that our competitors may also have heard of Kassen's discovery. If that is the case I shall know how to deal with them. The point to remember, however, is that behind Kassen is the Ixanian Government. Any indiscreet move on our part might mean failure."

Carruthers, in the role of the ingenuous Professor Barstow, nodded vaguely. Privately he wondered if "failure" were not a rather mild way of describing the receipt of a bullet in the back. Still, it was no part of Groom's policy to intimidate his new lieutenant. He changed the subject abruptly.

"Then we understand one another," he went on swiftly. "Now, Professor, we come to the question of your fee. I need hardly say that you will not find Cator & Bliss niggardly. As I said before, any reasonable demand on your part would receive our most sympathetic consideration. I take it you have given the matter some thought?"

Carruthers exhibited confusion.

"Well," he began uncertainly, "I am not a business man, Mr. Groom . . . I hardly know . . ."

"Perhaps," interrupted the other smoothly, "you will permit me to make a suggestion."

Carruthers registered relief.

"Just what I was about to propose."

Groom settled himself comfortably.

"As I have already pointed out, Professor, any work in this matter done by you on behalf of Cator & Bliss would remain our sole and absolute property. Further, we should expect you to place yourself under contract with us for a period of, say, five years; you will appreciate that we have to protect ourselves as far as possible. I imagine, however, that such a contract would not prove irksome. Your actual work for us will cease on the day our factories are in a position to produce the Kassen explosive."

"That is reasonable enough," admitted Carruthers.

"Very well then, Professor, we come to the financial aspect of the question. Here is my proposition. On the day I have already mentioned, when we are actually in production of the Kassen explosive, you would receive an honorarium of fifty thousand pounds. In addition—" He paused impressively. "In addition, you would receive ten thousand pounds a year for each of the five years of your contract. In the event of Cator & Bliss deciding to license other manufacturers to use the Kassen process, you would receive further honoraria of fifty thousand pounds for each licence. In other words, one hundred thousand pounds for you certainly, with the possibility of considerably more. Well, Professor, what do you say?"

Carruthers remained silent for a moment. His first impulse was to laugh. So Groom really took him for the simpleton of a Professor he was impersonating. One hundred thousand pounds—but only if Groom were able to create the opportunity for him to do the work and then only if that work bore fruit. Cator & Bliss stood to lose nothing; Professor Barstow stood to lose a great deal, even his liberty, possibly his life. Again there was no guarantee that, when he had fulfilled his part of the bargain, Cator & Bliss would acknowledge it. Certainly Groom would give him some sort of contract but, hedged about with "ifs" and "buts" as it would be, it would not be worth the paper it was written on. Besides, Cator & Bliss would undoubtedly refuse to define the exact nature and limits of his work in a written contract that might serve at some future date as evidence of the nature of their operations.

Groom was watching him closely. Carruthers affected a bewildered grin. "It's a lot of money, Mr. Groom."

The other smiled faintly.

"I told you, Professor, that you would not find Cator & Bliss niggardly. I take it that you accept our terms?"

"Of course, of course. I can only hope," he added apologetically, "that my work will justify the generosity of your treatment of me."

Groom's smile broadened.

"Then we'll take it as settled. The train stops for an hour at Bâle. That will give me time to arrange about your contract with our office there. Meanwhile—another brandy, I think."

"Ah, I see, a little celebration," said Carruthers with a

professorial giggle. "Well, Mr. Groom, I think I may exceed my allowance for once. Thank you!"

Groom's plump face was more congenial than ever as he ordered the liqueurs. When they came he turned to Carruthers, a broad smile on his lips, his glass raised for a toast.

"To the success of our . . ."

He did not finish the sentence. His eyes staring over Carruthers' shoulder suddenly narrowed. In a moment his face tightened into the bland mask of suspicion Carruthers had already seen once that day.

Two people had entered the restaurant car.

Groom's eyes followed them until they drew level with the table. The two passed on to a table a little farther down the car. Carruthers, his every sense alert, watched the retreating figures of a man and a woman with a growing feeling of excitement. As the two turned to sit down he glimpsed their faces. He had been right then. It was the man and woman of the Paris boat-train.

He became aware that Groom was talking to him.

"I beg your pardon, Professor," he was saying, "for the moment I thought I had seen a ghost."

Once more he raised his glass.

"As I was saying, Professor—to the success of our enterprise."

But his face had lost its geniality, his tone had lost conviction.

* * * * *

Back in their compartment, Groom's usual garrulity had deserted him. Muttering that he had some business to attend to, he disappeared behind what appeared to be a voluminous report and read steadily, pausing only occasionally to scribble a note.

Carruthers, for his part, was more than thankful for the breathing space. He found the rôle of the ingenuous Professor Barstow a little trying to sustain. Besides, he had much food for thought.

His fellow-travellers of the Havre-Paris express had certainly been recognised by Groom and, just as certainly, that recognition had proved an unpleasant surprise. Were this man and woman connected in any way with Groom's present enterprise? It was possible. They might conceivably be the Ixanian representatives from England. But in that case why should the sight of them surprise Groom? Once again he cursed Durand's shameful treachery. Durand might have known something. Durand—then an idea struck him. Representatives? Groom had spoken of only one. The woman might, of course, be the man's wife, or his "secretary." He found the hypothesis singularly depressing. He glanced in his mind's eye at the picture they had presented in the Havre-Paris train. The man, judging from the glimpses he had caught of him, certainly fitted the part of representative of the Ixanian Government. Neat, plump, dark, he reminded Carruthers of an Istanbul rug merchant he knew, not at all the sort of man, he thought, to capture the affection of such a woman. The man appeared to treat her, too, with a certain deference, as a superior. It occurred to him suddenly that the presence of the woman might be the unexpected factor which had caused Groom such dismay. Who was she? Obviously, Groom would give him no information. The less Professor Barstow knew, the better. He must find out for himself.

He rose and, murmuring that he was going for a stroll,

went out into the corridor, closing the door to the compartment firmly behind him. The first thing was to ascertain the whereabouts of the mysterious man and woman. If his conjectures had been right they would also be in the Roumanian coach bound for Zovgorod.

Giving way to the movements of the train in order to render his progress as slow as possible without arousing suspicion, he started to walk the length of the coach. As he passed each compartment he glanced casually at the occupants. He had almost reached the end of the corridor and the conclusion that his theory was wrong before he saw them. They were in a compartment by themselves, the man apparently dozing, the woman reading a book.

Carruthers did not pause and continued his way to the end of the corridor. There he stopped and, leaning on the handrail, gazed out of the window. By turning his head slightly he had an uninterrupted view of the entire corridor of the Roumanian coach: a few feet away was the entrance to the compartment of what he now felt practically certain was the Ixanian representative and his companion; beyond that, at the far end of the corridor, was Groom's compartment.

The train roared over a viaduct and into a cutting. Watching the embankment stream by, Carruthers considered his next move.

Obviously, he must make the woman's acquaintance, talk to her. But how? It was out of the question to reveal his true identity and business or even his imposture of Professor Barstow. He must, then, engage her in conversation as a fellow-traveller. It would not, he thought, be easy. She did not look the sort of person to encourage casual acquaintances. He considered several conceivable gambits only to reject them as clumsy and was still wondering how best to accomplish his purpose when Fate took a hand in the game.

The train had left the cutting and entered a long tunnel. Suddenly, he noticed that it was slowing down. By the time it emerged it was moving at little more than walking pace, while from below came a continuous and penetrating grinding. A few yards more and the train stopped with a jerk.

Immediately windows were flung open and heads appeared all along. A covey of officials descended onto the line and began peering beneath the coach. They were soon joined by the driver in his long blue coat. An excited conclave took place. The trouble appeared to be caused by the brakes of the Roumanian coach and the driver began plucking at a lever which projected from one of the bogeys. The officials followed suit and each in turn pulled the offending lever, to a running fire of facetious comment from the carriage windows.

Several passengers now took it into their heads to scramble down on to the line and gather round the group of officials. They were quickly followed by others. One or two waggled the lever with an air of understanding.

Carruthers, from his vantage-point at the window, watched the scene with amusement. Suddenly he heard the compartment door behind him open. "Pardon, Monsieur, will you please tell me what is the matter?" said a clear voice in English.

As he turned to reply, Carruthers gave no indication of his delight at this good fortune.

"Apparently," he said gravely, "an overheating brake. As you see,"—he waved his hand towards the commotion below—"the matter is now receiving attention."

A faint smile hovered on her lips. Her beauty was more than ever apparent.

"May I ask, Madame," pursued Carruthers, "how you knew that I was English."

The smile deepened.

"If this had been England," she answered, "the passengers would have waited patiently in their compartments for the train to start again. It would occur to no one to leave the train. Over here we order things differently."

Carruthers laughed.

"Madame is a psychologist," he said with a slight bow.

She did not respond but looked anxiously at the gesticulating assembly on the line.

"Tell me, Monsieur," she asked seriously, "do you think that we shall be delayed for long?"

"I think not, Madame," he assured her; "the brake, I gather, is already in working order. It is now, it seems, more an affair of the driver's honour."

"That, perhaps, is a matter not so easily disposed of."

As she spoke there was the blast of a whistle and cries of "*en voiture*" as the passengers hurriedly scrambled back into the train.

Carruthers cast about desperately for a means of continuing the conversation. The train was already moving and she was making as if to return to her compartment.

"Are you going to Bucharest, too, Madame?"

She was non-committal. To Bucharest, yes; but not to stay there. She volunteered no further information. Carruthers changed his tactics.

"I, too, am travelling beyond Bucharest. I am going to Zovgorod."

He sensed an immediate almost imperceptible change in her attitude towards him. She spoke softly.

"Indeed?"

"You know Zovgorod?" he said idly.

"I have been there." She paused; then, turning swiftly to meet his eyes, "You go on business, Monsieur?"

The sudden directness took him unawares. She was watching him closely. With an uneasy feeling that he had aroused her suspicions of him by his question, he smiled disarmingly.

"Fortunately, no. I am merely indulging my hobby—photography. There is, I am told, some unique scenery in the neighbourhood of Zovgorod."

She raised her eyebrows.

"So? I had not heard of it. Ixania sees few tourists. There is little of the picturesque in Ixania which is not reproduced, with the added advantage of adequate hotel accommodation, across her frontiers."

She spoke bitterly and remained staring out of the window as if her words had started an unhappy train of thought. Carruthers, only too well aware of the probable fatuity of his hastily improvised explanation, hoped that her thoughts had been deflected. He was disappointed.

She turned to him again.

"You have been misinformed of the attractions of Ixania, my friend," she said firmly. "I recommend you to change your plans."

Carruthers shrugged his shoulders.

"One seeks novelty," he said a trifle lamely. Mentally he resolved to make a camera one of his first purchases at Bâle.

"Change your plans nevertheless, Monsieur. Ixania is unhealthy for visitors—especially in the spring."

Again he encountered her highly disconcerting stare. He had no further doubts. He was being warned. In some mysterious way she had discovered his identity. Of whether she now knew him as Conway Carruthers or as Professor Barstow, technical adviser to Cator & Bliss, he was, however, ignorant. A lot might depend on how much she knew.

There was nothing to be gained by appearing too perceptive. He smiled incredulously and was about to reply when in loud, clear tones she interrupted him.

"Monsieur, would you have the goodness to tell me at what hour we arrive at Bâle?"

"Eight-thirty, Madame."

"*Merci, Monsieur.*"

With a gracious smile she turned and retired into her own compartment, shutting the door behind her. Out of the corner of his eye, Carruthers discovered the reason.

At the end of the corridor, watching them, stood Groom.

5

APRIL 20th *(CONTINUED)*

It was early evening and the train was racing through the rich fields of the Saône valley before Groom referred to the encounter in the corridor.

Leaning back in his corner, Carruthers had been endeavouring to piece the situation together from the fragmentary facts he had gleaned and the conjectures he had made.

Firstly, Groom, the representative of an arms firm, was out to prevent the manufacture of the Kassen explosive. Secondly, Groom wished to secure the process for his own use. Thirdly, he had engaged, or thought he had engaged, a technical expert to assist him in the latter task. Fourthly, the Ixanian representative from London was unwittingly leading Groom towards his headquarters in Ixania. Fifthly, the presence of one particular person on the train had disconcerted him. The rest was conjecture. It was almost certainly the woman in the Roumanian coach who was the source of Groom's particular anxiety. That woman had warned him, Carruthers, against entering Ixania. He closed his eyes. He was suddenly conscious of his complete ignorance of the business in which he was involved.

Groom had told a plausible enough story—it would certainly have satisfied the real Professor Barstow—but was it, after all, even plausible? Who was he? He felt himself lost, slipping, falling headlong, falling towards a mist which as it rushed towards him seemed peopled with vaguely familiar shadows. The voices in his head swelled into a roar until, quite suddenly, part of it died away into whispers, leaving only the thudding rhythm of the train embossed upon his returning consciousness. He could feel the sweat breaking out all over his body. With a start he pulled himself together. It was not like Conway Carruthers to doze.

Groom was talking.

"I am myself to blame, Professor," he was saying. "I should have taken you into my confidence. I should have put you on your guard."

"I'm afraid," said Carruthers, "I don't understand you." That, at least, was true.

Groom lighted his inevitable cigar before replying. Carruthers suspected that his constant preoccupation with a cigar was a device to give himself time to weigh his words carefully without appearing to do so.

"I will explain," he said; "but first tell me about the lady to whom you were talking this afternoon. Do you know her?"

Carruthers affected bewilderment. Actually, calm and collected once more, his moment of unaccountable weakness forgotten, he was thinking fast.

"Good heavens, no. She seemed worried about the breakdown to the train. I reassured her. We got into conversation."

"What did you talk about?"

Carruthers had been waiting for this question.

"Oh, generalities. She said she knew Ixania."

"You told her you were going there?"

"Certainly. Why not?"

Groom permitted himself an exasperated sigh.

"What reason did you give?"

Carruthers shrugged.

"I said I was going to take photographs of Ixanian scenery."

"Have you got a camera?"

"No."

"You must get one at Bâle. You will probably be searched for it at the Ixanian frontier."

Carruthers smiled grimly to himself at Groom's duplication of his own forethought. Meanwhile he had a part to play.

"I don't understand."

"I think you will. Ixania is, as you are probably aware, a republic with a president and a so-called chamber of deputies. The republic was the outcome of the revolution of 1921 against the monarchy. It was an unnecessarily bloody affair and, in that, typically Ixanian. The King, Mihail the Seventh, was only too ready to abdicate, the army was republican to a man and the people laboured under what must have been one of the last outposts of the feudal system in Europe. However, with the usual short-sightedness of revolutionary bodies, the republicans overlooked the fact that the business of government has, like any other business, to be learnt. A period of anarchy and confusion was the inevitable result. Equally inevitable was the re-introduction into the governing body of a section of its prevailing ruling class. I say re-introduction, but that is not perhaps the word. Insinuation would be nearer the mark. To do the republicans justice, a certain amount of discretion was exercised and the governing power was nominally invested in the President and Chamber. But the real power in Ixania to this day is in the hands of an oligarchy from the *ancien régime*. They are secure, for their responsibility is borne by the President and Chamber, although, in actual fact, the Chamber has not been summoned for three or four years now. The people have a superstitious respect for them. It takes more than a few months' madness to expunge the Ixanians' centuries-old reverence for titles and high birth."

He paused to examine the ash on his cigar.

"The situation," ventured Carruthers, "is not a novel one."

"Fortunately for our business no," said Groom calmly. "The novelty of the Ixanian situation is the way in which these people allow the most corrupt and incompetent bureaucracy in Europe to handle home affairs while they themselves spend their time annoying other nations. The royal blood, of course; there's a sort of seedy imperialist philosophy with a lacing of Fascism behind it all. That sort of fancy dress is splendid when the country concerned can pay its bills, but the peasants in Ixania are a poor lot and can't pay their taxes. The trouble with the aristocratic party is that they are fervent patriots and therefore, with one notable exception, stupid: well-intentioned perhaps, but irrevocably stupid." Groom shook his head sadly. "Somebody once called the munition industry the bloody international. He must have forgotten the flagmakers."

He looked up with his cold, faintly contemptuous smile on his lips. "You can't blame engineers for supplying what the world is so fervently anxious to buy. If I didn't, somebody else would. The only power that can legislate for fools is God."

"Or reason," put in Carruthers.

"Ah, but we were talking of patriotism," said Groom quickly. "And," he went on thoughtfully, "of one patriot in particular; the one who, heaven only knows how, manages to combine intelligence with patriotism. That person is the real ruler of Ixania. Her name is Countess Schverzinski."

Carruthers remained very still.

"An amazing woman, Professor," Groom continued. "I can think of few European diplomats capable of outwitting her. As a negotiator she is superb. She has all the Ixanians' love of intrigue and dissimulation with a Gallic sense of reality. Given a less sketchy background than that of her fatherland she would be a power in Europe. Even the best of card players cannot win with a hopeless hand. But with the Kassen invention as a trump card, the situation is materially altered. Last week Ixania rejected a customs union with a neighbouring state although the government had previously signified its agreement to the terms of the union. It was finally rejected as a result of representations made to the President by Prince Ladislaus, brother of La Schverzinski and titular leader of the aristocratic party. His instructions came, of course, from his sister. She has other plans for the restoration of Ixania's fortunes."

"Very interesting, Mr. Groom," said Carruthers politely, "but . . ."

"One moment, Professor. I will come to the point. I am, unfortunately, known to the Countess through past business relations. You will, I think, appreciate that under the circumstances my presence in Zovgorod would not be deemed desirable by the government. I had hoped to enter Ixania undetected. I have been disappointed. For some reason, the Countess is accompanying the London representative back to Zovgorod. She was the last person I expected to travel by this train. But there it is; she recognized me the moment she saw me. She gave no sign of having done so, but I am not such a fool as to suppose that she didn't. Her inspection of you confirms it."

"Then . . . ?"

"Exactly, Professor. The lady you were talking to in the corridor a short time ago is Magda, Countess Schverzinski."

Carruthers digested this information for a moment. He had played into her hands. Seeing him with Groom she had made it her business to find out where he stood. His lame talk of photography had been seen through immediately. He looked at Groom again.

"Will we be stopped at the Ixanian frontier?"

Groom shook his head.

"I think not. The relations between Cator & Bliss and the Ixanian Government are ostensibly cordial. The company's representative is *persona grata* in Zovgorod. The damage is that we shall no doubt be under close surveillance during our stay. Every precaution will be certainly taken to insure against our gaining any information concerning Kassen or his work. It is a nuisance, but it cannot be helped. We shall have to employ other measures."

"Such as?"

Groom smiled.

"Perhaps we had better not go into that, Professor. I think I have mentioned, however, that I should rely upon my knowledge of Ixanian officialdom to help us—that knowledge plus a large banking account. It is really quite simple."

With a chuckle he settled himself back in his corner and returned to his papers. He had the air of a man with something up his sleeve.

Left to his own thoughts, Carruthers gazed out of the window at the lights of a distant town. He was not pleased with himself. Conway Carruthers seemed to be losing his grip. He had made the mistake of underrating an opponent. More, he had failed even to perceive an opponent. Could it be because she was a beautiful woman? Impossible! Had he not resisted the wiles, the womanly guile of countless beautiful spies? Had they not possessed tawny hair and sinuous bodies? Had they not reclined provocatively on gilt divans? Had not their green eyes held promise of untold delights in return for the secrets he alone could reveal? And had he not gone on his way smiling with grim amusement at their baffled fury, their childish simplicity? Of course. Yet perhaps it was that this woman's eyes were dark, dark brown, that her hair was lustrous black, that her smile gave him a curious feeling in the pit of his stomach, that she was infinitely—as those appreciative Italians put it—infinitely *simpatica*. Perhaps, but he was mooning—mooning like one of those love-sick young Englishmen who always ruined his plans in chapter twelve by dashing frantically but indiscreetly to the rescue of their terrified woman. No more of it! From now on, he, Carruthers, would be the master.

* * * * *

Before the train reached Bâle an incident occurred which Carruthers dismissed at the time as unimportant, but which he was to remember later.

Groom did not go into dinner and Carruthers ate the first half of his meal in silence. Facing him was a lean-faced, rather untidy young man who spoke to the waiter in fluent French but with an unmistakable American accent.

There is nothing like a French restaurant car travelling at speed for promoting casual acquaintance. It is difficult to maintain a formal reserve with soup and wine splashing sociably over both sides of the intervening table.

"They tell me," said the American at last, dabbing ruefully with his napkin at the sleeve of his jacket, "that French railroad track is the worst in the world."

"This section of it is certainly one of the oldest."

"Then they ought not to serve soup *and* wine at the same time."

The discussion became general. The American had apparently travelled widely. The conversation turned to places. Seizing a possible chance to obtain some information, Carruthers brought the conversation round to Eastern Europe.

Belgrade was mentioned. Then: "Have you ever been to Zovgorod?" inquired Carruthers casually.

The American met his eyes for a fraction of a second before replying briefly, "No." He seemed disinclined to continue the conversation, called for his bill, paid it and with a nod to Carruthers rose and left the car.

* * * * *

As the train entered the outskirts of Bâle, Groom issued his first instructions.

There was a wait of several hours before the train to which their through-coach was to be coupled would leave for Bucharest. He, Groom, would go to the office of the Bâle agents of Messrs. Cator & Bliss Limited in the Badenstrasse and there have a letter prepared setting forth in detail the Company's offer to Professor Barstow. This he would sign and hand to the Professor until such time as the document could be superseded by a stamped agreement. Carruthers expressed his thanks dutifully.

The Professor would buy such things as he thought necessary—clothes, toilet requisites *and* a camera—and meet Groom on the train. Meanwhile, if he required any money, here were five thousand francs which he could regard as being on account of further honoraria.

Carruthers hesitated to take the money but, realizing that his own effectiveness might well be curtailed if he found himself short of funds, accepted it gracefully.

They parted company in the station yard, Groom disappearing into a taxi, Carruthers setting out to explore the city for an open store.

He found it no easy task. Except for an occasional café, Bâle was dark and silent. He soon hailed a passing taxi and consulted the driver. He was, he learnt, in the German quarter of the city. There were, however, stores open in the other quarters. Telling the driver to take him to the nearest outfitters, he sat back and watched sombre neo-Gothic façades change gradually into painted stucco.

Ten minutes later he set out with a brand-new suitcase full of his purchases to get a camera. The salesman was helpful and produced a remarkable little instrument that was not only capable of taking high-definition photographs in very poor artificial light but had the added advantage of being small enough to be carried in an inside pocket. He bought a supply of film for it and left well satisfied. He next thought of his automatic. Apart from the seven rounds in the magazine, he had no ammunition. He tried to buy some more, but there were, as he had anticipated, "formalities" to be gone through.

He had just over an hour left before the train went and made his way to a café. Seating himself at a table set back from the pavement, he ordered *vermouth-cassis* and glanced through a Swiss newspaper that had been left on the table.

A tradesman in Dijon had murdered his wife and her lover with a hatchet. The hotel proprietors of Geneva had condemned as "unethical" a suggestion that the League of Nations might be removed to Vienna. There had been a mountaineering fatality near Grindelwald. Then a small paragraph with a London dateline caught his eye:

MYSTERIOUS DISAPPEARANCE OF ENGLISH SAVANT

> *Mystery shrouds the disappearance of an English savant who left home several days ago on vacation. Two days ago, police discovered an overturned automobile deserted on a lonely road in the province of Cornwall. No trace of the owner could be found. Investigation showed the car to be the property of the eminent . . .*

"Verzeihung, mein Herr."

Carruthers looked up. An elderly German was endeavouring to squeeze himself through the narrow space between the tables. With a murmured apology Carruthers stood up to allow him to pass. As he did so, he happened to glance across the road.

A taxi had drawn up to discharge a passenger and was just moving off. A man walked away. As he moved out of the darkness into the light of a street lamp, Carruthers recognised him. It was Groom.

What was he doing in this part of the city? Hastily leaving some money on the table, Carruthers dropped the newspaper, caught up his suitcase and left the café. He could see Groom's paunchy figure walking briskly along the far side of the road.

Waiting until about seventy-five yards separated them, he started to follow, keeping to his own side. Suddenly Groom turned out of sight down a narrow side street. Carruthers raced for the corner. He reached it in time to see Groom disappearing into a passage on the right of the side street. Moving quickly and as quietly as possible over the sloping cobbles, Carruthers reached the passage and peered down it cautiously. Groom was nowhere to be seen.

The place was dark and evil-smelling. A single old-fashioned lamp on a bracket at the corner of the passage served to light both the street and the passage. The latter, which was formed by the side walls of two dingy buildings, continued for about six yards before debouching into an alley which appeared to be a cul-de-sac. In a moment he had gained the sheltering blackness of the alley. Along one side of its length ran what he judged to be a warehouse; on the other were three ramshackle houses, one of which Groom had obviously entered. They were, however, all shuttered and apparently deserted.

He glanced at his watch by the faint light of the lamp. He need not leave for the station for some time yet. Groom, too, had to catch the train. If Groom left soon he might have time enough to discover what brought a director of Messrs. Cator & Bliss to this sleazy alleyway.

He looked round for a hiding-place. The warehouse provided it. Two heavy double doors, obviously disused since the encroachment of the surrounding buildings had cut them off from the roadway, were set in large stone arches. Carruthers stepped in the shadow of the nearest of the arches and waited.

For a quarter of an hour he heard nothing but the

footsteps of an occasional passer-by on the cobbles of the side street. Then he heard the faint murmur of voices and a light gleamed for an instant behind the shutters of a window set high in the end house. Leaving his suitcase where it was, he glided quickly into the next arch. Whoever came out would have to pass close by him. Holding himself flat against the stonework, he listened intently.

The voices stopped. There came a sound of faint tapping. Straining his ears, he identified it as the sound of feet on bare boards. Someone was coming downstairs. He distinguished two sets of footsteps. They grew louder and then ceased. There was a pause as the feet crossed a stone passage, then the front door opened and two men came out into the alley and started to walk away.

As they came towards Carruthers he drew back. One of them was Groom, he had seen that much, the other was a slighter man. They were almost level with him and were talking in low tones. As they passed him, a gleam of light from the lamp at the end of the passage lighted for a second the face of Groom's companion. It was the Ixanian representative.

He caught a snatch of their conversation. They were talking French. Groom was speaking.

"You understand. The remainder will be credited to you at the Swiss Bank in Paris as soon as our technical adviser has approved the information."

The other mumbled what sounded like a grudging agreement as they passed out of earshot.

Nothing surprising after all. A bribe offered and a down payment accepted. Evidently Groom had already been making use of his "knowledge of Ixanian officialdom." Yes, the Countess Schverzinski was indeed badly served.

Suddenly he stiffened and flattened himself against the

wall. The door of the house that Groom and his companion had just left was slowly opening again. Then a man stepped out and closed it softly behind him. Although his face was in the shadow it was obvious that he was frightened, for he kept darting rapid glances to either side of him. Then, quickly and furtively, he followed the other two out of the alley. Carruthers caught a glimpse of a puffy, rabbit-like face as he went by. Once out of the alley, however, he turned in the opposite direction to that of Groom. Carruthers heard the footsteps die away, then collected his suitcase and found a taxi.

Groom was already in the train when Carruthers rejoined it. He handed Carruthers the promised contract letter with the air of a benevolent prince bestowing an honour. The foreign representative of Cator & Bliss was looking pleased.

6

APRIL 21st TO 23rd

The next thirty-eight hours passed without incident. From the windows of Groom's compartment, Carruthers watched the mountains of Switzerland and Austria pass in slow review. Then for some hours, they ran across wind-driven plains. On the second night, he again saw the lights of houses gleaming high up as they climbed into the mountain country of Transylvania. They stopped at stations of which he had never heard, but there were some familiar names—Budapest, Cluj, Sinaia, Ploesti. The places differed, however, only in name and in the language in which the advertisements were displayed. He experienced the boredom to which even the most hardened travellers are subject.

Occasionally he saw the Countess Schverzinski and the Ixanian envoy, whose name he had learnt from the sleeping-car attendant was Rovzidski, in the restaurant car. With the American acquaintance he exchanged remote nods. He endeavoured to pass the time with a Tauchnitz edition of Butler's *Erewhon* purchased hastily from a station bookstall; but his thoughts kept wandering from

Butler's stimulating conceptions to the more momentous business on which he was bent.

If Groom's plans went smoothly, it would not be long before Kassen's secret was in his possession. The time was near when he, Carruthers, would have to show his hand and deal with two groups of enemies. Neither group was to be despised. On one hand there would be Groom backed by the unknown, but no doubt extensive, resources of his international organisation. On the other, there was the Countess Schverzinski, an even more formidable enemy if Groom's estimate of her were true.

Mere possession of the Kassen secret was not enough. He must prevent its use in Ixania as well. That was an essential part of his task. What happened to it afterwards was another matter. If the peace of the world demanded that it should be destroyed, then destroyed it should be. But meanwhile there was this problem of preventing manufacture. Destroy some essential piece of laboratory equipment? It could be made again. Sabotage in any shape or form would merely serve to delay manufacture, not to prevent it absolutely. Kill Kassen? It was unlikely that the contingency of his death had not been anticipated and provided for.

They arrived in Bucharest early in the evening. Rain was lashing down when the train drew in. They had just over an hour to wait before the branch line train for Zovgorod left. They spent it in a small café near the station, where Groom related with some gusto a lurid account of a previous experience in the city.

The train for Zovgorod proved to be composed mainly of empty cattle trucks with two very dirty coaches and a mail van hitched to the rear. They were not due in Zovgorod until 7 A.M. the following morning and Carruthers did not look forward to the two-hundred-and-fifty-mile journey ahead. Groom tempered fastidious disgust with philosophic resignation and, to Carruthers' amusement, produced an atomiser and sprayed the upholstery with eau de cologne. It was, he declared, a powerful germicide.

Carruthers' first thought was to see if the Countess and Rovzidski, the Ixanian envoy, were on the train. They were, he found, in separate compartments in the next coach. He was mildly surprised to notice also that his American acquaintance was in the same coach.

There were, besides, two men whom he could not quite sum up to his satisfaction. They were roughly dressed, yet they had about them an indefinable air of authority. The elder of the two, a man about forty, had two deep scars on his forehead just above the right eye. His companion, who looked about twenty-five, wore a truculent expression and had the more usual type of duelling scars on his cheek. Both wore moustaches of an unmistakably military character. Neither of them, Carruthers noticed, carried any baggage. A few peasants with their families seemed to be the only other passengers on the train.

It was forty minutes late in starting. When finally it did get under way, however, the train rattled along at a fair pace. Lounging comfortably along the seat, cigar in mouth, Groom surveyed Carruthers with a benign smile.

"Well, Professor," he said heartily, "I'm sorry to have to subject you to all this discomfort, but I can tell you this much: our little business will take a good deal less time than I thought at first. In two or three days, if all goes well, we shall be on our way back with all the information we need in our pockets."

Carruthers looked as surprised as he could. Groom chuckled.

"You've heard of Sir Basil Zaharoff?" he went on.

Carruthers nodded.

"A competitor of mine," said Groom, "for whom I have the greatest respect and admiration. The biggest mistake he ever made was to let the newspapers get hold of him. 'The Mystery Man of Europe' they called him. Mysteries always mean one thing to the public—that there's something to be found out. What the newspaper man doesn't suspect, the public doesn't grieve over. Publicity may be the lifeblood of ordinary commerce, but it's poison to our industry. I flatter myself that there's not a reporter in the world who knows anything about me or my business."

Carruthers wondered how such a colossal conceit had managed to escape the attentions of even the most obtuse reporter.

"I mentioned Zaharoff," Groom continued, "because he once told me that in these days there was no such thing as a secret weapon—that it was an impossibility. It's true of course; why, you can usually find out all the details of every so-called secret weapon a few weeks after it has been made. The engineering and other technical journals publish them quite openly."

"But in this case . . ."

"Exactly. In this case, we're ahead of everyone else. That means that we shall be in a position to grant other firms licenses to manufacture. I believe I mentioned your position as far as licenses are concerned."

"But if it's so easy to discover the process, won't other nations ignore Cator & Bliss and manufacture on their own account?"

Groom looked shocked.

"Really, Professor, for an idealist your views on business ethics are extraordinarily cynical. Why, during the 1914 war, an English arms firm made an enormous number of a special type of fuse for the use of the British armies. After the war, the owners of the patent, a well-known German firm, claimed a large sum of money from the English firm by way of royalties. The matter was settled amicably as a matter of course. Out of court, naturally, but settled it was. And rightly so," he concluded austerely.

Carruthers pondered this new aspect of commercial probity. Such agile moralists would, no doubt, be more than equal to the task of reconciling the necessity for bribery and corruption of state officials with their other principles.

He looked across the compartment at Groom. Night was falling. Whoever was in charge of the train had apparently forgotten or been unable to switch on the lights, for they were in semi-darkness. Carruthers could see Groom, faintly outlined by the failing daylight behind the glowing end of his cigar, sprawled comfortably on the seat. Suddenly, a cold rage possessed him; a rage against these monsters who battened on the wretchedness, the weakness of mankind. Just for once, he resolved, they would be defeated—yes, even if it cost him his life.

He felt incapable of remaining in the compartment with Groom and, with a muttered excuse, went into the corridor.

Leaning on the window-rail he gazed out into the gathering darkness. Far away he could see a line of hills traced delicately against the strip of cold cerulean sky left by a dying sun. The clouds still hung, black and heavy, overhead. The sound of the train seemed to echo across the plain as if in a great waiting silence. He turned his head towards the freshening breeze.

* * * * *

They reached the Ixanian frontier at two o'clock in the morning.

Roused by the slowing of the train, Carruthers stretched his cramped limbs and climbed down on to the platform of the frontier station. The moon had risen and by the look of the surrounding country, Carruthers guessed that they were in a high-altitude pass.

It was bitterly cold and, burying his hands in the pockets of his thin overcoat, he walked up and down to restore his circulation.

Some slovenly-looking soldiers were grouped round a brazier at one end of the platform. These, doubtless, were the Ixanian frontier guards. Several corrugated-iron sheds flanked the station and as Carruthers drew level with them a disreputable-looking official appeared.

Carruthers was joined by Groom and the other passengers on the train, and the shivering group was ushered into one of the sheds. He looked round for the Countess, but she was not with them. The American vouchsafed a distant nod. Rovzidski stood just behind him. Then, through an open door on the far side of the building, he saw a large Mercédès saloon drawn up in the road beyond. A few seconds later, the Countess appeared, followed by one of the soldiers with her luggage. The official greeted her deferentially; she stepped into the car and was driven away immediately. He heard faintly the tyres of the Mercédès screech round a corner. The Countess was evidently in a hurry.

He produced his passport. As soon as the official saw it an unpleasant change came over him. His air of bored negligence gone, he ordered Carruthers to wait and glanced through the remaining passports hurriedly but carefully. Then summoning two of the soldiers, he announced that there would be a customs examination of baggage on board the train.

A murmur of surprise rose from the passengers as they returned to their compartments. Groom's eyes met those of Carruthers with a look of triumphant amusement as he turned to follow. Carruthers faced the official.

The man said nothing but, seating himself at a table, proceeded to copy out painstakingly the information contained in Carruthers' passport. Having done so, he handed back the passport with a flourish and waved Carruthers to the train.

Accompanied by the soldiers the customs official moved from compartment to compartment on his examination. Not even the peasants' bundles were immune. Waving aside the chorus of protests that rose, he inspected every piece of luggage in the train. Groom and Carruthers in the last compartment came in for the closest examination of all.

Groom, protesting with studied ill-humour, was made to open his two huge suitcases and submit them to the pummellings and proddings of one of the soldiers. It was Carruthers' turn next.

Following Groom's example, he complained vigorously in English, French and German. The official took no notice and ordered him curtly to unlock his suitcase. With a show of bad grace, Carruthers obeyed. The official undertook the examination himself, removing singly every article in it and keeping up a running fire of unintelligible comment as he did so.

Acutely conscious of the Browning reposing in his hip pocket, Carruthers was hoping desperately that they would not deem it necessary to search his clothes. He was soon reassured. With a grunt of satisfaction his camera was unearthed from the suitcase. A whispered colloquy with the soldiers followed. Then, turning to Carruthers, the official announced in hideous German that it was forbidden to bring cameras into the country and that his instrument was confiscated.

With a sigh, partly of relief, partly of annoyance, Carruthers surrendered his camera. The official wrote out a receipt and with a careless salute left the coach.

As the train steamed slowly out of the station Groom laughed.

"Well, Professor," he said genially, "how does it feel to have the Countess Magda Schverzinski interested in you?"

Carruthers smiled ruefully. He was very much the "Professor."

"I must confess, Mr. Groom," he said, "that after what you have told me, I am not entirely surprised. I do, however, wish that the Ixanian Government had been satisfied with a mere inspection of the instrument. I regret its loss. It was a nice camera. I should have liked to have taken some photographs in Zovgorod—as a memento of my visit. I have always been interested in architecture."

His answer seemed to amuse Groom.

"Well, Professor," he said solemnly and with evident intent to humour, "we'll see what can be done. I must say, I enjoyed the episode. That was probably the first time for years that they've had to conduct an ordinary customs examination at that station. The only goods contraband in

Ixania are bristles for brushes. That's about the only thing they export now that their lead mines have worked out; and they have a huge protective tariff on. However, looking for bristles must have dulled their faculties a little. Look!"

He struck a match and, reaching to his hip pocket, produced an exact replica of the camera that Carruthers had just lost.

"Keep it, Professor," he said in a matter-of-fact voice, "we may need it. At all events you can now take your photographs in Zovgorod."

Groom settled himself once more in his voluminous travelling-rug and, closing his eyes, was soon, to judge from his snores, asleep.

Carruthers, however, could not sleep. For a long time he tried, but the discomfort of the train and his thoughts kept him awake. The episode at the frontier had impressed him. Whatever doubts he had hitherto entertained concerning Groom's judgment of the situation had been dispelled. This was reality and he was dealing with powerful and decisive people. He must be decisive in his turn. Mistakes would be dangerous.

He must have dozed for a time. Suddenly, however, he was alert and wide-awake. He had an intuitive feeling that something was wrong. The train seemed to be travelling fast. Through the window, he could see a faint lightening of the sky in the east. Then, from the other end of the corridor, came the unmistakable sound of a shot, followed three seconds later by two more in rapid succession.

In an instant he was in the corridor. The moon had set and it was still too dark to see much, but he thought he discerned two figures moving in the corridor ahead.

An excited babel of voices told him that the shots had

been heard by others. At that moment there was a scream of brakes and he was flung forward off his balance. He saved himself by clutching at the rail. Screams and shouts from the other coach told him that others had not been so fortunate. The train ground to a standstill. Obviously, someone had pulled the emergency cord.

Between him and the place from which the sound of the shots had seemed to come, there were three empty compartments. As the train stopped he heard the click of the outside door of one of them. He slid into the nearest compartment and leant out of the window. He could just see two shadowy forms moving rapidly away across a field.

He withdrew his head and went back into the corridor. A guard with a lantern was approaching. Groom came out of their compartment and Carruthers told him what had occurred.

By that time the guard was near them, peering into each compartment in turn. Suddenly he stopped and shouted. The passengers crowded towards him. Pushing Carruthers aside, Groom elbowed his way to where the guard stood with his lamp held aloft and a look of horror on his face. Carruthers followed him.

There, sprawling half on the seat and half on the floor, was the body of a man with blood welling from a large wound on the forehead. The light from the lantern threw his face into ghastly relief. The teeth were clenched, the eyes stared wildly, the entire face was distorted by fear: but the dead man was easily recognisable. It was the face of Rovzidski, Ixanian envoy to London.

Groom was the first to turn away. Carruthers followed him back to the compartment. For a time the plump, white-haired man, ignoring the hubbub, stared out of the window in silence. Carruthers, marvelling at the man's self-possession, heard him swear once under his breath. Then he turned and sat down.

"I regret to disappoint you, Professor," he said bitterly, "but I spoke too soon. Our stay in Zovgorod may be longer than I expected."

With that he settled himself once more in his rug. When they woke him some fifteen minutes later for questioning, he wore an air of tired martyrdom.

* * * * *

By seven, the time the train was due to arrive, they were still some sixty kilometers from Zovgorod. Thoroughly unnerved by the murder, the train officials had lost their heads and showed it by alternately browbeating the passengers and demanding their moral support.

This much was clear. Whoever had shot the man had left the train via the door which was found open. Carruthers refrained from saying anything about the two men whom he had seen making their escape. They had been seen by another passenger and this, in conjunction with the fact that the two passengers with the military moustaches whom Carruthers had noticed were nowhere to be found, seemed to reassure the chief interrogator. Carruthers was glad that it did.

Obviously, Rovzidski had been suspected of trafficking with Cator & Bliss while he was still in London. The Countess Schverzinski had escorted him home to Ixania not only to ensure that he did not get into further touch with Groom, but also probably because the best place to deal with him was in Ixania where drastic measures could be hushed up if necessary. Rovzidski, if he had found that he was suspected, might have been tempted to remain abroad. True, the Countess had not been able to prevent his meeting with Groom in Bâle, but—he remembered the rabbit-faced watcher—the meeting had doubtless not gone unreported. Rovzidski's executioners had boarded the train at Bucharest. Having delivered the traitor, the Countess had discreetly left the train at the frontier, leaving them to do their work. They had done it, stopped the train and made their escape in a part of the country where immediate pursuit was impossible. One thing was evident. The Countess Magda Schverzinski did not stand on ceremony where her enemies were concerned.

Groom, brooding in his corner, was reticent on the subject.

"He knew too much," was his guarded rejoinder when Carruthers attempted to discuss the motive for Rovzidski's murder.

Regarding the two men who had done it, he vouchsafed an opinion.

"You may remember the Society of the Black Hand which flourished in Macedonia some years ago. Ixania has a parallel organisation today. It calls itself, a trifle ridiculously, the Society of the Red Gauntlet and the members, as in the case of the Black Hand, are mostly of the officer class. They call themselves a patriotic society, but their speciality is political terrorism. The Black Hand wielded enormous political power at one time. They had a finger in practically every governmental pie and numbered even judges, generals and cabinet ministers among their members. The Red Gauntlet, however, is far less impressive. It is, I believe, largely the tool of the aristocratic party. The business looks like their work."

He lit a cigar and added petulantly:

"The real trouble with this damned country is that they don't put restaurant cars on the trains."

Carruthers found himself wondering whether, when the time came, his own elimination would be received so calmly. His eyes met those of the man opposite. Groom was smiling his faint contemptuous smile; but in his eyes there were other things. Carruthers shuddered involuntarily. For the first time he felt afraid.

7

APRIL 23rd TO MAY 8th

The city of Zovgorod is well situated. Set in the bowl formed by the junction of three valleys, it is protected both from the winds that sweep down from the cold north and up from the hot, dry south. The climate is temperate for Eastern Europe. If Nature had had the forethought to make the River Kuder navigable, Zovgorod might have had commercial importance. As it is the city has had strategic importance instead; an unfortunate distinction for a Balkan city. It lies in the path of a force utilising the valleys to strike northwards from the south; it lies at the point where that force can be most readily intercepted from the west. Turk, Slav, Latin and Teuton fought over the ground for centuries. The waves of conquering armies, sometimes from the west, sometimes from the east, have broken over it and receded, leaving always a dross of alien blood and alien culture behind them.

The latter was by far the more desirable inheritance. Everywhere in Zovgorod is evidence of its chequered history. The infusion of many Western influences into an architecture predominantly Byzantine is, for the most part, strangely pleasant in its results. An astringent quality saves it from the sentimentality of the merely picturesque. The new civilisation has had little opportunity to mix its blessings in Zovgorod and the older streets still have a sinister dignity of their own; a dignity, be it said, that not even the faint smell of medieval cess-pools that pervades them can wholly dispel.

The smell of Zovgorod was always the main impression of the city carried away by those 19th century travellers who had the curiosity to visit it. Nature, so provident in the matter of Zovgorod's prevailing winds, made no ready provision for sewage disposal. The Kuder might have been induced to serve the purpose, but before the electric power concession was granted to a Swiss syndicate who built a dam across it, it was a nuisance of a river, alternately flooding the cellars of the city and dwindling to a sluggish typhoid incubator. When Carruthers arrived it had been for years a fairly inoffensive stream steadily bubbling down from the sluices higher up the valley. But the old quarters still smell. Only the modern city centered upon the Presidential (formerly royal) Palace, the ministry of Defence, the police barracks and the Chamber of Deputies enjoys the privilege of main drainage. In the modern city, too, are the apartments and offices of the great Ixanian middle business class of traders and commission men as well as the town houses of the landed families (tobacco, essential perfume oils, wolfram mines) and the old nobility, those, according to Groom, who counted. The Ixanian peasant is no lazier and no more lacking in moral fibre than his counterpart in other countries. He has, in addition, the ability to cultivate from the hides of his beloved hogs some of the finest brush bristles in the world, and, until recently, a major business in Zovgorod was the provision of a buying, selling and distribution service of unrivalled dishonesty, rapacity and inefficiency to handle these and other products of the peasants' industry. Every young Zovgorodian aspired to be a business man. That is, unless he belonged to the officer caste. In that case too, the peasants supported him; but through the more formal machinery of taxation.

All this and more Carruthers had learned from occasional conversations at mealtimes with Groom. At other times he saw little of him.

They had taken rooms at the Hotel Europa. As Groom pointed out, almost its only advantage was that it was situated in the centre of the city and was therefore readily accessible. Groom occupied the Royal suite; so called, it seemed, because it included a sitting-room. Carruthers had an adjoining bedroom along the corridor and the luxury of a bathroom.

Soon after they arrived Groom had intimated that it would be unlikely that the services of his technical adviser would be required for the moment and that Carruthers might consider his time his own.

As far as Carruthers could see, Groom spent most of his time receiving an assortment of furtive-looking visitors in his sitting-room. These he presumed were Groom's agents in Zovgorod. From their purposeful looks as they left the Royal suite, he concluded that Groom was making generous promises.

For his own part, he decided that he could not do better than sustain his role of amateur photographer. Camera in hand, therefore, he wandered about the city taking an occasional photograph. Much of his time he spent in the Kudbek, the main street of the city, sitting at a café and attempting to decipher, with the help of an Ixanian-

French dictionary he had bought, Zovgorod's leading newspaper. He was thus occupied on his fifteenth day in Zovgorod when an incident occurred which was to have an important sequel.

The Kudbek, so called because it contains a small bridge across the Kuder, is one of two or three wide thoroughfares in the city. Most of the buildings in it are offices, with cafés and shops below them. The Chamber of Deputies scars the horizon at one end; facing it at the other is the Presidential Palace. Carruthers was sitting at a café near the Chamber of Deputies end. He was in a despondent mood. He had discovered nothing of value and had no prospect of doing so. He seemed as far away from accomplishing his purpose as when he boarded the ferry at Southampton. The significant happenings, the coincidental encounters, the fortuitously overheard plans that had always kept Conway Carruthers active before, were unaccountably absent. The incident in Bâle had certainly seemed true to form: but what was it? Nothing but a furtive meeting between a business man and a corrupt official. True, there had been a second watcher and the corrupt official had been murdered, but it was all so logical. Everybody connected with the business seemed to be behaving with such baffling directness and practicality. There was no cunning with which to grapple. He could not even listen to Groom's conversations with his agents; there was no connecting balcony between the windows. He had no more idea of where Kassen and his laboratory were than when he started. If he knew even that, at least it would be something to work on.

He sighed and looked out across the wide pavements of the Kudbek. There were the usual chattering passers-by, the usual green-uniformed police, the usual seller of lottery tickets. Then his eye was caught by the more unusual sight of an Ixanian farm cart ambling slowly along the tram-lines.

It was a two-wheeled vehicle, its contents completely shrouded by a large tarpaulin. The driver was slouched over the reins sucking a straw. Slowly it drew across the road until its wheels obstructed both tram tracks.

Two trams were coming in opposite directions. The drivers of both trams rang their bells. The cart stopped. The trams slowed down, their drivers shouting. The driver of the cart seemed to be asleep. The trams pulled up with a squeal of brakes.

Suddenly, the tarpaulin was thrown back. Two youths sprang from under it. Shouting defiantly, they gathered up bundles of leaflets from the floor of the cart and began to scatter them wildly in the air. Borne by a slight breeze, the leaflets fluttered about in all directions until the street was littered with them. Carruthers secured one that alighted near him.

Pandemonium broke loose. The whistles of the police and the aimless shouting of the crowd which immediately gathered were punctuated by the cries of the young men in the cart and the angry ringing of the tram bells.

With equal suddenness it all ceased. A squad of police at the run with revolvers drawn dispersed the terrified crowd, while others dragged the agitators, still shouting, from the cart. One who resisted was ruthlessly clubbed. All three were removed in a hastily commandeered private car.

Carruthers looked at the leaflet he held. It was in Ixanian. He managed, after a little difficulty, to translate.

It was, he gathered, a manifesto from a body calling itself the Young Peasants' Party, exhorting the people of

Ixania, a trifle vaguely, to take "action." What the contemplated action comprised and what it would accomplish were left apparently to the imagination and personal taste of the recipient. The Young Peasants' Party, Carruthers opined, was all things to all men.

He was contemplating the effusion with some amusement when a voice behind him said "Pardon me." He turned. It was his American acquaintance of the train.

Carruthers greeted him with some restraint. He had not forgotten the other's curious behaviour on the train. The American drew his chair up to Carruthers' table and smiled disarmingly.

"I guess I owe you an apology, Professor," he said gracefully.

Carruthers raised his eyebrows.

"You see," explained the other, "my name's Casey—Bill Casey of the *Tribune*."

"How do you do, Mr. Casey," said Carruthers politely. Casey looked crestfallen. "Never heard of me, I guess. You see, Professor, when we got talking on the train and you started asking about Zovgorod, I was thinking you might be a British newspaper man."

Carruthers smiled.

"I gather that you have taken steps to find out that I am not."

"Sure, it cost me a quarter at the Europa."

"I always thought that newspaper men had a sort of Freemasonry of their own."

"Oh, we get together as a rule. But this time it's a bit different. Somebody got a hunch that a big story was due to break in Zovgorod pretty soon. That's why I'm here. And that's why I'm not particularly anxious to have any more of the boys around."

Carruthers was thinking hard. He would not give himself away a second time. He leant back in his chair and nodded amiably.

"Very nice of you to mention the matter at all," he said.

Casey was clearly hoping for a more interested reception of his information.

"Have a drink," he invited.

Carruthers accepted. The drinks were ordered. There was a pause.

"Curious about that guy on the train," said Casey chattily. "Who was he, do you know? The one who got shot?"

"His name was . . ." Carruthers broke off and shrugged. "I've forgotten," he said.

Casey glanced at him for a moment.

"They didn't publish it," he said briefly.

Carruthers was silent. Casey lit a cigarette. He went on as though Carruthers had volunteered a relevant comment on the subject.

"Any idea why they bumped him off?"

"None at all, Mr. Casey; have you?"

"Yes," said Casey.

"You ought to tell the police."

The drinks arrived. Casey raised his glass.

"Well, here's to Ixania." He looked up from his glass. "Do you know the Countess Schverzinski?"

Carruthers sipped his drink.

"Never heard of the lady."

"You were talking to her soon after you left Paris."

"Really? It's amazing the curious people one meets in trains."

Casey grinned.

"OK, you win, Professor." He leant across the table.

"I suppose," he said earnestly, "you wouldn't care to make a statement."

Carruthers looked mystified.

"What about?"

Casey ignored the question.

"Naturally," he went on persuasively, "I wouldn't use it until I had your OK."

"I can't imagine . . ."

"Sure, I know," interrupted Casey grimly; "you're just here on holiday taking snapshots."

"Exactly," said Carruthers.

"Now, now, Professor," said the *Tribune* man reproachfully, "no kidding. Listen. Someone gets a hunch that there's going to be trouble in this part of the world. Fine! *Tribune*'s ace foreign correspondent dashes to scene of impending trouble. What does he find? Exhibit A: member-of-Ixanian-Government Rovzidski rubbed out by Red Gauntlet mob three hours after arrival in country of his fathers. Exhibit B: Ixanian Government fail to take action against slayers and killing reported as accidental in Ixanian press. Exhibit C: bird named Groom, big shot munition boss, receiving local gunmen in hotel apartment. Exhibit D: well-known and respected scientist in retinue of said big shot, doing . . . doing what?"

"Is that all you know, Mr. Casey?" said Carruthers, amused.

"No," said Casey promptly.

Affecting to consider this intelligence, Carruthers was silent for a moment or two. Casey clearly possessed information that would be useful to him. He must not miss the opportunity of getting it.

"Have another drink, Mr. Casey," he said.

Casey accepted with an expectant air. Carruthers lit his pipe.

"Now, Mr. Casey," he said heavily, "what do you want to know?"

The other leant forward again.

"Firstly," he said briskly, "why was Rovzidski killed? Secondly, what are Cator & Bliss after in Zovgorod?"

Carruthers examined the bowl of his pipe. He prepared to lie convincingly.

"I can't answer your first question, Mr. Casey, because I don't know. I can answer the second, though in absolute confidence. I warn you, if you publish this information it will be denied."

"OK, shoot," said Casey.

"Cator & Bliss are selling field guns to the Ixanian Government. I am here as consultant on questions of ballistics."

Casey's eyes hardened. Slowly he put his hand in his pocket and produced a bundle of papers. He singled out one.

"Your record, Professor," he explained curtly. "New York cabled it to me a week ago." He started to read: "Henry Barstow, Fellow of the Royal Society, Doctor of Science, etcetera, etcetera, what's all this? University of so-and-so Chair of Physics: Fellow of Royal Society, 1925: ah! here we are: publications: *An Examination of the Atomic Theory, Collected Papers on the Lorentz Transformations, An Examination of Einstein Dynamics,* author of essay on 'Atoms, structure of,' in *Encyclopaedia Universalia,* new edition. Well, well, well! nothing about ballistics here, Professor."

Carruthers laughed, not very comfortably.

"You're a very thorough man, Mr. Casey."

"Thorough enough to know, Professor, that Cator &

Bliss's ballistics technician is Major-General Lanceley-Pinton. He used to be in the British army."

"Interesting, Mr. Casey, but I fail to see . . ."

"And the Ixanian Government aren't buying field guns. They placed an order with Skoda three months ago." He rose to his feet. "I'll be seeing you, Professor," he said, and was gone.

Carruthers looked after him down the street with mixed feelings. True, he was now free of Casey's questioning, but, equally, he had failed to get the information he sought. Besides, his estimate of Casey had convinced him of one thing; that the *Tribune*'s foreign correspondent would not be content to abandon the Professor altogether as a possible source of information. He might even discover his, Carruthers', impersonation and use the threat of exposure as a lever to secure the story he sought. There was only one aspect of the interview that gave him the least cause for satisfaction. Groom's boast that he was unknown to the press of the world was, to say the least of it, an exaggeration.

The gentleman in question was already at dinner when Carruthers returned to the hotel. He appeared less preoccupied and a trifle more self-satisfied than at any other time since Rovzidski's murder. Carruthers seized the opportunity to inquire after his progress.

Groom did not resent the question. "I can understand your impatience, Professor. Zovgorod is not an entertaining city. I think I can promise you that I shall soon be in a position to enlist your help. I am in touch with the right people. I shall know within two or three days whether my efforts have been successful or not."

He hailed with unqualified approval the arrival of the *wiener schnitzel* he had ordered.

"At any rate, Professor," he said, selecting the German mustard from the tray of condiments held before him, "they do know how *wiener schnitzel* should be cooked. Just a few more capers and thirty seconds less in the oil and it would be perfect. A German cook, thank heaven. Whoever originated the notion that French chefs were the best in the world didn't know good German cooking."

He returned reverently to his food. Carruthers ordered a *tyroler rostbraten* and did some quick thinking.

That Groom was in touch with "the right people" probably meant that he had managed to reach someone able and willing, as Rovzidski had been, to surrender vital information in return for a substantial bribe. The implications of this possibility depressed him. Obviously, if so many people were in the position of knowing enough for Groom's purpose, his own difficulties were enormously increased. It would be harder than ever to prevent manufacture of the Kassen explosive permanently. He could probably hinder Groom's plans by pretending that any account of the process submitted for his inspection was worthless, but that was only playing for time. It accomplished nothing definite. His thoughts revolved round the problem again and again without reaching any conclusion.

Groom laid down his knife and fork with a sigh of satisfaction.

"You may or may not know," he said, "that Zovgorod boasts an Opera House. Tonight they are doing *The Magic Flute*. I have told the head waiter to get me two seats. If you are fond of Mozart you might care to join me. I asked for grand tier stalls. Dress is not necessary."

Carruthers accepted with alacrity. Half an hour later they stepped into a taxi.

They were about to move off when Groom suddenly

ordered the driver to wait. He turned to Carruthers apologetically.

"You will excuse the delay, Professor, but I don't want to lose our bodyguard."

With a chuckle he drew Carruthers' attention to two men on the pavement a few yards from them. They were gesticulating wildly to a passing taxi.

Carruthers turned to him.

"Cator & Bliss?" he inquired facetiously.

"No, our friend the Countess," said Groom solemnly. "She is taking no chances, you will observe."

Seeing that the "bodyguard" had secured the taxi, he nodded to the driver. They drove off.

The first act was nearly over when they arrived at the Opera House. In the interval, his companion drew Carruthers' attention to the Countess Schverzinski sitting in a box with a man wearing formal evening dress and a sash of office. Carruthers watched her, fascinated by her beauty and the ease of her manner, as she received visitors to her box. He found it painfully difficult to identify her, however indirectly, with the murder of Rovzidski.

Her companion in the box was, he was told, her brother Prince Ladislaus. A benevolent old gentleman with a single order on his shirt-front in the next box kissed her hand over the intervening ledge. Groom whispered that it was the President. Carruthers noted the arms of Ixania on the front of his box. An insignificant little man with a monocle was pointed out as the Minister of the Interior. He was, Groom explained, the son of a café proprietor, a fact which accounted, no doubt, for his assumption of a monocle, the symbol of military caste.

The roar of conversation died away as the lights

dimmed. The leader of the orchestra raised his bâton. There was silence. Then Mozart began again.

It was music that was to remain with Carruthers for many days afterwards; flowing through his mind, a constant soft-voiced obbligato to the thoughts that crowded there; gently guiding and directing them as the banks of a river guide and direct the swollen stream that rushes between them to the sea. When it was finished he sat through the wild applause that broke out in silence. A sudden calm confidence seemed to fill him. It was as though he had been granted a new lease on life. But somewhere in his brain words were forming. They took shape for a moment and faded; but in that moment he saw a semblance of the truth. For he saw that the days of the man who called himself Conway Carruthers were numbered and that he was soon to die. Under his breath he whispered urgently to himself, "I must hurry."

The company crowded on to the stage to take their final curtain. More bouquets were handed up to them. The applause was subsiding. A few *"Bravas"* still hung in the air. The orchestra leader raised his bâton. The drums rolled. The audience rose to its feet. The first triumphant chord of the Ixanian National Anthem shattered the silence. At that moment, every light in the Opera House flickered once and went out.

8

MAY 9th

Carruthers was awake early the following morning. As he lay in bed contemplating the sunlight already pouring through his window, the incident at the theatre was still impressed upon his mind. The picture of Groom fighting madly for the exit, the terrified faces, the vision of all he had seen in a few seconds by the light of a hastily struck match, floated before his eyes. Yet it was now not so much the panic itself that occupied his thoughts as the cause of it all, the electricity failure. That sudden flicker before the light went out was curious. It suggested a gradual overload rather than a sudden power surge.

He pressed the bell for the Swiss waiter, ordered breakfast and then called the man back as he was going.

"You heard about the electricity failure at the Opera House last night?"

"But yes, Monsieur, terrible."

"Has it happened before?" he asked. "Except in bad storms, I mean. Do you have many power failures?"

"No, Monsieur, I remember only one before. But that was in the night. I could not sleep and switched on the light to read. It went out for about ten minutes only. The electricity is very reliable here. It is in charge of Swiss engineers."

"When was that?"

"About two months ago, Monsieur. I remember well. My wife was having a baby."

Carruthers was thoughtful. The waiter hastened to reassure him.

"There is no cause for alarm, Monsieur. It will not happen again." He went on at length. Doubtless, if it had not been for Ixanian stupidity there would be no breakdown at all. Swiss engineers were of the finest. But these pigs of Ixanians . . .

Suddenly Carruthers had an idea, a strange idea. Waving the waiter away he leapt out of bed and hurried into the bathroom.

By the time his breakfast had arrived he was half-dressed. In ten minutes he had finished both his breakfast and his dressing.

Stuffing his wallet into his pocket, his fingers encountered a piece of paper. He drew it out. It was the Young Peasants' Party's "manifesto." Without thinking, he returned it hastily to his pocket and left the hotel.

His first thought was for a newspaper.

The electricity failure of the night before was mentioned in a few lines chiefly taken up by the names of the distinguished persons who had experienced what was described, a trifle extravagantly, as "the Y.P.P. outrage." But it told him what he wanted to know.

He hailed a taxi and told the man to take him to the National Library. There he asked for the *Encyclopaedia Universalia*. The library was able to produce it and, moreover, in an English edition. The brief biography of Professor Barstow that Casey had quoted so ironically in the café, told him where to look. He turned to "Atoms, Structure of."

It was a long article occupying nearly three columns in the *Encyclopaedia*'s six-point type. He read it through carefully. He found it surprisingly easy to understand and was soon in possession of the information he sought. There, in Professor Barstow's careful prose, were the sentences that instinctively he had known he would find:

It has been shown that this change in atomic structure can be effected under these given conditions. In an experiment carried out recently, a charge with a pressure of one and a half million volts was built up in a succession of specially designed oil dielectric condensers. Ionisation of the air in the vicinity of the electrodes took place at a comparatively low potential and difficulty was experienced in . . .

Carruthers shut the book and left the library.

His next step was to buy a panorama map of Zovgorod and the surrounding country. Armed with this he retired to a public garden and found a quiet seat. As he did so, he noticed a man whose face seemed vaguely familiar, seated a short way away. Then he remembered. It was one of the men whom Groom had pointed out the previous evening; one of the "bodyguard." Obviously, this man had been set to watch him alone. His colleague was Groom's shadow. He, Carruthers, must have had his movements followed for the past fortnight; stupid of him not to have noticed it before. He dismissed the matter from his mind for the time being and opened his map.

His objective was the electricity distribution station at Zovgorod. He quickly found it on the map. It was on the outskirts of the city on the north-east side. He sat back and thought.

Zovgorod, like most other towns, would be fed with electricity distributed from the central station by means of several subsidiary mains each carrying the supply for a different quarter of the city. Each subsidiary would carry its own system of fuses and "breakers" to deal with short circuits, overloads or surges. It was thus obvious that an overload such as might well result from anyone utilising the process referred to by Professor Barstow in the *Encyclopaedia,* would, if applied anywhere inside the city, cause an electricity breakdown only in the quarter served by the subsidiary main in question. Now the Opera House and the Hotel Europa were set far apart on the map. With the evidence of the newspaper, which reported a failure throughout the city, plus that of the Swiss waiter at the hotel, he concluded that Zovgorod's electricity failures were not confined to any particular quarter.

From this it followed that the source of the overloads must lie between the Zovgorod distribution station and the hydro-electric power station at the dam higher up the valley. Once locate that source and the chances were that Kassen's laboratory would be found. The times of the failures were suggestive in themselves. In the case of the waiter it had been in the early hours of the morning; in the case of the Opera it had been close on midnight. Both were times when the city's electricity requirements were small; times, therefore, most likely to be chosen by Kassen for his experiments.

He considered his plan of action.

The power from the dam would almost certainly be carried down into Zovgorod by means of overhead lines. Somewhere along those lines there must be a branch main to the laboratory. The lines would lead him to it. He would start at the distribution station.

The first thing, however, was to get rid of the man following him. He glanced at his map again, then rose and left the gardens. A quick glance as he stopped to light his pipe told him that the Countess's agent was about twenty yards behind him.

Walking leisurely, he turned towards the Kudbek and, hailing a taxi, told the man to drive to the Greek Church which the map had shown at the opposite end of the city to the electricity station. Out of the corner of his eye he noted that the agent had also found a taxi.

As they bowled along the Kudbek, Carruthers looked through the small window at the back of the cab at the taxi behind him. The agent, evidently bored by a fortnight's uneventful pottering, was lounging back, leaving it to his driver to keep Carruthers' taxi in sight. Carruthers, too, sat back and awaited his opportunity.

They turned out of the Kudbek into the tangle of side streets south of the Palace. Choosing a moment when his taxi was nosing its way between a thronged pavement and a stationary cart facing in the opposite direction, Carruthers softly unlatched the left-hand door and, tossing a note for the fare on the seat, slipped out into the roadway behind the cart, gently shutting the door of the taxi again as it left him behind.

It was all over in a few seconds. Mingling with the crowd he saw the unwary agent driving away towards the Greek Church. Carruthers himself was soon back in the Kudbek where he chartered another taxi, this time to take him to the distribution station. He paid the taxi off at the end of the road in which it stood and walked down.

Zovgorod, like many other European cities, still retains

the sharp line of demarcation between town and country which is the legacy of the walled-city period. The road to the distribution station started in the city and went out over a hill among fields. The station itself, a box-like concrete building, lay some way back from the road. A spiked fence surrounded it, but Carruthers could see enough. Through the windows he made out the outlines of two large oil-cooled transformers. It was, as he had thought, only a distribution plant. On the far side, supported by a large steel structure, were the insulators and oil-immersed switch-gear for the main power intake from the overhead lines. He moved a little higher up the hill and was rewarded by the sight of a long procession of pylons striding away up the side of the valley until the curve hid them.

He looked about him.

High above the grassland and the dark green patches of fir woods rose massive snow-capped peaks that cast long shadows down the sunlit slopes below them. Here and there he could discern shepherds' huts, their flaked stone walls almost invisible against the grey-brown hills from which they had been quarried, and mountain streams looking like white smudges as they rushed down to the river. But he had no time to contemplate the grandeur of the Kuder valley; he must follow the pylons.

He turned and went back into the town. It was then about eleven o'clock. He would need food on his journey. He bought some provisions and a bottle of red wine and set out.

For the first hour he kept to the road which ran along the bottom of the valley by the river and for some distance along which he could keep the pylons well in view. The valley wound in a series of S bends. The power lines, taking the shortest practicable route from one end of each S to the other, crossed and recrossed the valley, alternately rising five hundred feet or more up the hillside and descending almost to river-level. If the sides of the valley had been regular and the path of the pylons had been consistent, he could have followed them entirely from the road; but soon a huge buttress of rock obtruding into the valley deflected the lines which took a sharp turn upwards and disappeared behind a belt of firs.

Carruthers halted and surveyed the side of the valley. About a hundred yards farther on there was a path leading up. He walked towards it. It was a rough track about eighteen inches wide and obviously very little used; but it led in the right direction and he began to climb.

Tweeds, he soon found, are not in warm weather the ideal clothes for mountain climbing, for that was what his progress soon became. The track grew almost precipitous and he was still further hindered by the loose surface and his package of food and wine. He had been climbing for half an hour when he stopped, ate his lunch, drank his wine and smoked a pipe. Some forty minutes later, much refreshed and free of encumbrance, he continued the ascent in better style. By the time he reached the belt of firs it was afternoon. His footsteps on the stones sent lizards, basking on the sun-drenched rocks, scuttling away in staccato terror. There was no other sound but the soft chirping of grasshoppers and the monotonous drone of a cicada some distance away.

He rounded the trees close to a pylon, strengthened and guyed to take the double pull sideways caused by the left-hand turn of the lines. From where he stood he could see the lines where they ran horizontally for about a mile along a ridge. Thankful that he could once more take up the chase on level ground, he went forward.

His way lay for the most part through clearings which had been made through the trees, and only occasionally did he catch glimpses of the valley below. He covered the distance rapidly. At the end of the ridge the lines dipped away to the right, out of sight again from where he stood. He walked straight on a little way to a promontory from which he could take his bearings.

It was an awe-inspiring sight that met his eyes. He had climbed higher than he had supposed and the valley lay before him like a map. To the right he could see the pylons leaving the trees about half a mile away. He traced them down and up the other side of the valley where they disappeared once more into the middle distance. Then, far away before him where the valley narrowed into a gorge, he saw the dam, a wedge-shaped gash of white against the dark rock background. To the left of it, perched precariously at the foot of a mass of rock towering above it, was a cluster of buildings which, Carruthers guessed, housed the turbines and generators that supplied Zovgorod with electricity.

So far, although he had scrutinised every yard of the overhead lines carefully, he had failed to detect any branch connection. If there was such a connection it must be made at a point on the line in the hidden part of it to the right of him or in that on the opposite side of the valley near the power station. That Kassen's laboratory was actually at the power station or on the farthest side of the dam, he thought unlikely. At the power station, Kassen would lack the privacy necessary for his experiments; to erect special power lines for the sole purpose of carrying electricity to a laboratory on the shores of the lake beyond would be a very costly business. No! His objective was in the valley somewhere.

He retraced his steps to the point at which he had left the lines and followed them on down a gradual slope. On his right, the great firs towered against the sky. On his left, they grew from roots so far below him that his eyes were level with their foliage. A rough path, probably worn by the foresters who kept the way cleared for the lines, made it easy going for a time. Then, once again, the track ended, the lines bore to the left and he was forced to negotiate what appeared to be a disused stone quarry. To do this he had to make his way down along the edge of the quarry to where it was shallow enough for him to cross the bottom which was about a hundred yards wide. Once across, however, he had not far to climb up to where the lines, considerably lower down the hillside than before, were descending to cross the valley. There remained only a thick clump of trees between him and the end of that unexplored section of the lines. He was already resigning himself to returning on the following day to explore the last section of lines on the power station side of the valley when he saw the gleam of insulators through the trees ahead of him and knew that his search was ended.

He went forward cautiously to the foot of the tall pylon. Beside it stood a short steel gantry carrying two huge steatite insulators to take the strain of the heavy covered cables which led, almost at right angles to the power station lines, straight down the hillside through a copse.

He moved slowly in their wake. They did not go far. Almost before he noticed it he had come to the edge of a deep gully which the trees had masked. He looked over the edge. There, below him, hidden from curious eyes on every side, was a brick building into one end of which the branch power cables disappeared.

It was an oddly shaped structure. At one end rose a large square tower. This was about eighty feet high, but the size of its plan gave it a squat appearance. A single long window in the side showed that, in spite of its height, it had no floors. It was into the tower that the cables led. He guessed its purpose. He had seen such buildings before. It was a High-Tension laboratory.

From where he stood no entrance to it was visible. It was doubtless entered from the long, low, glass-roofed building that abutted upon it. One thing puzzled him. On the roof of the tower was a searchlight encased in tarpaulin. He decided to take a closer look at the laboratory.

To his left, the lip of the gully ran sharply downwards. He worked his way down carefully. Once, he dislodged a large stone which clattered down into the gully with a terrifying noise; but it drew no response from the occupants of the laboratory buildings, and after waiting for a minute or two he went on. Soon he was on a level with the laboratory. He could see the top of it over the heads of some young rowans which grew in a large clump at the foot of the gully. He gently pushed his way through them for about a dozen yards. Then he stopped. Barring his way was a wire fence.

It was not the fence that made him pause; he could have squeezed through it easily enough; it was the sight of a dead owl suspended between two of the wires. A few feet away there was a post supporting the wires. He examined it closely. The fence was an electric one. Anyone coming into contact with it while the current was on would be instantly electrocuted.

Retreating behind the screen formed by the rowans, he

considered this new obstacle. The owl had obviously been dead some hours, probably since the previous night, for owls rarely flew during the day. It was doubtful if the current was switched on unless there were experiments in progress. He would have to find out for certain.

He took off his watch chain and, attaching it to the end of a twig, went back to the fence. If the fence were alive, the metal chain held across adjacent wires would short-circuit the current and cause a tell-tale flash. It was likely, too, that it would also sound an alarm bell, but that he had anticipated and decided to risk. He brought the chain into contact with the wires, but nothing happened. The current was off. A moment later he was inside the fence and in the shelter of some bushes.

By taking a rather circuitous path, he found that he could approach the lower building without breaking cover. This he did and was soon in the shadow of the end wall. He moved slowly along to the corner and peered round. About twelve feet away was a window. Once out of the cover of the bushes he stood a fair chance of discovery. In that unhappy event, he would not improve his chances of avoiding Rovzidski's fate by being found behaving furtively. Making as little sound as possible, he strolled, hands in pockets, round the corner of the house and glanced through the window.

Inside was a laboratory. It ran almost the entire length of the building. At the far end was a door which, he guessed, connected through another room with the High-Tension laboratory.

The room into which he was looking presented a curious problem. At one end was a small ore crusher, such as is used in metallurgy, and a cathode ray oscillograph. One corner was decorated with all the paraphernalia of the analytical chemist and, inexplicably, a small hydraulic press with a circular ram. A small treadle lathe completed the equipment of this strange room.

He was moving on to find some way of inspecting the High-Tension building when he heard the unexpected sound of a car approaching in low gear from the valley below. Then he remembered the disused quarry. There would be a road leading up to it that could be used for approaching the laboratory. The car stopped. He returned to the end window and, flattening himself against the wall, waited.

Soon an electric bell pealed. Through the window he saw a man in dungarees come through the door at the far end and exit through another door almost opposite to him. A moment or two later the man in dungarees returned, holding the door open for a woman who swept in past him. Carruthers drew back before he had had time to see the newcomer's face, but he had guessed that it was the Countess Schverzinski.

He heard her address a few imperious words to the man in dungarees, who went back into the room from which he had come. A few seconds later another man entered. Carruthers heard him exchange what sounded like a greeting with the Countess. His voice had a curiously vibrant tone which made even the ugly Ixanian gutturals sound liquid. Carruthers moved his head slightly and the owner of the voice came into view.

He was a short, narrow-shouldered little man, with a large brachycephalic head sparsely covered with straight black hair. His mouth was twisted as though he were perpetually on the point of ridding himself of a bad taste. He wore a white dust coat. This man, Carruthers concluded, must be Kassen.

To his great relief the Countess broke into French, obviously to render her words unintelligible to the man in dungarees who stood at the door. The man went out leaving the door ajar.

"You must be more careful," she was saying; "if the lights had failed during the performance it might have been really serious. As it is, there were three women injured in the panic and the President has announced that he will make inquiries."

"That imbecile!"

"My dear Jacob," said the Countess coldly, "if I didn't know that, outside your work, you were a fool I should be angry with you. I could if necessary persuade the President that an investigation would be unwelcome, but it would immediately make him curious. The less mystery there is, the greater the secrecy."

"But what can I do?" retorted the other angrily. "Between one A.M. and five A.M.! Four hours out of every twenty-four! What's the use of that to me? Already it has lost us months."

"It cannot be helped. We are all impatient, but you must do the best you can. Remember, Jacob, this is an order. You must not use the power before one o'clock in the morning. Last night it was a quarter to twelve. What happened?"

The Countess was very domineering. Kassen answered sulkily.

"You treat me as if I were a child, Magda. I could not help it. Things were going well. I did not think of the time. It was only when Kortner telephoned from the power station in a panic that I realised that it was early."

The Countess seemed mollified. She said something in a

low tone which Carruthers missed. Kassen laughed shortly.

"And now, my friend," he heard her say, "tell me your news."

"The affair marches," answered Kassen; "the consignment of ore from the old Grad mine was much better; it has less lead in it. How many tons have they brought up?"

"About eighty. But there is more lower down the seam if you need it. I hope not. There has already been a lot of talk about it in the village and there are rumours about that we are going to smelt lead there again."

"Dear lady," said Kassen blandly, "eighty tons will make enough magdanite to blow up Europe."

"What do you mean, magdanite?"

Kassen laughed softly.

"My new name for our little secret. In honour of you. Of course, you guessed that. Your name, Magda, will go round the world linked with mine. It is so appropriate. Power and beauty go hand in hand. Magdanite shall be their envoy. It is exquisitely appropriate, Magda. My brains contribute to your beauty. Tell me, Magda, what will beauty give in return?"

His voice had grown husky. Carruthers heard a quick movement. There was a pause.

"You are foolish," she said, but there was pity in her voice; "let me go, Jacob."

She was silent for a moment, then she went on: "As for this name of yours, I do not like it. This stuff you have made is but the means to an end. It will be a bloody means and it disgusts me."

There was a sneer in Kassen's voice.

"And yet you will not hesitate to use it, Countess?"

"No."

"And Colonel Marassin, does he share your disgust?"

"Colonel Marassin is a soldier. His enthusiasm is academic."

"And yours, beloved Magda, is the sentimentality of the patriot."

"No, Jacob, the impersonality of the surgeon. But I did not come here to argue with you. I want to know how soon it will be ready."

"Nothing can be done until the mixers arrive. There is no hitch I hope."

"None. Rovzidski did that part of his work satisfactorily. The credits were arranged this week. But I want as little experimenting as possible. The presence of this man Barstow with the Cator & Bliss man makes me uneasy."

"They can do harm?" Kassen spoke anxiously.

"No, I think not. They are being watched constantly. Without Rovzidski they are powerless. There is no one but you or me from whom they could get their information."

"The man Barstow is a fool, but he has been working in his lame dog way along the same lines as myself. A glance at the manufacturing instructions for the conditioning process would be all he needed. You are sure Rovzidski's copy has been destroyed?"

"You need have no fear. Colonel Marassin searched Rovzidski's papers himself."

"Then why do they remain here?"

"This Groom is very tenacious. He has many agents in Zovgorod. They report to him every day. He seems to be trying to bribe one of the President's staff, a man named Prantza. I employed him for a time as a secretary."

"Who is he?"

"He knows nothing. I am allowing the affair to go on. If it will keep Groom busy pursuing shadows, I am content."

"How shall we replace Rovzidski?"

"For the moment it is unnecessary to replace him. The factory is ready. When the machinery arrives from England we will consider the question. I have been thinking that Kortner might be removed from the power station when the time comes. He is, I believe, a capable engineer."

"But can we trust him? I tell you, since the Rovzidski affair, I am uneasy."

"Colonel Marassin will look after Kortner. A word to the police in Berlin and it would be all up with him. As for your unhappiness, my friend, forget it and think of Bonn and Chicago."

Kassen laughed. It was an unpleasant sound.

They had lapsed into Ixanian again. Carruthers waited for a moment, then, deciding that there was nothing more to be learnt there, silently worked his way back to the shelter of the bushes.

He had a lot to think about. The disquieting Colonel Marassin was obviously the man responsible for Rovzidski's death and probably a prime mover in the Red Gauntlet Society of which Groom had spoken. There were other things, too: the mention of the factory, the news that only two persons now held the Kassen secret, the possibility that Groom was doomed to failure. At last he had something to work on.

He arrived back at the fence and squeezed through it again without mishap. He dare not risk being seen on the valley road by the Countess returning to Zovgorod and started to climb back the way he had come.

He had gone about six paces when he heard a rustle ahead. It might be a bird starting up, but he was taking no chances. He stopped, then, bending double to move clear of the tell-tale leaves, he crept forward, using the loose stones that lay about to steady himself. He heard the rustle of the descending blow just in time. With a quick movement he turned. His assailant was caught off balance. Carruthers straightened as his arm shot out. The man crashed into a bush and was still.

Carruthers looked at the stone that he still grasped. There would be no more trouble from the unknown yet awhile.

His first instinct was to run. But the noise of loose stones falling might betray him where the noise already made might pass unnoticed. Also, he wanted to see who the attacker was. He stayed absolutely still. There was no sign from the laboratory. He parted the leaves and looked through.

There, spread-eagled in the undergrowth, a thin trickle of blood oozing from a cut on his forehead, lay Casey, the representative of the *Tribune*.

9

MAY 9th AND 10th

Carruthers looked down at the unfortunate Casey in some confusion. What was he doing there? Was he acting for the Countess? Was he the representative of another armament manufacturer? Or was he merely a go-ahead young newspaper man after a story? It was, to be sure, unlikely that he was working for the Countess. He would certainly have raised the alarm if that had been the case. But he might well be either of the other two alternatives. But which? If he were the former, it were wiser to know him for an enemy; if he were really a *Tribune* man, then he might prove a useful ally.

Carruthers hoisted him carefully out of the undergrowth and laid him down on level ground. His pulse was almost normal. His eyes showed that the concussion was not serious. There was no water within easy reach, but the cut was not bleeding badly. Carruthers sat down to wait. It was not long before Casey's breathing became stertorous and his eyes opened.

He looked at Carruthers and then as memory returned to him he tried to rise. Carruthers motioned him to be silent and pressed him back. Then, leaning down, he whispered:

"Don't talk or they'll hear. Wait until you're feeling better and then we'll move."

Casey closed his eyes again. It was half an hour by Carruthers' watch and days in his thoughts before Casey raised himself painfully on his arm and whispered that he was "OK."

Carruthers led the way back to the top of the quarry. Casey was still dizzy and had to be helped part of the way, but once on the path they were able to travel fairly quickly. Carruthers remembered a stream he had crossed on the ridge and mentioned the fact to Casey. Otherwise, they plodded up in silence.

It was not until Casey had bathed his head and they had both drunk from the stream that the silence was broken. Producing a crushed packet of Lucky Strike, Casey offered them to Carruthers. The latter, however, produced his pipe. They both lit up.

"Well, Professor," said Casey thoughtfully, "I guess there ought to be a bit of explaining."

Carruthers nodded.

"Yes, but not now. Before we go any further, though, perhaps you'll tell me why you tried to hit me."

"I thought you were one of the inmates of that place come out to take a poke at me. I wanted to get mine in first."

"I had the same ideas about you," admitted Carruthers.

"Say, Professor, do you know what that place is?"

Carruthers thought for a moment before replying non-committally, "We'll talk about that later."

"OK. Let's go."

As they emerged from the belt of trees which had been

Carruthers' first objective, he pointed to the valley below. A car was bumping along the road back into Zovgorod.

"All clear now," he said, and started the climb down.

"The Countess?"

Carruthers nodded.

It was dark when they reached the outskirts of the city. They found a taxi and drove immediately to a restaurant, for they were both ravenously hungry.

By mutual consent, they postponed conversation until the more pressing need of food was satisfied. Then, lighting a cigarette, Casey leant back in his chair.

"Well, Professor, what about it?"

Carruthers, busying himself with his pipe, did not look up as he answered.

"You know, Mr. Casey, I've been thinking that in discussing this matter with you I may be committing a very unfortunate indiscretion. Unfortunate for me, I mean, and my particular interests."

Casey nodded.

"I see what you mean, Professor. You'd like to know just who this Casey is and what he wants before you talk."

"That," admitted Carruthers, "is my feeling. Foolish perhaps, but understandable, I think."

"That's all right, Professor. I'll give an account of myself. Before I do, though, there's just one question I want to ask you."

"Go ahead."

"These interests of yours, Professor. I suppose they wouldn't, by any chance, be identical with those of Messrs. Cator & Bliss?"

"No, Mr. Casey, strange as it may seem, they are not."

"Fine," said Casey. "Now we know where we are."

He fished about in his pocket and produced a passport, from which he drew a small folded card.

"First," he said briskly, "there's my passport. You'll find that all in order, I think. Next, here's my press warrant from the *Tribune*. OK? Right. About three weeks ago our Bucharest correspondent reported that there was something peculiar going on in this state. Nothing definite, mind you, but a lot of small items which pieced together made up a sizable query. For instance, they had one or two almighty big explosions, big enough to make craters eighty feet across and nearly as deep in solid rock. Inquiries were made by Bucharest and they said they were blasting for stone. They picked some curiously inaccessible places to do it in. Places where there are no means of transporting stone available. Again, they've been recruiting for the army by offering increased rates of pay. They've also had some manoeuvres. There was something funny about those manoeuvres. Ixanians are generally reckoned pretty poor soldiers; but it seems that these manoeuvres were even dumber than usual. They looked fishy to the people in Bucharest. Have you ever heard of an army attacking with telephone exchanges? Well, that's what this one was doing. I know a bit about tactics and I saw their maps. Where their supporting artillery should have been they had telephone exchanges. What's more, they manoeuvred in every case for retirement. Can you explain that?"

"As a matter of fact, I think I can," said Carruthers, "but go on."

"There were one or two other things, mostly political. The general impression, however, seemed to be that little Ixania was trying to make her presence felt, that she had been manufacturing excuses to be an unfriendly neighbour, sabre-rattling in fact. There was nothing much doing in Paris so, thinking that there might be some meat here, the office sent me along to write a series about the Balkan powder keg. Well, what with one thing and another, I figured that there might be meat for more than a series. I said so and they told me to stick around for a week or two.

"The first thing that puzzled me was Rovzidski's death. The Countess Schverzinski is the government here and he was a friend of hers. She'd travelled back with him, too, I remembered that. Why was he killed? I found out that he was to have been in charge of a new factory they've built up on the shores of the lake above the dam. Nobody seemed to know what they were going to make there. My guess was that it was something to do with munitions. The arrival of Cator & Bliss in force seemed to point that way too. Were Cator & Bliss selling arms to Ixania? It cost me a bit in graft to find out, but I did find out. They weren't; nor had Ixania any intention of buying arms from them or anybody else. They had already placed an order with Skoda for routine items, as I believe I told you. I was puzzled. Particularly I was puzzled about you, Professor. You so obviously knew something, but I couldn't make out what about or why exactly you were here. I'm hoping to know before the night's out. Anyhow, I came to the conclusion that the Countess was the focal point of the whole business, so I kept my eyes on her. It's been a nice job, she's easy to look at, but I didn't find out much from that source. What I did find out was that there's a group of army officers calling itself the Red Gauntlet Society who were responsible for killing Rovzidski and a few more besides; and that there's a laboratory of sorts hidden up in that valley on the subject of which they are very touchy. I was up there today having a look for myself when you slugged me."

"Excuse my interrupting, Mr. Casey," put in Carruthers, "but I should be very interested to know just how you found that out."

"If you're thinking that I've done anything smart you're wrong," answered Casey frankly. "I had a piece of luck. Have you heard of the Young Peasants' Party?"

Carruthers thought for a moment, then searched his pockets. He found the "manifesto" and laid it before Casey.

"You mean the authors of this?"

"That's it. It's run by a bird named Andrassin. He was exiled by the old monarchist government for sedition and went to New York. I got to know him there. He had a bookshop over on the East Side. I used to buy off him sometimes. He once sold me a calf-bound copy of Florio's *Montaigne* for a nickel. He was that way if he liked you. He's a good little guy and pretty intelligent. I used to talk to him for hours. He taught me a lot one way and another and I was able to help him out over one or two things. He's a socialist and used to get very hot under the collar about the peasants' burdens. When the republic was declared he threw his hat in the air and rushed back to the fatherland. Now he says that the republic's even worse than the monarchy. To hear him talk about his fellow-countrymen you'd think that oblivion would be about the best thing for them. All the same he tries to organise them and hammer a little sense into their thick heads. They're cretins, he says, and you've got to talk to them in cretin language or they won't understand."

"Hence the quasi-religious tone of this pamphlet," inquired Carruthers.

"Ideals," said Casey, "are the principal produce of America. That's why we had to invent salesmanship and publicity. Without them we should never have been able to make the ideals racket pay. When he was in the States, Andrassin fell hard for the hot gospellers—technically, so to speak. He reckoned that they knew all there was to know about recruiting public opinion. For all that, he is, as I say, a pretty intelligent man. I ran across him soon after I arrived. He put me wise to a lot of things. He gave me all the dope on Rovzidski and the other things. But he said that there was a lot going on he didn't understand. Nothing specific, unfortunately, but his idea was that the capitalist party—he's got all the jargon—were starting something that was going to be mighty unpleasant for someone or other. He probably knows more than he'll tell even me. He says that the Young Peasants' Party will be ready when the time comes. I never heard of a political party that wasn't going to be ready when the time came. The trouble is," he concluded gloomily, "they never know the right time."

He lit another cigarette and exhaled thoughtfully for a moment; then he turned once more to Carruthers.

"I guess you're wondering," he said, "why in the world the *Tribune* is interested in Ixania's domestic affairs."

"I am," said Carruthers.

"The Ixanian Government is trying to negotiate a big loan back home. If there's a likelihood of big trouble coming here, the time to know about it is now."

"But no one, surely, would lend Ixania money?"

"You wouldn't think so, would you? But apart from the fact that bankers love to lend money they haven't got to their creditors so that the creditors can pay back what they don't really owe, Ixania has hinted that there's oil here."

"They could sell the concession."

"They could, but they won't, for the simple reason, Professor, that there isn't any oil; at least, that's my guess. They won't allow any drilling and they won't reveal just where the oil is. I suppose that their proximity to Roumania is supposed to lend colour to the idea. If there isn't any oil they must need money pretty badly to try to get away with a bluff like that. Nobody but an international banker would fall for it. Those birds don't need reasons for lending, they want excuses to do so."

"They do need money badly," said Carruthers.

"What for?"

"To make confectionery with."

Casey looked bewildered.

Carruthers leant forward.

"Large candies," he said slowly, "just a little larger than a Mills bomb; candies, Mr. Casey, that will make craters eighty feet across and nearly as deep in solid rock; candies that kill men by the hundred."

Casey frowned incredulously.

"Are you trying to tell me, Professor, that the charges that made those craters were no larger than Mills bombs?"

"Only a little larger, Mr. Casey."

Casey sighed.

"Well, Professor, I guess you know a lot that I don't. I'll certainly be interested to hear it."

Carruthers hesitated for a moment. Then he made up his mind.

"What I'm going to tell you," he said, "may strike you as absurd and fantastic. I admit that it may sound so. But I believe it to be the truth. For that reason I am going to ask you to forget the fact that you are a newspaper man. This is a truth which must not be published until it is history. I have heard it said that a newspaper man is a reporter first and a man afterwards. I am asking you to reverse that situation."

Casey was looking at him curiously.

"OK, Professor," he said briefly.

"In the first place, Mr. Casey, I think I ought to tell you that I am not Professor Barstow."

Casey received this information calmly. He produced a cablegram from his pocket.

"Before you go on, Professor, I guess I ought to show you this cable." He handed it over.

Carruthers read it. It was twelve days old.

BARSTOW DISAPPEARED WEEK AGO MYSTERIOUS CIRCUMSTANCES STOP SUICIDE SUSPECTED STOP

The cablegram was signed "NASH."

"I suppose," said Casey, "you wouldn't care to let me see your passport, Professor?"

With a grim smile Carruthers passed it to him across the table. Casey glanced at it and passed it back.

"Looks all in order to me, Professor. I suppose you won't tell me about those mysterious circumstances?"

Carruthers was silent for a moment. His thoughts were groping their way back through a dark fog. For a moment he forgot Casey. He had come to a wall in the fog. He could not see it nor yet touch it, but he knew it was there. He turned away and his mind became clear again.

"I'm afraid I don't know, Mr. Casey. I have never had the pleasure of meeting Professor Barstow, nor do I know anything of him. This passport was given to me by certain responsible persons. What I really am does not matter. My name is Carruthers."

Casey met his eyes for a few seconds; then he nodded. "OK," he said, "we'll skip that bit for the moment."

Carruthers filled his pipe again and lighted it.

"It was quite by accident that I met this man Groom," he began. "He mistook me for this Professor Barstow. There must be some facial resemblance between the two of us. At all events I did not disillusion him."

He drew at his pipe, blew out a cloud of smoke and went on.

"It was at an hotel at Launceston in Cornwall . . ."

PART TWO

REVOLUTION

The narrative continued by Casey

10

MAY 10th

When first I heard the story of the man who called himself Carruthers, I did not believe it.

That is understandable. Even now, as I sit writing in the pitiless glare of a Parisian wallpaper, it is difficult to realise that what has happened has not been a dream—by dyspepsia out of repressed reflexes. But my eyes wander back to a scar on my wrist and I remember vividly how painful that bullet graze was as I toiled down the hillside in the Kuder Valley. "Only a flesh wound," say the novelists. Let them try it for themselves. But I grow diffuse. The reference to the dream-like confusion of my thoughts is no mere conceit. It is apologetic; for I find it difficult to begin at the beginning, to sift impressions from facts and to present a logical account of those breathless days I spent with Carruthers.

For Carruthers I shall call him. Whoever he was before he came to Zovgorod, whoever he is now, has no bearing upon my picture of him. It is as Carruthers that I think of him.

His was a strange patchwork of a personality. You received the impression that you were seeing him through binoculars that moved in and out of focus of their own volition. In the everyday affairs of life he was a nonentity, a blur. I can, indeed, remember little of his life in relation to them. It was only in moments of crisis that he became an individual. At such moments he was immense. He had a sort of full-blooded theatricality about him that never failed to win my complete confidence. It would not have occurred to me to question his ability to deal with the most desperate situation. Yet, once the mood was past, I invariably found myself amazed by the way in which sheer luck had converted what, in cold blood, seemed asinine decisions into strokes of genius. I see now that in thinking this I was mistaken. The play of action upon circumstances must be determined by some universal law. Carruthers must have been gifted with subconscious understanding of it. The character he had so curiously borrowed was but a highly stylised mask; a motley that was significant only against its special background.

By the time Carruthers had finished his story that night in Zovgorod, the waiters were switching out the lights. Somewhere it was striking one o'clock. I had all but finished my cigarettes and the table was littered with ash and Carlsberg glasses.

"And that," he said, leaning back, "is all."

I lit my remaining cigarette without replying. A host of questions rose to my lips. I examined them one by one. To most of them I found the answers readily enough. This man whom Carruthers knew as Groom was not unknown to me by reputation. He was an arms agent with many *noms-de-guerre.* The official list of directors of Cator & Bliss contained twenty names. Any of them might be the man in question. If he were Grindley-Jones in China, Harcourt in South America, and Coltington in the Near East, he might well be Groom in Europe, and would no doubt reserve yet another identity for the boardroom and general meetings. As for his encounter with Carruthers, it was, after all, perfectly understandable. A business man feeling rather pleased with himself over a deal he's putting through meets a man who's an expert on the subject of the deal in question. What a stroke of luck for him! What could be more feasible than that he should secure the services of the expert to protect himself against trickery. Rovzidski's death was an inevitable corollary of the whole affair. It was a typical Red Gauntlet job. I had examined these and other questions to my satisfaction, but I was still in the dark on one point. I put it to him.

"Those telephone exchanges," I said, "you told me you could explain that."

"I imagine," he replied, "that the Kassen bomb is electrically detonated. The telephone exchanges served as a practice means of centralising the firing of it. That accounts, too, for the retirement tactics. You trick the enemy into advancing and then blow him sky-high. Your offensive consists of mining the enemy. I expect that they had some means, too, of projecting the explosive charges. That field gun order to Skoda probably supplies the clue there; but the charges are so small and easily laid that the mining method is probably regarded as the simplest. It would be quite easy to launch a rather feeble attack, leave your charges and retire before the counter-attack."

"Wouldn't the enemy get used to that pitch?"

"Yes, they would. When they did, you would launch a real attack and hold your position. They would hesitate to counter-attack and face the magdanite, while if they did decide you were bluffing and attacked, you would retire again leaving your charges as before. Think, too, of the amount of magdanite one aeroplane could carry. It would be an almost infallible method of prosecuting a war. The enemy's losses would be enormous; those of the magdanite users would be small because they would never attack in strength."

I had to admit the probable truth of this.

He was thoughtful for a moment and then asked me once more and very gravely for my assurance that I would not send the story to my editor.

"You needn't worry," I told him, "they'd think I was crazy if I did."

He seemed satisfied and asked me if I believed him.

I answered, frankly, that I didn't know what to think.

He assured me that time would show that he had spoken the truth.

"Mr. Casey," he went on, "I have been thinking over what you have told me. May I suggest that we join forces."

I hesitated. I must admit that I had been impressed by his arguments for the necessity of the task to which he had set himself. But I always make a point of mistrusting my emotions and said so. He smiled.

"I do not ask for your emotional support. I fancy that an alliance would be mutually advantageous. You will get your story; I will carry out my purpose."

We shook hands on it. As we did so, the proprietor informed us that the restaurant was closed and asked us to leave. We apologised and Carruthers tipped the man extravagantly. "An offering to the Gods," he explained when I told him that an Ixanian never says "thank you" unless he thinks you a fool.

We left the restaurant and Carruthers proposed a walk back to the Hotel Bucharesti where I was staying. He was silent on the way. I asked him if he had a plan of action in mind, but he was evasive. We would, he said, make our plans in the morning and we arranged that he should call at my hotel. He refused to come in for a drink and we said good-night at the entrance. I watched his spare, lank figure walk away along the sidewalk until the darkness hid him. Then, from a doorway, another figure appeared and walked slowly after him. His escort had found him again. It was not until I turned to go inside that I realised that my head was aching abominably.

* * * * *

I was still asleep when Carruthers arrived. He was sitting in my armchair waiting when I opened my eyes.

"How's the head?" he inquired a little abstractedly.

"Fine." It wasn't, but I thought it might save a lot of talk to say so.

"Good." His eyes gleamed. He lit his pipe and leant forward. "Groom says he'll have the Kassen secret by tomorrow."

I sat up in bed and lit a cigarette.

"But I thought you heard the Countess say he was on the wrong track."

"I think she was mistaken. Groom has more up his sleeve than this man Prantza. Don't forget that affair might well be a blind to put the Countess's agents off the scent. He's very confident and talks about our leaving the day after tomorrow."

"What are you going to do, wait until he's got it and then steal it from him?"

"No. If we do that we are adding to our difficulties. Remember, there are very probably only two copies of the process left. One is with Kassen and the other with the

Countess. If Groom gets one of them, a third copy will be made and they'll be more than ever on their guard. Besides, we might fail to get Groom's copy and he is almost certain to make a duplicate himself. The more copies of that conditioning process there are, the more trouble we're going to have disposing of them."

"What's your idea, then?"

"I believe that Groom intends to steal one of those two copies. I should think that it will be the Countess's; Kassen's place is too well guarded. Where does she live?"

"She's got a big house not far from the Palace. It stands in its own grounds."

He pursed his lips thoughtfully. "She may keep her copy there. I don't think she'd risk leaving it in the care of anyone but herself. Do you know if the place is guarded?"

"I didn't see any guards."

"That probably means that it's very well guarded."

"Then I don't see . . ."

"You're quite right, this speculation is useless. We've got to know how Groom proposes to get his information and stop him."

"How?"

"This afternoon at four o'clock he's having a conference with his agents."

"How do you know?"

"I overheard him telling the waiter to take drinks and cigars to his room at four. He's had these conferences before. I recognise the symptoms."

"You mean his bunch of tough guys?"

"As you say, the tough guys."

"Well, Mr. Carruthers," I said, "I don't see how, short of hiding in the closet, you're going to get much out of the conference."

"That's where you can help me, Mr. Casey. Will you come round to the Europa at three o'clock sharp and ask to be shown up to my room?"

"Sure, but . . ."

"On your way there, Mr. Casey, I would like you to execute a small commission for me. I would do it myself only I should first have to go to a lot of trouble to get rid of the gentleman shadowing me."

I nodded resignedly.

"I want you to go into two telephone booths and remove the receiver from each. Just cut the wire at the point where it enters the box arrangement so that there's a length attached to both receivers when you've got them."

"Supposing I'm caught?"

He seemed to recognise the possibility.

"Yes," he admitted, "it will call for circumspection on your part. But it is essential that we have them."

"I suppose you're going to hook up a detectaphone?"

"Yes."

"How are you going to do it with two telephone receivers? You need a microphone."

He smiled cryptically.

"I will show you when you arrive," he said. "Meanwhile, I have work to do—at three o'clock then, Mr. Casey."

He walked to the door. Suddenly he stopped and listened intently. Then, with a quick movement, he flung open the door. Outside, a waiter was bent double by the keyhole. He straightened himself with a start.

"Your breakfast, Monsieur," he said in French.

"What were you doing outside that door?" I asked.

"Bringing your breakfast, Monsieur." His face was blank.

"I didn't ring."

"Pardon, Monsieur, they told me you had." He made a movement to go. Carruthers stopped him and put his hand on the coffee-pot.

"Lukewarm," he said in English. "Must have been outside for about ten minutes. Does he speak English?"

"I don't think so."

"I don't suppose our friend the Countess would employ anyone who didn't for this job. Most waiters know a little. We'll have to stop his mouth. Attract his attention."

I started to complain angrily that the coffee was cold. The man leant forward apologetically to pick it up. Carruthers glided behind him. The unsuspecting waiter made no defensive movement. I waited for the blow. Carruthers made no move but straightened himself and nodded with satisfaction as the man went out.

"He's all right," he said, "he doesn't understand. I expect he told the Countess he knew English. Hotel English wouldn't help him with the subject of our conversation. The key was in the door, too. He can't have heard much."

"He may not even have been trying to listen," I said maliciously.

Carruthers smiled. "Still sceptical, Mr. Casey? I wonder for how long you will remain so."

He poked his head back round the door as if he was going. "By the way, Mr. Casey," he said, "I should very much like to meet friend Andrassin. Will you arrange it?"

I nodded with my mouth full, and he went.

My breakfast finished, I dressed slowly. There were some hours to go before the three-o'clock appointment, but I had to secure the telephone receivers and wanted to leave myself plenty of time. It was eleven when I left the hotel and walked towards the Kudbek. I remembered that there were some booths in the post office there.

I reached the post office all too quickly. Outside, I stopped and stood there for a minute or two feeling rather foolish. There is nothing so damaging to a man's self-esteem as the thought that he has been too credulous. It is a charge against his intelligence that he finds the greatest difficulty in defending. There is no excuse, no self-justification that he may use as balm to this wound to his pride. Brought face to face with the necessity of acting, and acting, I thought, rather childishly, upon my hasty estimate of Carruthers' story, I was acutely conscious of behaving like a cub reporter on his first assignment. The foreign correspondent of the *Tribune* in Europe stealing telephone receivers to listen to what would probably turn out to be a perfectly ordinary business conference, at the behest of a crank with a penchant for ten-cent shockers, was a picture that made me blush. Atomic bombs! Secret papers! Secret agents—the blush deepened until I was glowing with self-contempt. But, such is man's hatred of knowing himself for a fool, I knew that, credulous or not, I should keep that appointment at three and that, reposing uneasily in my pockets, would be two telephone receivers, the property of the Ixanian Government. In the end, only the evidence of his senses will convince a man, especially should he be a newspaper man, that he has actually been deceived by a lunatic.

I pulled myself together and entered the post office. The line of telephone booths seemed terribly conspicuous. I chose the remotest of them and stepped inside, opening my penknife in my coat pocket as I did so. Lifting the receiver from its hook, I asked for the first number that came into my head and started sawing at the flex where it entered the box. It was surprisingly tough and I was additionally handicapped by a blunt knife and having only one hand free to use it. I managed at last, made a show of replacing the receiver and slipped it into the pocket of my raincoat which I carried over my arm. I stepped out of the booth and walked rapidly away in a cold sweat of fear. I did not like to go back to the same post office for the second receiver and after some difficulty found another booth where I repeated the process.

I walked back to the Kudbek with the receivers bumping against my side and made for the nearest café. I felt I had earned a drink. The café was crowded, but an unmistakable head of wild white hair caught my eye. It was Andrassin. Beside him sat a middle-aged man with a narrow intelligent head, a black moustache and dark-blue eyes. I made my way to the table. Andrassin greeted me enthusiastically and begged me to take the vacant chair. Holding my overcoat carefully in my lap, I sat down gratefully and ordered brandy. Andrassin flourished his arm expansively in the direction of his companion.

"Mr. Casey," he said, beaming, "I'd like you to know Toumachin."

He addressed a few rapid words of Ixanian to Toumachin who bowed gravely and surveyed me with a pair of shrewd eyes. Andrassin beamed at us both and then turned to me with an apologetic twinkle.

"Mr. Casey, we are at the moment plotting the overthrow of Capitalism; you will excuse us for a moment?"

I reassured him and for two or three minutes the two conversed in rapid undertones, Andrassin doing most of the talking, the other listening solemnly. They presented a remarkable contrast. Andrassin, shock-headed, voluble and bright of eye with enthusiasm and vitality, was admirably offset by the grave, level-headed, deliberate Toumachin. Each, it was easy to see, was the complement of the other. What Toumachin lacked in freedom of imagination, Andrassin supplied; what Andrassin lacked in executive force was brought by Toumachin: common purpose and sincerity bound them together. Andrassin had told me of Toumachin as a young man talks of a hero. Toumachin, it was obvious, held Andrassin in the same high regard.

With a final rush of words from Andrassin, their conversation ceased. Toumachin stood up, bowed to me and shook hands. Then he walked gravely away.

"He goes," said Andrassin unnecessarily; but his remark lent a touch of drama to the departure. That was Andrassin's way. He might have been another Reinhardt.

He became suddenly serious. "Mr. Casey," he said slowly, "we are in the midst of great happenings."

"More mysteries, Andy?"

"No, Mr. Casey, no more mysteries. We know and we are ready to act."

"Know what?"

He shook his head grimly.

"Well, well," I said good-humouredly, "you'll give an exclusive when the story does break, I hope."

He smiled, a trifle wanly, I thought.

"Toumachin has forebodings," he said with unusual gravity, "and when that man has forebodings, I, too, am apprehensive."

"Whatever it is," I urged him, "forget it."

"You are right, Mr. Casey, I am growing old. Tell me, what have you been doing with yourself in our so gay and prosperous Zovgorod?"

"Trying to be a good newshound, Andy—which reminds me; I've run across a Britisher who wants to meet you very badly."

He gave me a quick glance and smiled. "I know," he said slowly. "His name is Professor Barstow. He is a friend of Groom, the arms-maker. He called on you this morning."

"You know him?"

He shook his head. A light dawned on me.

"I suppose that waiter at the Bucharesti isn't a friend of yours?"

He nodded somewhat diffidently.

"I am a little disappointed in Petar," he said with a smile; "his knowledge of English cannot be as good as he says. He reports that you are enamoured of the Countess Schverzinski and that with the aid of the Englishman you will attempt to seduce her this afternoon at three o'clock."

When I had recovered from the effects of this intelligence, I returned to the attack.

"What's the idea of setting your bloodhounds on to me, Andy?"

He reddened a little.

"You must forgive me, Mr. Casey, but I am your friend and it is for your own good. You are on the edge of a conspiracy that at any moment may blow up." Metaphor was never Andrassin's strong point. He grew redder. "Mr. Casey," he said earnestly, "you will please go back to Paris. God himself could not give you better advice."

I stopped laughing and looked at him. I had never before seen him so quietly serious.

"Andy," I said gently, "you realise, don't you, that you're as good as telling me not to leave on any account?"

He snorted impatiently.

"When will you Americans realise that there are times when a little, just a little, discretion is necessary?"

"It's no use, Andy, if there's a ghost of a chance of

anything happening here, I stay. You can tell me it's my own fault afterwards. What is it, a revolution?"

"You talk childishly, my friend," he said wearily.

We sat silent for a time; Andrassin was behaving curiously. Obviously, he had something really serious on his mind. I caught his eye. He grinned.

"You must forgive me, Mr. Casey," he said. "I am very worried and should have known better than to imagine that you would have returned to Paris."

"OK, Andy, no bones broken. Now, what about getting together with this guy Barstow?"

His expression changed again. He shook his head firmly.

"No, Mr. Casey, that I am afraid I cannot do." He was very positive.

"Why?"

He looked round and lowered his voice.

"This Barstow," he said, "is a marked man. What you call on the spot."

I suspected exaggeration. Andrassin was inclined to be shaky on his American idiom.

"Do you mean someone's going to kill him?"

He shrugged.

"I do not say that, but he is, nevertheless, in a very delicate position. I would not consider him the ideal subject for a life insurance."

Carruthers' story loomed large in my mind. I experienced a wave of excitement; but I affected exasperation. "Look here, Andy, for goodness' sake tell me what all this mystery is about."

Andrassin shook his head again. "You will learn nothing from me, Mr. Casey. Already, perhaps, I have said too much." He paused, then added: "I know more than is good for me?"

I made a last effort.

"Tell me one thing. Is Professor Barstow in any way involved in this conspiracy you talk of?"

He hesitated, then shrugged his shoulders.

"He is. Whether he knows it or not, he is. That is why I will not see him. I do not take unnecessary risks. As for you, my friend, have nothing to do with him. It will be better for you."

I knew that it was useless to pursue the matter. He changed the subject abruptly and spoke of days in New York with a nostalgia in his heart as apparent as it was infectious. He quoted Goethe, Hobbes and, as he rose to leave, Nietzsche.

"Action has no sense," he said. "It merely binds us to existence. I have wasted my life, Mr. Casey," he added sombrely.

We exchanged farewells and I watched him walk away until his short sturdy figure and his white shock of hair were hidden by the passers-by.

I never saw him again.

11

MAY 10th AND 11th

At five minutes of three that afternoon I arrived at the Europa and asked for Professor Barstow.

Carruthers received me enthusiastically, shut the door carefully behind me and bolted it. Then he asked me eagerly if I had brought the receivers. I produced them from my pockets. He pounced on them with a cry of satisfaction.

"Have you your knife?" he asked.

I handed it to him. He went to the bell by his bedside and cut the wire near the push. He next proceeded to strip about twelve feet of it from the wall and bared the ends of insulation.

I watched these preparations with some misgiving. It was evidently apparent in my face, for he glanced at me and smiled.

"You needn't worry, I'm not going mad."

"What are you doing?"

"We're going to listen to that conference. That's why I asked you to bring the second receiver. We can both listen."

"What are you going to do for a microphone?"

"I'll show you in a minute."

He finished his work on the bell-wire, opened the door of the room softly and pointed to a door along the corridor.

"That's Groom's room. In it there is a telephone. That will be our microphone."

He took the end of the bell-wire and showed it to me.

"Now then, the telephone wires run out of the room just by the door there. What I want you to do is to stand at the end of the corridor and whistle if anyone comes."

"But . . ."

"I'll explain in a minute."

I went to the end of the corridor and waited. A waiter appeared in the distance and I whistled at Carruthers who was bending down doing something to the telephone cable. He disappeared into the bedroom. The waiter went away again and Carruthers reappeared. I saw him thrusting the wire under the carpet into the corridor; then he stood up and beckoned.

I went back into the bedroom with him. He drew the end of the bell-wire in and shut and bolted the door again.

"I've tapped the telephone wires," he said. "We shall hear the conversation through the telephone transmitter."

"Is the telephone on its hook in Groom's room?"

He nodded and smiled. My heart sank and I sighed rather irritably.

"Then how do you suppose we're going to hear with the transmitter out of circuit?"

"If the telephone were off its hook someone might notice and put it back. The transmitter, however, is not out of circuit. While Groom was at lunch I took the precaution of jamming a couple of matchsticks under the hook—not enough to see, but just enough to raise the hook."

This was better; then a thought struck me.

"Is there a private exchange in the hotel?"

"Yes."

"Then what about the operator?"

"I'd thought of that. The telephone's worked by the clerk at the reception bureau, so I sent him to get me a time-table. While he was away I fixed a pin on the indicator disc so that it can't signal the fact that the hook is up."

"Supposing Groom tries to make a call?"

"In that case we shall hear him and draw our lead in under the door. I've fixed it so that a slight pull will disconnect it."

I congratulated him again and my words were none the less convincing because I was also congratulating myself. The man was not a complete fool.

The receivers were soon connected and we sat down by the door to listen and wait.

At three-thirty, Groom went into his room. The telephone proved a sensitive one, and we could hear him moving about. Then there was silence for a long time and I thought the connection had broken, but at about three-fifty-five we heard the waiter arrive with the drinks and the voice of Groom telling him where to put his tray. He spoke French with a curiously clipped accent, quite unlike any British-French accent I had heard.

The hands of my watch had moved to ten after four and I was wondering whether Carruthers hadn't jumped to conclusions about the conference when we heard the first arrival being greeted by Groom. The language was French. Groom's ignorance of Ixanian was a stroke of luck. The name of the first arrival was not mentioned and Groom merely told him to help himself to a drink.

Several more arrived during the next ten minutes and we could hear them talking together in low tones. A pair near the telephone transmitter seemed, I thought, to be using Greek. By half-past four the party was complete, for we heard Groom's voice calling them to attention. There was silence. Then Groom started to speak.

"Now, my friends," he said, "you know what I want and how I want you to get it. There must be no mistakes. You know where the safe is. Prantza has provided Nikolai with the details. I want all the papers in it, that is all. If there is money or jewellery there, take it and divide it amongst yourselves. I am not concerned with money." I detected a note of contempt for the men to whom he spoke in his voice. "In fact," he went on, "the more like an ordinary burglary it looks, the better I shall be pleased. As to the main purpose of your visit here, I shall give you half your pay this afternoon and the remaining half when Nikolai delivers the papers."

There was a murmur of protest from his audience as this was translated to them. One man spoke up.

"We must be paid now, Monsieur."

"I am not a fool, Nikolai." Groom's voice was cold. "I have already given you money for Prantza from which you doubtless extracted a generous commission for yourselves."

There was another murmur—not quite so expressive.

"I may add," continued Groom silkily, "that it will be quite useless for you to attempt to satisfy me with any worthless documents or to extract more money from me by keeping back any essential part of the papers you find in that safe. Before the second half of the money is paid, my expert who is here in Zovgorod will examine the papers and see that they are what I require."

There was silence. He went on:

"The moment the papers have been secured, Nikolai will bring them straight to me here. The others will scatter to other parts of the city. That should be soon after two a.m. tomorrow morning providing that the safe gives no trouble. Nikolai can then remain here with me to safeguard your interests until later in the day when the papers will have been approved and your money paid. I have only one thing to recommend to you; that is, that you endeavour not to kill any of the guards unless it is absolutely necessary. That will be all. I will give the money here to . . ."

I heard no more. Carruthers had twitched the wire away and was hauling it into the room.

"Quick," he said, "we'll go to a café before they come out. I don't want to risk Groom coming in with you here."

He rolled up the wire and, thrusting it into his pocket, opened the door. There were sounds of movement from the room opposite. I dropped the receivers back into my coat pockets and we left the hotel. A taxi took us to the Kudbek where Carruthers insisted on leaving the receivers in a telephone booth before we went to a café.

He ordered strong black coffee and produced his pipe. I had beer and lit a cigarette.

"Well," said I, "what's the next item on the programme?"

He gave me an amused look.

"Confess, Mr. Casey," he said, "that you came in a mood of complete scepticism."

"OK, I'll admit it. But I'm convinced now." I did not tell him that it was as much as a result of my conversation with Andrassin as through our eavesdropping expedition.

He looked pleased.

"Good, now we can go ahead."

"How?"

"There can be no doubt, I think, that they propose to go after the copy of the conditioning process in the possession of the Countess. She evidently overlooked the fact that Prantza knew where her safe was. They may have got the combination from him, too. At all events, we must not spoil their game. Our primary object is to prevent manufacture of the explosive. Every copy of that process must be destroyed, and while those copies remain in Ixania we've got a chance of destroying them."

"But what about Kassen? Short of bumping him off, I don't see how you can do anything about it."

"You can leave Kassen to me," he said with a faraway look.

"If that means that you're going to kill him yourself," I said warmly, "you can count me out."

He shook his head. "I'm not going to kill him," he said slowly, "I have a better idea."

Whatever his idea was I did not like it and said so. He clapped me on the back, a thing I detest, and told me heartily not to worry. I stuck to my guns.

"Look here, Carruthers," I said, "it seems to me that you've bitten off a good deal more than you can chew. I'm for informing the American Legation of the situation and leaving them to act as they think fit. This is an international matter. When I came here, I was prepared for revolution and God knows what, but I wasn't prepared for this sort of a mess. I tell you, if we fall down on this and it gets known that I had anything to do with it, it's me for the high jump. Mind you, I'd risk that if I thought we had the smallest chance of success, but frankly, I don't think we've got an earthly. Why, take this business of the robbery; how do you suppose we're going to stop a mob of eight dagger-packing Greeks?"

"Eight? I should say that there will be at least ten."

"Eight or ten, what difference does it make? We haven't an earthly. I suggest, and I guess you'll realise the sense in what I'm saying, that we both get in touch with our respective Embassies or Legations now and let it go at that. If they don't care to do anything about it, then no one can blame us. We'll have done our best. You can square it with this guy Groom, stall him, say that the dope is incomplete, anything you like to give our people a chance to take diplomatic action. Tell the League of Nations maybe."

I sat back and finished my beer. I had got what I wanted to say off my chest and felt better. I glanced at Carruthers; he was lighting his pipe. He blew out a cloud of smoke and his eye caught mine. For some inexplicable reason I found myself regretting my outburst, feeling that I had in some way uttered a heresy. I tried to clear my mind of prejudice, told myself that I was right, that my proposal was sane and sensible and that I ought to have been ashamed of myself for even considering Carruthers' crazy plans. His pained silence became oppressive. "Well," I said at last.

"There are just two drawbacks to your suggestion," he answered. "In the first place, do you imagine that the American Minister would believe you?"

"Why not?"

"Think."

I thought; and the more I thought, the more I knew that he was right. I pictured myself trying desperately to convince a hard-headed State Department careerist that I had discovered in a laboratory in the Kuder Valley a serious menace to world peace in the shape of an atomic explosive. I imagined his weary demand for confirmation, the righteous indignation of the Ixanian Government at his apologetic requests for explanations of the existence of the Kassen laboratory, the curious army manoeuvres and the electricity failures. Worst of all, I anticipated the angry notes from my editor that would surely follow the inevitable complaints from Washington. The Bucharest correspondent had provided me with certain information, my job was to report, not to manufacture mare's nests; thus they would run. "What's the second drawback?" I asked.

He did not answer me for a moment. When he did, he had dropped his professorial air, and seemed to exude an enormous self-confidence. The change impressed me. I found myself hanging on his words.

"Supposing you persuade your Minister that you are not a lunatic and that he reports the whole business to Washington and supposing they accept the facts at your valuation? What are they going to do? Send Ixania a note? The only result of that would be to put these people on their guard. Besides, I don't suppose the Government here knows what the Countess is planning. The President is probably in the know, up to a point at any rate, but he will do what Prince Ladislaus tells him. Can you imagine the United States dispatching an expedition to Ixania on the strength of your story? Even if the League of Nations was brought into the picture nothing could come of it but disaster. There is no precedent, no international machinery which can serve as a basis for action. How could you expect a lot of statesmen sitting round a table to legislate for criminal tomfoolery like Kassen's? What's more, if the affair did become a matter for League inquiry and the nations heard about it, every one of them would be tumbling over itself trying to get the secret in the sacred name of its own security. The only body that could deal with this affair would be an international police force, and, unfortunately, there isn't such a thing."

I was beaten and knew it. I temporised. We were, I reminded him, hopelessly outnumbered. He admitted it with relish. We ought, I maintained, to enlist help if we were to have even the faintest hope of success.

He considered this proposal for a moment, then shook his head.

"Numbers," he said, as though he were addressing a military academy, "will destroy our essential mobility. In principle, however, I agree with you. We need allies, or rather an ally. I have been thinking of your man Andrassin."

I had been waiting for this and told him of Andrassin's refusal, holding my peace, however, concerning the remainder of Andrassin's conversation. Carruthers took the news calmly.

"For the moment," he said, "it does not matter. When the time comes I shall know how to persuade him."

I doubted it but did not argue the point.

"Meanwhile," I said provocatively, "there is the difficulty of finding a way in which two men can stop ten men without making a noise about it."

"I have a plan," he replied simply. "After I left you this morning I had a look at the house of the Countess. It is absurdly vulnerable. The appearance of the place from the square in front is deceptive. The grounds stretch back a considerable distance to the river. There is an old stone quay there, and I should imagine that it used to be used as a way to and from the Palace, which has a similar quay. The river is the obvious way of approach."

"Sure. If you have a boat."

"There is a way to the quay from the land; a passage

from the square. Once on the quay, the rest is plain sailing."

"What about the guards?"

"I saw two men in the grounds at the back and there's certain to be another in front of the house, but the place is so overgrown with shrubs that it should be easy to avoid them. The only snag will be the man posted on the quay."

"How did you get a look at the grounds, then, with a man on the quay?"

"There was no man on the quay when I went. But I guessed that there must be one at night time. There's a brazier there and a shelter arrangement."

"That's fine, but I still don't see how we're going to hijack Groom's men."

"We know the approximate time of their arrival. Does that suggest nothing to you?"

"Nothing at all."

"I'll explain."

He leant forward and talked rapidly for about ten minutes. When he had finished I think I felt more miserable than ever in my life before. My opinion of Carruthers sank to zero.

"And do you believe," I said bitterly, "that we're going to get away with a crazy scheme like that?"

"Why not?" He seemed genuinely surprised.

The man was fantastic. I made up my mind once and for all.

"I'm sorry, Carruthers, but I guess you'll have to count me out. I don't mind taking risks, but there isn't any risk about your scheme, it's a surefire ticket to the Zovgorod penitentiary and they don't treat their prisoners any too well, I'm told."

He smiled. "All right, I'll go by myself."

I felt a sudden wave of irritation with him. He must see that his plan was utterly and absolutely crazy. I raised every possible objection to it, and there were many; I argued and reasoned with him for nearly an hour. It made no impression on him. I sank back in my chair and ordered another beer. He grinned at me. I gave up.

"All right," I said desperately, "when do we start?"

The words were out of my mouth before I knew that I had uttered them. It was the involuntary acquiescence of exasperation. I let it go. I believe Theodore Roosevelt himself would have done the same. Carruthers had a way of making you behave and think like a dime novel.

* * * * *

The next few hours were, I think, among the most unpleasant I have ever spent. The nearest parallel to them that I can remember is the hours before the Yale-Harvard game in '22 when I was wondering if my ankle would hold out.

We were to set out at twelve o'clock. The fact that Nikolai was expected by Groom at the Europa soon after two A.M. meant that the operations of the gang would commence soon after one. According to Carruthers we had to be there when they arrived.

First, however, we had to lose Carruthers' "bodyguard." We had dinner and sat at a café until eleven-thirty. Then we rose and walked about until we found a lonely side street. We strolled down it and had the satisfaction of observing the Schverzinski agent turn the corner and proceed in a leisurely manner in our wake. We stopped at the corner.

"I think it's a different man," said Carruthers. "If so, I'll work the taxi dodge again."

Telling me to meet him outside the post office in twenty minutes' time, he seized my hand, wrung it heartily and in a loud voice bade me good-night. I responded and he departed to hail a passing taxi. I saw the agent scuttling after him and made my way back to the post office. Within a quarter of an hour he had joined me with the comforting news that the agent was speeding after an empty taxi on its way to the red-light district.

Another taxi took us to the Palace. From there we walked to the square in which our objective lay. It was a fine night, but cold, and we walked briskly. The moon had yet to rise and there were few street lamps. The almost imperceptible light of the stars was our sole illumination. We soon came to the square. It was deserted. We could see the black bulk of the Schverzinski house. It was in darkness except for a faint chink of light coming from a heavily curtained room on the first floor. Carruthers led the way along that side of the square which ran to the left of and at right angles to the house, until we came to a narrow passage-way between the boundary of the Schverzinski grounds and a walled garden. A wrought-iron lintel carrying an unlit lamp bridged the space between the two walls. Below it was a wrought-iron gate. It was locked.

Carruthers fumbled in his overcoat pocket, produced something that gleamed faintly in his hand and attacked the lock. A few minutes later I saw him twist his hands. There was a grating noise and the gate swung open with a slight squeak. Carruthers cursed under his breath and motioned me to keep still. My heart in my boots, I waited for the alarm. To my taut nerves the noise had seemed ear-splitting, but it passed unnoticed by the front guard.

We remained still for about five minutes; then Carruthers led the way down the passage.

It descended sharply. On either side of us the walls towered higher and higher, shutting out almost every vestige of light. We felt our way along the wall. My hand encountered a wooden doorway. Carruthers whispered that it was the entrance to the servants' quarters and that I must go carefully as there was a flight of stairs ahead. A little way on I asked him how he had got through the gate in broad daylight. He answered that it had been open but that as it had shown signs of use he had provided himself with a pick-lock fashioned from one of the Hotel Europa's forks. This piece of ingenuity encouraged me, and, for the first time, I felt a pleasurable sense of excitement.

We reached the bottom of the steps and I was relieved to find that the walls were lower there and that we could see our way. We went a little faster and must have covered a quarter of a mile before Carruthers halted, cupped his hands and brought his head close to mine.

"Go carefully now," he whispered, "we're near the quay."

I listened and could hear the sound of water. The walls seemed to dissolve into a black pool of shadow ahead. Carruthers drew me into the shadows and whispered that we were at the foot of the stairs leading up to the quay. The passage had obviously been made for the use of boatmen and servants belonging to the house to obviate the necessity for their going through the grounds.

I followed Carruthers up two or three stairs and saw the top of his head outlined against the skyline. A glow from a fire lit up one side of his face. Someone coughed close at hand and I heard the sound of a match striking. It was the guard. Carruthers turned round and motioned me down the stairs again. We retreated a little way up the passage.

"He's about twelve yards from the top of the stairs," he said. "I'm going to get him over to the far side of the quay by lobbing a stone into the water. When I give the signal come on quickly. Turn right at the top and you'll come to some more steps leading down into the garden. The quay was built high to stop the flood waters. There's quite a drop on the other side."

He picked up a large stone from the path and we went back to the steps. I heard the swish of Carruthers' arm and a loud splash some way ahead. There was a pause; I heard a movement from the quay and Carruthers' whispered "Now." I followed him on my toes. The glow from the brazier seemed like a searchlight, but I dared not pause until I felt Carruthers' hand on my arm steadying me. We were at the top of the steps into the garden. The next moment we were in the shadow once more.

We stayed there for several minutes before Carruthers once more led the way into the blackness. I could feel grass beneath my feet and leaves brushed against my face. We seemed to be zigzagging. Once the black form in front of me stopped and I heard the crunch of feet on a gravel path and saw the gleam of a lamp. It disappeared and we went on until the house loomed suddenly above us. We stopped in the shadow of a wall and, whispering to me to stay there until he returned, Carruthers stole silently away.

I was shivering and turned my coat collar up. There was a lightening in the sky that foretold the rising of the moon and I could make out the shape of a low balcony above my head. I tried to see the time by my watch, but it was still too dark. Once I heard a slight scraping noise from the house, but that was all. It must have been about ten minutes later that I jumped as Carruthers touched me.

"I've been inside," he whispered, "through a window in

the servants' quarters. The room at the end of the balcony is the one we want, I think."

"How do you know?" I whispered back.

"It's the only one with a locked door. Come on."

"What about the guard in front?"

"Asleep like a good Ixanian."

At the end of the wall he paused and I saw him drawing himself up on to the balcony. I went forward, felt a drainpipe against the wall and followed suit. I crouched beside him by a pair of tall French windows.

"This is the one," he said.

It was locked—naturally. Once again I found myself cursing the childish absurdity of this crazy adventure. But I had reckoned without Carruthers' preposterous accomplishments. He pressed the window top and bottom.

"It's one of those double fastenings," he said softly; "a handle turns in the middle and shoots the bolts top and bottom. When the wood warps they're child's play to open."

Once more the mutilated fork came into play and a minute later I heard the bolts ease back and saw the door swing inwards. We stepped in on to a soft-carpeted floor. Carruthers shut and bolted the windows behind us.

The first thing I noticed was a strong perfume. Carruthers struck a match which he shielded carefully with his hands and I saw the reason, a large bowl of lilies on an eighteenth-century writing-desk in the middle of the room. Besides this there were two easy chairs and a bookcase, little else. I had time to see that the heavy window curtains were undrawn before Carruthers blew his match out.

"Behind the curtains for us, I think," he said.

We enveloped ourselves in the heavy lined velvet folds

and stood with our backs pressed against the wall, about two feet from the window. A large pelmet supported the curtains away from the wall, so that by holding ourselves flat there was nothing to betray our presence to anyone in the room.

"What now?" I whispered.

"We wait."

Wait we did. The moon had risen and sent a shaft of light through the window into the room when I stuck my arm out cautiously and saw by my watch that it was after one o'clock. Carruthers had forbidden the slightest movement and my feet were numb and my calves aching with the strain. I began to think that we had presumed too much in believing that we had anticipated Groom's intentions. I was soon to learn that Carruthers had been right.

I was wondering whether it would be possible to ease the pain in my legs by raising myself up and down on my toes when there was the crunch of a step outside the window. I felt Carruthers stiffen. A moment or two later there was the sound of a tool being used on the window. There was a pause, then the handle of the fastening turned jerkily and the window swung inwards against the curtain behind which we were standing. Groom's men had arrived. I held my breath.

A man stepped slowly into the path of the moonlight and stood still. He glanced over his shoulder, then peered forward. He moved out of my range of vision. I felt Carruthers' shoulder leave mine as he leaned sideways. From his side of the curtain he could in this way command a view of the room. A sudden glow of reflected light told me that the visitor had a flashlight. I could hear my watch ticking in the silence and pressed my wrist against my leg to deaden the sound.

Whatever the man was doing, he was very quiet about it. I put my hand out to touch Carruthers and met his hand moving slowly out of his coat pocket. There was something cold and hard in it. I felt the outline. It was a gun. Suddenly there was a distinct click from the other side of the room. I put my hand out again. Carruthers had gone. The next instant I heard a thump on the floor and Carruthers' voice near the curtain saying "Quick."

I came out of hiding and saw Carruthers bending over the man he had slugged. Above his head was a small circular safe. It was open. Carruthers looked up.

"See if there's anyone down below."

I tiptoed to the window, bent double and edged out cautiously on to the balcony. There was plenty of light now. Through the balustrade I could see just below me a man's head. I crept back and reported to Carruthers. I found him, flashlight in hand, poring over the pages of a hand-written manuscript clipped in a black folder. The writing was in Ixanian, but several pages consisted almost exclusively of chemical formulae unmistakable in any language.

Suddenly there was a "hsst" from outside the window and a voice softly called, "Nikolai." Carruthers doused the flashlight instantly and, thrusting the papers into the safe, swung the door to and twisted the combination lock. My eye caught the gleam of the knife just in time. The man on the floor, Nikolai, had come to and was gathering himself for a spring when I jumped. I landed right on top of him and we rolled over on the floor. We finished up with him on top and his knife went back to strike when Carruthers intervened. I saw the man go hurtling back against the desk. There was a crash as the bowl of lilies went over.

"The window!" snapped Carruthers.

As I scrambled to my feet I heard him re-engaging Nikolai. I saw the shadow by the window and ran towards it. Attracted, evidently, by the noise, the man was on the balcony. My fist caught him on the side of the face and he went down. He was up again in an instant, but before I could follow up my attack he was over the balustrade. I heard him land on the path below and rushed back into the room. I was just in time to see Carruthers deliver a short-arm jab which sent Nikolai flying into an overturned chair. Carruthers did not wait for the man to get up but grabbed my arm and pulled me behind the curtain again. I soon discovered the reason. Behind the panting of the man on the floor I could hear footsteps. I made an involuntary movement to go, but Carruthers held me.

"Wait," he hissed in my ear.

Nikolai had evidently heard the sound too, for he straightened himself and started towards the window. There was the sound of a key in the lock. Carruthers drew me back against the wall. I saw Nikolai outlined against the window and heard the door open. An instant later I was deafened by the sound of two shots from the door. The man at the window stopped and swayed, and I caught a glimpse of a wolfish face contorted with pain in the moonlight. The next instant he was gone and I heard him stumble as he landed on the path. There was a shout from the front of the house. The shots had evidently woken the guard. I heard running footsteps and further shots sounded from the grounds. Then the lights in the room went up.

My heart thumping, I waited breathlessly for discovery. There was no sound in the room. Then I heard a familiar click. The safe had been opened again. I turned my head slightly. Carruthers could see into the room. I heard the safe shut again and the door of the room swing to. The owner of the gun had gone out.

"Now," hissed Carruthers.

Ten seconds later we were out of the room and standing under the balcony. Carruthers listened. I saw the flash of a shot in the grounds and a shout.

He turned to me. "If once we get in that passageway we're trapped for a cert," he whispered, "Nikolai and Co. are there. We must go by the front."

We skirmished our way round the side of the house and Carruthers went forward and reconnoitred. A minute or so later he reported that the coast was clear. There were further shots from the rear of the house as we dashed down the grass verge of the short drive, but we gained the square without encountering any further trouble.

It was not until we were seated in a taxi and my breath was returning that I asked the questions that were perplexing me.

"What happened to the guards in the grounds? And ten men couldn't have passed the man on the quay as we did."

"You didn't imagine, did you, that those cut-throats would take Groom's injunction seriously? The poor devils were knifed," he answered. "There's nothing like the knife for that sort of job. It's silent and certain and it's the favourite weapon in this part of the world."

"Very probably. But the thing that's bothering me is: who fired those shots and then calmly went to the safe? It couldn't have been the Countess."

"It was, all the same. She gave me the last piece of confirmation I needed. The second copy of the Kassen process is in that safe. She flew to it immediately to make sure it hadn't gone. Did she hit Nikolai?"

"Winged him, I think."

He looked thoughtful. "I wish she'd killed him. He saw my face in the moonlight. It may mean trouble with Groom sooner than I had bargained for." He turned to me suddenly, a new light in his face. "An amazing woman that," he said softly. "Did you see? She fired from the hip and winged him." He paused; then with a comically elaborate air of carelessness went on: "Her head has an almost Madonna-like quality, don't you think?"

I was silent. It may have been that the tension of the past few hours had produced a violent reaction. I had an almost irresistible desire to roar with laughter, for a fantastic idea had entered my head. This incredible man had fallen in love.

* * * * *

I arrived back at my hotel at two forty-five. About an hour and a half later two men entered Andrassin's lodging, dragged him from his bed and beat him to death.

Only one man in the house saw them leave. Roused by the noise he opened his door and saw two men disappearing down the stairs. He caught a glimpse of the face of one of them, not enough to enable him to recognise the man again, but enough to notice that he had pronounced duelling scars.

12

MAY 11th

Carruthers brought me the news.

We had arranged before we parted the night before that we should meet at a café in the Kudbek at eleven in the morning. Hearing of Andrassin's murder he had come straight to the Bucharesti. He arrived at about half-past ten.

He had learned about it from the waiter who had brought him his breakfast. He had been pumping the man to find out whether anything was known of the fracas at the Schverzinski's house and the whole story had come out. The government-controlled newspaper had devoted a few unimportant inches in a late edition to the affair; but Andrassin, it seemed, was held in respect by the people and rumour and gossip were busy. According to Carruthers' informant the murder was a political move by Andrassin's enemies and a blow to freedom.

To say I was horrified would be to put it mildly. I behaved, in fact, a trifle melodramatically, as most of us do under the stress of a strong emotion, and was enraged by Carruthers' calm acceptance of the situation. I called violently for immediate action. "I'll get those dirty thugs," I raged, "if it's the last thing I do."

"It will certainly be the last thing you do," said Carruthers quietly, "if you attempt to do it at the moment."

I calmed down eventually and Carruthers waved my apologies aside, but the feelings of horror and anger at the wanton and brutal destruction of the good man who had been my friend still haunted me. I paced the room restlessly. Carruthers sat in my armchair deep in thought. As I walked, my mind ran over my last meeting with Andrassin. It was only yesterday. Ages ago! He seemed now an infinitely tragic figure. I saw him once again receding into the crowd, his brisk, alert figure, his white mop of hair bobbing, a man who knew more than was good for him. I stopped suddenly and turned to Carruthers. The events of the night had driven my conversation with Andrassin out of my head.

Carruthers listened intently while I told him of Andrassin's hints and forebodings. When I had finished he in his turn sprang up and began pacing the room.

"You ought to have told me this before," he said at last; "the affair becomes clear."

"Does it?" I was in no mood for riddles.

"Why, yes, the reason for Andrassin's murder. What Andrassin knew was what we know. Andrassin was the first person they thought of after the attempt of last night. Groom is supposed to be pursuing a shadow. They wouldn't reckon with him. Andrassin was the danger. He knew and he wasn't going to hold his tongue. He had to be disposed of quickly. Notice the time. Robbery at one-thirty or thereabouts; two hours later Andrassin is murdered and, from what my man told me, by the same men that got Rovzidski—the Red Gauntlet. The whole thing's obvious.

It sounds, too, from what you've told me, as though Andrassin was planning to put a spoke in the Kassen wheel." He stopped suddenly. "Casey," he said, "we've *got* to get in touch with this man Toumachin. It's our big chance."

"How are we going to get in touch with him? I don't know where Andrassin lived and even if I did it wouldn't be much good; I don't suppose you'll find a Young Peasant within a mile of the place by now."

"Well, we'll have to find them somehow. Things are getting serious. I didn't see Groom this morning, they told me he had gone out early. If Nikolai gets a look at me or if Groom identifies me by his description, it's open warfare in that quarter. What's more, I've got a double guard now. Two of them followed me here this morning." He thought for a moment, then snapped his fingers. "I've got it. The waiter, Andrassin's man, the one you say he put to keep an eye on you. He'll know what we're after. What's his name?"

"Petar."

"Let's have him up."

I rang the bell. Carruthers went to the window and stood with his back to the room. I dropped into the armchair and lit a cigarette.

There was a discreet knock and Petar came in.

By nature he possessed the pallid complexion common to waiters, but this morning he was livid. His eyes were swollen and looked as if he had been weeping. I told him to come inside and shut the door.

"Petar," I said gently, "we were friends of Andrassin."

He looked from me to Carruthers' back, but did not speak.

"We want to know," I said, "where we can find Toumachin."

His lips tightened, his face became blank.

"I do not understand, Monsieur. I know nothing of these men of whom you speak."

"You are of the Young Peasants' Party, Petar?" I asked.

"No, Monsieur."

"Come, Petar, we are friends and we know that you are a member."

He shook his head vigorously. I could see the sweat on his forehead.

"Look here, Petar," I said soothingly, "yesterday morning when I left here, I went to a café. There I met my friend Andrassin, who told me that you were a friend of his, and Monsieur Toumachin. We wish to avenge Andrassin's foul murder. But we must talk with Toumachin first."

He looked at us again, this time in hesitation.

"My friend here is English," I added quickly, "and I am an American citizen. I met Andrassin in New York. We were close friends."

The waiter still hesitated. Then he seemed to make up his mind.

"Sa' Maria prospek eleven," he said quickly, "and may the Holy Mother bless the steel of your daggers." There was a sudden gust of passion in his voice. Then he recovered himself, bowed slightly and went out.

I looked at Carruthers.

He nodded. "Now," he said.

I dressed hurriedly. Ten minutes later we descended the steps of the Bucharesti. A thought struck me.

"What about your bodyguard?"

"I hadn't forgotten them," said Carruthers; "we shall have to try another game this time."

He was looking up and down the street. His face became suddenly grim. "Let's walk," he said.

We walked for about a quarter of a mile. Then Carruthers stopped.

"I don't like it," he muttered.

"What?"

"They're not following us and I can't see them."

"Nothing much wrong with that. They've probably decided that it's a hell of a job and slid into a café for a drink."

He shook his head. We walked on a bit. Then we stopped again. The only thing in sight was a cruising taxi. Carruthers shrugged his shoulders.

"You may be right," he said doubtfully.

We hailed the taxi. It drew up alongside and we got in. Carruthers had found by reference to his map that the Sa' Maria prospek was near the Opera and told the man to put us down there. The door was slammed on us and we started off.

We had been going for about three minutes when Carruthers suddenly shouted that we were going the wrong way. The windows of the taxi were shut tight and I felt unaccountably drowsy. A blanket of cottonwool seemed to be enveloping my brain. I saw him as if in a distorting mirror groping for the window and struggling vainly to open it. His arm went back to break the glass when I felt him fall back on the seat beside me. Then I lost consciousness.

* * * * *

The first thing I saw when I opened my eyes was a bust of the late Czar of Russia. I opened my eyes farther and saw an Ixanian army officer's uniform. The wearer was a tall young man with an enormous moustache and eyes unpleasantly pink, like those of a bull terrier. He was leaning against a table with his legs crossed and a long thin cigar drooping from the centre of his mouth. He looked at me without speaking. My eyes repassed the Romanoff and I examined the room.

I was lying on a sofa. On the floor beside me lay Carruthers. His eyes were open and he was gazing at the painted ceiling. The room was beautifully furnished. About three inches from my right eye was a lovely old brocade. It was the window, however, that gave me the clue to our whereabouts. The shape of it was unmistakable. We were in the house of the Countess Schverzinski.

Carruthers levered himself up on to one elbow and turned his head in the officer's direction. The latter exhaled a cloud of smoke and, cigar in mouth, lounged over to the door. He opened it and exchanged a few words in Ixanian with someone outside it, then returned to his post by the table.

I nodded to Carruthers and my head throbbed with pain. He sat up.

"The Countess?" I said.

"Yes. Demand the American Consul."

"*Taisez-vous*," said the officer sharply. He had a thick and atrocious accent. I guessed that his French was limited. The fact was soon confirmed for someone opened the door, said a few words and he snapped an order at us in Ixanian. We remained uncomprehendingly prone. He shouted "*Venez*" in a parade-ground voice and we crawled to our feet and followed him out of the room under the suspicious eye of another officer who stood at the door, revolver in hand.

We were led across a large wood-floored hall towards a small door at the far end. We were about halfway across when a huge pair of double doors on the right swung open and a tall, thin, imperious-looking man of about fifty appeared. He rapped out an order and our party came to a standstill. The pink-eyed officer stepped a pace towards the man at the door and saluted. A short dialogue ensued. The pink-eyed officer was evidently accounting for us, for I heard our names given as *Barstof* and *Carsej*. The man at the door nodded curtly, scowled fiercely at us and withdrew, slamming the double doors with a crash behind him.

I glanced at Carruthers.

"Prince Ladislaus," he whispered.

The pink-eyed officer said "*Taisez-vous*" again and we moved on to the small door. This was opened carefully and we were ushered into a room which I recognised instantly as the scene of our adventure of the night before. But I had not time for more than brief recognition. Seated at the desk facing us was the Countess. She gave a curt instruction and the door closed behind us.

She gazed at us for a moment or two in silence. I had not seen her at close quarters before. At a distance she had been a handsome woman, but now I saw that she was beautiful. My mind was busy, but I found great difficulty in associating the murder of Andrassin with this exquisite creature. Even today I am still inclined to attribute the revolting ferocity of the band of cut-throats that called itself the Society of the Red Gauntlet to the late Colonel Marassin rather than to the Countess. Toumachin once endeavoured to sum her up by saying that while detachment of mind in a man is an excellent quality, it becomes in a woman a cosmic catastrophe. But Europe has a weakness for that sort of superficial man-woman generalisation. The Countess was beyond such ready-made psychological simplicities. And so, for that matter, are most other people.

But there was no time for psychological assessments, simple or otherwise, as we faced the Countess across her desk that morning. Carruthers attacked.

"What is the meaning of this—this assault, Madame?" he asked.

Her red lips moved ever so slightly into a smile. "You are making progress with your hobby, Professor?" she asked.

"Apart from the fact that one of my best cameras was, for some inexplicable reason, taken from me at the frontier, I am. May I ask," he went on, his voice trembling with indignation, "who you are and what this intolerable outrage means? I remember you, Madame, we met on the train to Bucharest. You seemed sane enough then."

I remembered my part and got to work.

"I don't know who the hell you are, lady," I blustered, "but this'll take a helluva lot of explaining away to the United States Consul, and I guess the same thing goes for the Professor here."

I went on to speak of my newspaper connections (how Nash would have blushed), a mythical relative at Washington and the inviolability of the American citizen abroad.

She listened in silence, twiddling a fountain-pen impatiently until I had finished. She contemplated it thoughtfully as she answered me.

"Any complaint to your consul, Mr. Casey, will be met with the counter-complaint, supported by witnesses, that you forced your way in here uninvited. Our *chargé d'affaires* in Washington will request your Government to inform your employers that if they must be represented in Zovgorod they must make other arrangements. You will, furthermore, be conducted to the frontier and deported as an undesirable alien."

I drew a deep breath and was about to reply, but she silenced me with a contemptuous flick of the hand and turned to Carruthers. I held my peace. I had plenty to think about.

"And you, Professor Barstow?" she queried coldly. "What do you propose to do?"

"I shall certainly complain," declared Carruthers; "you cannot pervert international justice in this high-handed manner."

She regarded him interestedly. "I wonder if you are quite the ingenuous fool you seem to wish to appear," she said; "but let me set your mind at rest, Professor, I have no desire to exchange tiresome correspondence either with your Government or with that of Mr. Casey. I merely wished to make it clear that I could have both of you outside Ixania within twenty-four hours if I wished to. In your case, Professor, even less ceremony would be necessary than in the case of Mr. Casey who belongs to the press. There must be no question of complaints."

"I am at a loss, Madame—" began Carruthers again.

She held up her hand. "Spare me your indignation, Professor. I had you brought here for a purpose. Mr. Casey will explain who I am, unnecessary though it doubtless may be."

"The Countess Schverzinski," I said coldly.

She looked amused. "A revelation, no doubt, Professor?"

"A revelation indeed, Madame," announced Carruthers brazenly. "Your behaviour is all the more inexcusable."

A frown gathered on her forehead.

"This play-acting has ceased to be entertaining. I will explain why I have had you brought here."

We waited, for all the world like a pair of schoolboys before their master. Then she picked up what had been a fork from her desk. My heart sank. It must have fallen from Carruthers' pocket during the struggle.

"As you are probably aware," she said, "there was an attempted burglary in this house last night."

"Obviously I cannot be aware of it," interrupted Carruthers promptly. "I cannot read the Ixanian newspapers."

She smiled again. "Still play-acting, Professor?"

Carruthers said "Pah!" disgustedly and she continued.

"This fork was found on the scene of the burglary. It is from the Hotel Europa. You, Professor, are stopping at the Europa. You, Mr. Casey, visited the Professor there yesterday afternoon. The burglars arrived here at about half-past one this morning. I interrupted them at their work. Neither of you was in his hotel until about half-past two. Where were you when the burglary took place?"

We were silent.

She did not seem to expect an answer to her question, but examined the fork thoughtfully. A single sapphire glowed on her right hand. She looked up and went on.

"These are troublous times and at such times men may disappear without anyone being the wiser. I wished you to have no illusions on that point; that is why I had you brought here. Also I wished to warn you. You, Professor, are suspect. You are, I am sure, a worthy man. I hear that you are a clever one. But you are playing a dangerous game. The laboratory is the place for the exercise of your talents. It is a pity that you left it to meddle in affairs that do not concern you. I suggest that you part company with Mr. Groom and return to England forthwith. Moreover, I give you twenty-four hours in which to do so. After that you will be a marked man and I shall not be responsible for the consequences. As for you, Mr. Casey, you may stay in Zovgorod on one condition. That is, that you confine your activities strictly to the conduct of your profession. You may come and go as you please. I shall, in fact, welcome the opportunity of presenting to you myself the Ixanian Government's views on the new Eastern pact of non-aggression. One indiscretion on your part, however, will mean your immediate deportation."

She pressed a button. The door was flung open. We made as if to go, but she motioned us to wait. An officer stood in the doorway.

She gave a sharp order in Ixanian and the door closed again. She turned to me.

"Andrassin, I believe, was a friend of yours, Mr. Casey?"

I nodded. I could not trust myself to speak.

"A pity he had to die. A most intelligent man; I have had some delightful conversations with him. He held some interesting views on the international banking system which I shall make it my business to propagate at some future date. But he remained curiously immature—like a youth who has just read Paine's *Rights of Man* for the first time—he had no sense of proportion." She said the last six words very slowly.

I made no comment. She looked me in the eyes. She seemed to have forgotten Carruthers. "Death is very lonely, Mr. Casey. It is best that it should remain so."

The door opened behind me. I turned round. A man stood in the doorway. He was tall and thin. His small eyes were pale blue and dull like pebbles; not even the heavy moustache he wore could conceal the thin cruelty of his mouth. Above his right eye were two deep duelling scars.

"This gentleman," said the Countess, "is Colonel Marassin—my aide-de-camp."

The man bowed slightly. We returned his bow.

"I wanted you to see Professor Barstow and Mr. Casey," said the Countess in French, "in order that you may remember them. The Professor here has decided of his own free will to leave Ixania within twenty-four hours. Mr. Casey tells me that he plans to devote himself exclusively to journalism in the future."

Marassin's pale eyes flickered from one to the other of us.

"I shall myself be on the train to the frontier tomorrow morning," he said. His voice was pitched in an unexpectedly high monotone.

"The Colonel will have no objection if I select a crowded compartment?" said Carruthers blandly.

There was a dead silence. I saw Marassin's eyes flicker towards the Countess and her barely perceptible nod. I cursed Carruthers' stupidity.

"On the train by which I arrived in Zovgorod," continued Carruthers affably, "a poor fellow, whose name I do not know, was shot. You know, Colonel, I can't help thinking I've seen you before somewhere."

I saw Marassin's hand move quickly to his pocket, but he stopped and his expressionless eyes turned to the Countess.

"Unlikely, I think," she said coldly. "The Colonel rarely appears in public." She stood up and addressed Carruthers. "You will meet Colonel Marassin at the station at ten o'clock tomorrow morning, Professor. That is all."

The interview was ended. Marassin stood aside. We walked to the door.

"Good-bye, Professor," said the Countess.

Carruthers looked back. He bowed slightly. "Good-bye, Madame," he said.

But my eyes were for Marassin.

*   *   *   *   *

An hour later we sat over the remains of our lunch, and held a desultory council of war.

"There's not a shadow of doubt in my mind," said Carruthers in reply to my question, "that Marassin was responsible for the deaths of Rovzidski and Andrassin. What's more, I'm the next on the list."

"But what grounds can they have?"

"You heard what she said. I am suspect. My association with Groom, the suspicion that I was somehow mixed up in last night's affair. These people don't wait for judicial proof, they act."

"But why get you on the train?" I asked. "They could have finished you off easily this morning. That hoodlum, Marassin, was itching to do it. What on earth induced you to make those cracks about having seen him before?"

He grinned. "It made no difference. My death warrant had already been signed."

I temporised. "Look here, Carruthers, aren't you dramatising the situation a bit? If they wanted to get rid of you, that was their opportunity. As it is, they want to get you out of the country with as little fuss as possible."

He shook his head. "No; they wouldn't feel safe even if I were out of the country. I might talk. They don't know how much Groom's told me. As for this morning, they obviously couldn't kill me in the Countess's house and with you knowing I was there. The fact that you are a pressman would make it additionally risky for them. The idea probably is for me to take my leave of you under ordinary circumstances. Then, when we've lost touch, exit Professor Barstow, shot up by bandits or something like that; letters of regret, criminals will not go unpunished, a peasant or two hanged."

I felt that he was right. "The curse of it is," I said bitterly, "that she's got the whiphand of us. I'm not supposed to get myself deported."

He nodded absently and sucked at his pipe for a time; then he said: "What do you think we ought to do?"

I felt that the question was purely rhetorical, but he seemed to expect an answer.

"I take it that you have no intention of trying to leave Ixania?"

"Not the slightest. Apart from the fact that I have no intention of being killed, I have work to do here."

I asked a question that had been troubling me.

He became vague. "Who I really am is unimportant at the moment. Perhaps I shall be able to tell you soon." He lapsed into a thoughtful silence and I saw a puzzled frown gathering on his face. Then his hand moved ever so slightly in a gesture of dismissal. He turned to me.

"I must go into hiding. There's nothing else for it."

"But where?"

He shrugged. "We must see Toumachin at once. He may be able to help."

I had almost forgotten Toumachin. But the position seemed hopeless. I barely knew the man. In any case he would probably be far too busy looking after his own life to bother about our affairs. I said so.

Carruthers ignored my comment. He spoke almost to himself. "It was bound to happen sooner or later. Perhaps it's just as well; now, at least, we do know where we are."

My headache, the after-effect of the drug that had been administered in the taxi, was wearing off. I began to sit up and take notice.

"Look here, Carruthers," I said. "Don't you think we're being rather foolish? Wouldn't it be better if we took the Countess at her word and laid off?"

He shook his head. "No, Casey," he said quietly, "it wouldn't. I, at least, am too deeply in it to draw back now, even if I wanted to do so, which I don't. I can't ask you, of course, to risk your job and possibly your life, seeing the business through, but, if you do feel like going on with it, I shall be glad of your help."

It was an appeal to my feelings which both irritated and impressed me in its moderation. I argued round the point. Then he casually broached the subject of Andrassin's murder and I knew that, willy-nilly, I would commit myself again. When, ten minutes later, we started on our way, walking this time, to visit Toumachin, I had forgotten everything but the enterprise in hand. That was the last occasion on which I tried to make Carruthers or myself see sense. It was, I had seen at last, a waste of time.

We played the now-familiar game of spotting the shadower before Carruthers announced that the "bodyguard" had been withdrawn. This was a piece of good luck. The Countess had evidently decided that we were sufficiently chastened. Carruthers insisted, however, on taking me past the American and British Consulates. That the sprinkling of loungers in the vicinity of each were planted there for a purpose was apparent even to my sceptical eye. We made no attempt to enter either. I was not sorry.

After a good deal of trouble we found the Sa' Maria prospek. It was one of the innumerable narrow streets that honeycombed the older parts of the city. Number eleven formed part of a large flat façade that embraced three other houses—all, judging from a rickety signboard, divided into one- and two-room lodgings. There was a bell at the side of the door and we heard it peal faintly in the distance as we pulled it.

A minute or so elapsed before the door was opened by a dishevelled woman of about fifty. She had obviously been struggling unsuccessfully to do up her corsets for the ceremony, for she was clasping her solar plexus in a peculiar fashion.

"Toumachin?" I said.

The door was slammed sharply in our faces. I thought I heard the purr of an electric buzzer immediately afterwards. I looked at Carruthers. He grinned.

"Being careful," he said.

We waited for a moment or two. Then I looked up and caught a glimpse of a head being withdrawn hastily from a window. A little while later the door was opened again, this time by a man. He was short and thick-set and dark. His protruding jaw and creased forehead gave him a grim look, as though he had just done, or was about to do, some very dark deed. His brown eyes stared at us suspiciously. His hand was in his pocket.

"Toumachin?" I said again.

We were subject to another searching stare, then, reluctantly I thought, he motioned us in with a movement of his head. As the door closed behind us I saw his hand come out of his pocket holding an old-fashioned nickel-plated revolver. He waved us up the stairs ahead of him. We climbed about three flights before he called on us to halt.

We were on a small landing. He flung open one of the two doors leading off it and we went inside. He followed us and shut the door. It was a low room with a long narrow window at one end stretching from the ceiling to within a foot of the bare floor. A bed, a table, a wash-basin and several chairs furnished it. At the table, revolver in hand, sat Toumachin.

As we came in he stood up. Then he recognised me and, putting his revolver down on the table, came forward and greeted me politely in French. I introduced Carruthers. I saw his eyes gleam as I did so, but he only hesitated a moment before asking us to sit down. His solemn face did not betray the curiosity and uneasiness he must have felt.

"We come," I began, "as friends of Andrassin."

"How did you know where to come?"

"From a friend of Andrassin's. I will explain in a minute."

He nodded. "Andrassin spoke of you to me," he said, "but," he indicated Carruthers, "this man is not a friend. He is, I think, an ally of Groom, the munitions maker."

I nodded.

"Monsieur Casey," he said without emotion, "if this visit is an indiscretion, you will not, I am afraid, leave here alive."

"There is no indiscretion, Monsieur."

"That remains to be seen."

"Perhaps," interposed Carruthers, "we should explain our presence to Monsieur Toumachin."

Toumachin inclined his head. "It would, no doubt, be best."

"We have come to you, Toumachin," I said, "because we believe, firstly, that much of what we are about to tell you, you already know; secondly, because we believe that we can help you, and thirdly, because we ourselves need help. I think that you know sufficient of me to believe me when I say that if Andrassin had not been murdered we should have put our trust in him. It is to you as his friend and successor that we turn now."

I had thought over my speech carefully. I intended to play on his undoubted affection for Andrassin and I succeeded to an unexpected degree. He sprang up and walked to the other end of the room. When he turned, his eyes were filled with tears.

"Even now," he said quietly, "when Andrassin is cold and his friends dare not go to his mutilated body for fear of their lives, I cannot believe that he is dead. Nor, for me, will he ever die. What good there is in the party that he has built is of his spirit. Those who have cut him down shall pay with every drop of their blood." His voice rose in a sudden tempest of anger. After his previous impassivity, the change was all the more impressive. We sat silent. At last he turned to me gravely, his face once more calm. "Tell me why you are here," he said briefly.

I waited for a moment marshalling my thoughts. Then I began. I made no attempt to refer to Carruthers by any other name than Professor Barstow. The prospect of trying to explain and justify what I still regarded as a most unsatisfactory aspect of his story was more than I could face. For all Toumachin knew it might be the custom of English professors to indulge in Wild West antics once loosed from the restraint of their laboratories. I noticed him once or twice, however, looking curiously at Carruthers placidly smoking his pipe as my recital progressed. Nearly an hour had passed before I came finally to the events of the day, told of them briefly and sat back in my chair to light a much needed cigarette.

Toumachin looked across the room questioningly at the man who had ushered us in and who had been an intent listener. The latter nodded slowly. Toumachin stroked his chin thoughtfully for a moment or two, then he looked up at me.

"As you said, Monsieur Casey, much that you have told us was already known. But we have also learned much. The Professor here is certainly correct in his conjecture that Colonel Marassin intends to kill him tomorrow. We will talk more of that later. What I am anxious to know is: what does the Professor desire? Does he desire the Kassen secret for himself?" He swung round suddenly and faced Carruthers.

Carruthers answered him.

"The only thing that I desire is the complete destruction of all practicable records of the Kassen process. I wish to render impossible the use of this gift of science for the perverted ends of the old civilisation."

"You have no qualms about destroying the evidence of this discovery?"

"None. What man has discovered once he can discover again. I believe that next time Kassen's secret is discovered the world may be ready to receive the knowledge of it as a blessing. It may not be in our lifetime, but the time will come."

Toumachin turned to me.

"It was the Professor's idea that you should come to me?"

I nodded.

"I thought so," he said. He turned to Carruthers. "It was my intention to preserve the discovery of Kassen in a safe place, to keep it hidden until I judged that knowledge of it could do no harm."

Carruthers looked at him for a moment, then shook his head. "My way is the better, Monsieur," he said. "While that secret remains even remotely accessible to mankind, there is danger. Men build for themselves battleships and guns. They tell you that these arms are only defensive and that they do not intend under any circumstances to use them offensively. But there always comes a time when fear robs the people of sanity. Then the people appeal to their leaders. Their leaders, if they are strategists, know that the best defence is attack. The damage is done. The weapons that were prepared never to be used are fulfilling the inevitable function of their existence. We cannot make a new world while men, however well-intentioned, so much as possess weapons of destruction."

Toumachin stroked his chin and looked from me to the man in the corner. There was silence in the room. I could hear the faint sound of a woman singing in another part of the house.

"You are right, Professor," said Toumachin at last. "My reason tells me so: but that part of me which is a politician tells me that all would be well if the Kassen discovery were entrusted to Toumachin. You will answer, and rightly, that other men have had similar thoughts and that while an ordinary man may be true unto himself, a leader of the people is motivated by the fears and hopes of the masses that stand behind him. It is true. The conclusions of reason indicate the only true practicable decision. The united mind of a people is the mind of a child. That is why you will notice a child-like quality about most successful politicians. They reflect the mass mind." He paused, stroked his chin and smiled slightly at Carruthers. "Very well, Professor," he said, "you shall play adult to us children. You will throw the knife into the river lest we cut ourselves or other children." He turned to the man in the corner and held a brief conversation with him in Ixanian. Then he turned to me.

"You and the Professor have done well in this affair. The

Young Peasants' Party acknowledges your efforts. More, we welcome you, Mr. Casey, as a representative of the American press. You can, if you will, be of inestimable service to us. We are about to make a bid for power in this country."

"A revolution?"

"A revolution if you wish to call it that. It is badly needed. You, here in Zovgorod, can have no conception of the plight of the peasants in the country. It is, let me tell you, a terrible one. The character of the present Government you know. The Chamber of Deputies has not been summoned for years. It is a travesty of democracy. I will not weary you with a history of the economic blunders committed since the republic came into being with such high hopes and such inferior abilities. The Countess Schverzinski is aware of them, for she is a clever woman, but her political creed is based partly on her inherited instincts and partly on her personal ambition. She desires power and glory for Ixania. The peasants ask no more than food for their bellies. A new order is long overdue."

"You will succeed?"

"I believe so. I am having great difficulty in restraining a section of the party from attempting violent reprisals for the murder of Andrassin. There was a stormy meeting this morning. To show our hand thus would be fatal. Meanwhile, however, the peasants are being organised. It is now a matter of days before we shall be ready to effect a *coup* to coincide with their march on Zovgorod. We shall, I think, take them by surprise. Our plans have been kept secret from all except the council of the party. They can all be trusted, for they are good men and they have daggers at their backs. Only one thing impedes us—the army. Many of the soldiers are sympathetic; they are themselves drawn from peasant stock. But we cannot be sure of them yet. If their officers order them to fire, they may obey. A man in uniform loses the ability to think for himself. The . . ."

"One moment, Monsieur."

We turned to Carruthers. I felt a trifle impatient of his interruption.

"Monsieur?" said Toumachin politely.

"How many are there in the army?"

"Twenty thousand."

"Where are they quartered?"

Toumachin told him.

Carruthers drew at his pipe. "I presume, Monsieur, that the army owes its allegiance to the Government in power?"

"Yes, monsieur."

"It seems then that if the army could be concentrated in a remote part of the country while the *coup* was carried out in the city, the new Government could establish itself and claim the allegiance of the army as its constitutional right and order their return. There would thus be no question of disobeying orders."

There came a sudden crackle of excited speech from the man in the corner. Toumachin listened to him, then held up his hand for silence and turned back to Carruthers.

"How would you effect the removal, Monsieur?"

Carruthers drew his chair up to the table, demanded a map of Ixania and talked steadily for about ten minutes. The man in the corner leaned over his shoulder and gave vent to sharp ejaculations of approval.

When he had finished, Toumachin sat back in his chair and stroked his chin. For fully fifteen minutes he sat there deep in thought, his hands caressing his jaw, his finely proportioned forehead creased into a frown. We waited. At last he sat up and turned to me.

"Who is this man, Monsieur Casey?"

"Professor Barstow," I said and blushed.

He gave me one of his rare smiles and shook his head. Then he stood up and his voice descended two octaves at least.

"No," he thundered firmly, "this man has been sent by fate. You have brought to me the saviour of Ixania."

He turned and, clasping Carruthers in his arms, kissed him loudly on both cheeks.

It was some time before Carruthers managed to explain that it was the tobacco that had made him choke.

13

MAY 11th TO 21st

It was early evening before, to the accompaniment of extravagant precautions against our being observed, we left Toumachin's lodging.

Much had been done. Carruthers was to install himself in a vacant room in Sa' Maria prospek eleven late that night and remain there in hiding. I was to take advantage of my comparative immunity and for the time being act as a sort of general intelligence bureau for Toumachin, Beker—the sinister little second-in-command who had let us in—and other fugitive members of the Young Peasants' Party lying low in the district. Toumachin seemed anxious, however, that I should move to the Sa' Maria prospek when the trouble started. I was not unwilling. If I came out of the business alive it would make a whale of a story. If I didn't, well, it wouldn't matter much. Arrangements were to be made by Toumachin for keeping a tab on Groom's activities, and Carruthers' plan was to be put into action. That I doubted the practicability of the famous plan goes without saying. Its favourable reception by Toumachin would have impressed me more if I could have rid myself of the thought that, although Toumachin seemed to possess more than ordinary ability, revolutionaries were, for the most part, notoriously unsuccessful at their business.

As we strolled towards a café, Carruthers asked me what I thought of the chances.

"Fifty-fifty," I answered diplomatically, "but I should think that the biggest danger is among Toumachin's own followers. You heard what he said about those birds demanding immediate reprisals for Andrassin's murder. That man Beker told me that there were two schools of thought on the question. One bunch wants to assassinate the President. Another lot are all out for blowing up the Kuder dam—making their presence felt like."

Carruthers stopped dead in his tracks.

"What's the matter?"

"Had an idea."

"Good one?"

"I don't know."

We walked on in silence and found a bar near the cathedral.

I had a beer, Carruthers his usual sweet black coffee. He grunted absently when I asked him a question. I gave it up and returned to my own thoughts. These consisted chiefly of a survey of the more recent revolutions. I had succeeded in depressing myself to an almost suicidal degree before Carruthers came out of his trance.

"What do you think of Toumachin?" he said suddenly.

The question surprised me. I gave him my rather sketchy impressions, but I soon saw that he had lost interest. He seemed to have something on his mind. I waited.

"A pretty shrewd judge of men I should think," he said after a bit.

"Must be."

"Seemed pleased with that idea of mine." It sounded more of a question than a statement.

"So he ought to be. It's most ingenious."

He shook his head deprecatingly. My bewilderment increased. I looked at him curiously. He fiddled with his empty coffee-cup and looked away. There was something about his attitude that I found faintly reminiscent—but of what? Suddenly, he emitted a short self-conscious laugh.

"Emotional blighters these foreigners. Saviour of Ixania, eh? If he wasn't such a shrewd sort of chap you'd say he was a bit sentimental."

I could hardly believe my ears. If the man hadn't been sitting beside me I would have sworn that I was listening to the ham lead of a third-rate stock company playing the Englishman in a crook melodrama. I jumped. That was it. I had remembered now why his attitude had been familiar. My mind went back to the première of a new play in New York and to a party that had followed it. I had been introduced to the lead, a quiet man with a faraway look. He had been glad to hear that I had enjoyed the play, but had expressed surprise. As we had talked I found the conversation leading almost imperceptibly to the subject of his own performance. I remembered the way in which he had seemed to avoid discussion of it, by enthusing over the performances of other members of the company. Now, in Carruthers odd performance, I recognised the same sort of phony bid for approbation.

"He'll probably revise his opinion of it when he cools down," I said brutally.

He shrugged. "You're probably right." But I knew he didn't think so and felt like kicking him.

The subject was dropped and we returned to the business in hand; that of Carruthers' removal to the Sa'

Maria prospek. After some discussion it was decided that the less Carruthers was seen about the Europa the better. I was for abandoning his belongings, which could have easily been replaced, but it turned out that he had left the bulk of his money, four thousand francs in Swiss and English currencies, locked up in his suitcase. The possession of plenty of ready cash was essential in the circumstances and I volunteered to collect it with his other gear if he would give me a note to the manager of the hotel. I soon regretted my offer. I might have known that such mundane simplicity would not appeal to Carruthers. He raised all sorts of objections to the proposal, none of which I could answer to his satisfaction. I might be seen leaving by Groom. The Countess's agents might have given instructions to the management. There were lots of other similar obstacles to which I gave in, finding myself finally committed to entering his room furtively—he still had his room key—and lowering his case by means of a cord out of the window. He would be waiting to receive it on the pavement below.

As we set off Carruthers explained to me that it would be a simple matter for me to reach the staircase leading to the rooms unobserved as the night porter who came on duty at ten was rarely at his post. Should I, by any outside chance, be questioned, I was to pretend to be a foreign bristle buyer, as there were a number of such gentlemen staying there. The prospect of excusing myself for snooping about somebody else's apartment and lowering his bags out of the window on the grounds that I was a bristle buyer did not commend itself to me; but it was a waste of time to argue with Carruthers. By the time we reached the end of the street in which the Europa stood it was dark.

With a jauntiness that I did not feel, I walked on alone to the palm-flanked entrance.

I had decided to put a bold front on it. No front was needed. Not at first, anyway. I reached Carruthers' room without meeting anyone and let myself in. Carruthers had warned me against switching on the light and the first thing I did was to fall over an overturned chair which lay in the middle of the room. I cursed, struck a match, shielding it carefully with my hands, and looked around.

The room was in a state of indescribable confusion. The bedding had been turned on to the floor and the mattress slit open. The pillows had been similarly treated and there were feathers everywhere. Drawers were open and as I moved my foot caught in a picture-frame stripped of its contents. I went into the bathroom, crushing glass under foot as I did so. Another match showed me Carruthers' case, the locks smashed and the contents strewn on the floor. A rapid search showed that the money had gone. Suddenly I thought I heard a faint sound from the bedroom. I put the match out and stood still. There was dead silence for a minute or two and I concluded that I had imagined it. The place was beginning to get on my nerves and I picked my way back to the window in the bedroom. I opened it gently and looked out. Carruthers was below me and looking up. He waved his hand. I took a piece of paper and a pencil from my pocket, scribbled: "Room ransacked, money gone," and uncoiled the cord. I attached the note to one end and lowered it down to him. Then I dragged what remained of the bed to the window and lashed the other end of the cord to the frame. I had just completed these preparations when I felt a sharp tug on the cord and leaned out. Carruthers motioned me to haul the cord up again. I did so. On the end was my note to which Carruthers had added: "Leave everything and clear."

I let the rope down again and was just buttoning up my coat for the descent when I heard a faint "click" from the door. I flung my leg over the sill. I got no farther. The door flew open and a stab of light from the corridor illuminated the room.

"If you move an inch you'll be shot," said a familiar voice.

I remained motionless. I was still half-blinded by the unexpected light and all I could see was two figures silhouetted in the doorway. Then the door shut and the room lights were switched on. It was Groom and Nikolai and in the right hand of the latter was a heavy automatic fitted with a Maxim silencer.

Groom regarded me steadily for a moment: Then: "Get back into the room," he said.

I did so.

"Put your hands behind your head."

I obeyed. Nikolai stood beside him glowering at me. He was a tough-looking Greek with a dirty complexion, a wet clumsy mouth and a nose that drooped nearly to his chin. He had his left arm in a sling. The fingers of his useful hand twitched longingly at the hair trigger of the gun. Groom addressed him without taking his eyes off me.

"Is this one of the men?"

"Yes, Monsieur."

"Where's Professor Barstow?" he said to me.

"I don't know."

"You're lying." He spoke coolly. "Where are the papers you stole the other night?"

"I don't know what you're talking about."

"Who are you?"

I told him.

"You're a very foolish man, Mr. Casey. I think I ought to explain, if you entertain any doubts on the subject, that if you do not tell me what you have done with those papers you will be shot dead inside five minutes."

His florid face had lost none of its benignity as he uttered the threat. He was smiling slightly, not very pleasantly, but smiling. Only a faint twitching of the muscles at the side of his mouth and a deadly quality in his eyes betrayed the fact that he was very much in earnest. My spine crept.

"Look here," I said hastily, "I haven't got your papers, they were put back in the safe."

"The copies then, please, Mr. Casey."

"There are no copies."

He shook his head impatiently and his fleshy cheeks quivered grotesquely. "Bluff, Mr. Casey, will do you no good," he said and his voice had become curiously husky. "I am going to count five," he said, suddenly dropping into French. "If you haven't told me by then I shall know one of two things; either that you really do not know or that you are a fool. In either case, Nikolai will shoot you. You hear, Nikolai?"

The Greek's wet lips opened a little, showing his gums. I saw the muzzle of the silencer drop slightly until it was pointing at my stomach. Groom glanced sideways at him.

"No, Nikolai," he said, "not the stomach. He will scream and that will attract attention."

The gun tilted a few degrees.

"*Un,*" said Groom.

"You won't get away with this."

"*Deux.*"

"They hang murderers in Ixania, don't they?"

"*Trois.*

I was silent.

"*Quatre.*"

He paused a little longer. I saw Nikolai's forearm bracing to take the recoil. I bit my lip to stop my mouth trembling. Then, with a click, the lights went out.

As I hurled myself sideways, I saw the flash and heard the sharp thud of the silenced gun. I sprawled on the floor. There was the sound of a scuffle, a cry of pain and the lights were up again. Standing with his back to the door, automatic in hand, was Carruthers. Facing him were Groom and Nikolai, the latter holding his wounded arm. I scrambled to my feet.

"See if Groom has a gun," said Carruthers curtly.

I found a small Belgian six-shot automatic in Groom's breast pocket. Nikolai gave a howl of agony when I touched him, but I took no notice. There was only an empty holster under his arm, but in his pocket I found twenty pounds in English notes which I took. Carruthers did not take his eyes off the pair.

"His gun's on the floor behind you," he said. "Put it in your pocket."

I obeyed. Carruthers smiled at Groom who was staring at him, a puzzled look on his face.

"I find this behaviour a little odd, Professor," he said at last. He indicated the panic-stricken Nikolai. "This gentleman and I discovered this man," he nodded at me, "burgling your room."

"I told him to," answered Carruthers grimly.

"Ah, in that case," said Groom, "there's nothing more to be said." He took a step towards the door.

"Stop where you are," snapped Carruthers.

Groom stopped. "Certainly," he said mildly. "But I do

wish you would point that pistol somewhere else. They go off so easily if one isn't used to them."

"That, Mr. Groom, will be unfortunate for you."

The lips of the other man curved in a genuine smile.

"You know, Professor," he said slowly, "I think I must be getting old. This is the second time that I have made a mistake about you." A sudden thought seemed to strike him. "You are, I suppose—er—Professor Barstow?"

Carruthers grinned. Groom's eyes hardened.

"I shall not make a third mistake," he said.

"No, you won't," said Carruthers, "because I'm going to shoot you. Give me the gun you picked up, Casey—the one with the silencer."

"But . . ." I began.

"Give it to me. Wait. See if it's loaded first."

It was loaded and I handed it over. I saw him level it, then I looked at Groom. A change had come over him. The round, genial, florid face had turned a dirty grey. The plump cheeks had fallen in. The lower lip trembled as though he were striving to say something. Suddenly he turned away with a choking sound, retched and vomited. Carruthers looked at him for a moment, then raised his arm again. Nikolai went down on his knees. I turned away, but no shot came. I felt a touch on my arm.

"Come on, let's get out of this," said Carruthers.

We went. I felt a trifle shaky. We reached the street without meeting a soul.

"How did you get in with the key in my pocket?" I asked him.

"Took the master key from the night porter's office. As I told you, he's never there when he should be."

I said nothing. We walked on, our feet echoing on the deserted pavements. After a while I said: "Lucky for me you jumped to what was happening when I didn't come down. Thanks a lot."

"I didn't wait for that. As soon as I knew that the room had been searched I realised that they'd be waiting for me to come back. Naturally, Groom thought I'd taken the Kassen papers for myself. I heard the last part of your conversation through the keyhole." He paused, then added irrelevantly: "Groom's a strange man, isn't he?"

"Hm. Do you think he meant to shoot me?"

"Of course he did."

"Why didn't you shoot him?"

"I found I couldn't do it." He sounded more surprised than ashamed.

We came at last to the Sa' Maria prospek, where we halted. I gave him the money I had retrieved from Nikolai and then fished Groom's gun out of my pocket. He shook his head.

"You may need it," he said; "it's best to be prepared."

I pocketed the automatic with a sigh. The transition from newspaper man to desperado is a more arduous process than some people would have you believe.

* * * * *

It was ten days before I saw Carruthers again. The day after our encounter with Groom, the pink-eyed officer from the Countess called and cross-examined me in his ludicrous French concerning Carruthers' whereabouts; but I denied all knowledge of him and, after a last threatening "*Où se trouve cet homme, Barstof*?" he departed with an ominous promise to return. I was, however, in touch with the affairs of the Young Peasants' Party. It had been arranged that Beker should telephone to me every day at different times and from different public booths. With the likelihood of my telephone being tapped, our conversations were necessarily non-committal, but I gathered that everything was going according to plan—Carruthers' plan—and that developments might soon be expected. Of the Countess and Marassin, I heard nothing. I must confess that I felt a trifle out of it. The events of the past few days had accustomed me to dramatic action. The uneventful backwater in which I now found myself, beyond allowing me to make up some arrears of sleep, held no attractions for me. There was, besides, little information that I was able to pass on to the Young Peasants, and I suspected that Toumachin was keeping me wrapped in cellophane and out of the way while his plans matured. He was probably right for at that time I was endeavouring to restore my self-respect by cabling guarded reports to New York. They were, under the circumstances, useless pieces of work and I was not surprised to receive an urgent cable demanding, in effect, to know what I thought I was playing at. I was in a difficulty here. To cable back that I was waiting for a revolution to break was out. There was certain to be a censor at work. I thought round the problem a bit and then sent a message which would, I hoped, look dumb enough to be cryptic. It ran:

> ARTICLES ON IXANIAN BIRDS TO FOLLOW SOON. PREPARING TO LEAVE NESTS. OLD BIRDS SHY. CASEY.

The next day I received a reply. It was encouraging.

> WILL CREDIT YOU IN ZOVGOROD IF MONEY NEEDED. NASH.

I considered the sentence and decided that it was a request for information concerning the projected New York loan. I sent the following reply:

HAVE ENOUGH TO GO ON WITH. SEND NO MORE. MIGHT GET LOST. YOUNG BIRDS ALSO SHY. CASEY.

The reply from New York was quietly encouraging.

HOLDING FUNDS FOR YOUR SAYSO. NASH.

For the next two days I went about in a much more buoyant frame of mind. I even went so far as to seek the promised interview with the Countess on the subject of the Eastern Pact, but was told that she was away. I was seen instead by Prince Ladislaus. He was, I decided, one of those dumbbells who made a uniform look good and no more. If the Countess had been in the vicinity he would not, I felt, have dared to open his mouth. As it was, he sat me in a chair and talked pompous inanities at me for an hour and a half. I was thankful when it was over.

A further two days doing nothing, however, soon made me long even for an interview with the Prince. I spent most of the time when I wasn't waiting for Beker's telephone calls sitting in cafés reading back numbers of *Time* forwarded by the *Tribune* man in Bucharest. I was thus engaged one afternoon when a man sat down beside me. I turned and recognised Beker. I was surprised to see him and said so as I returned his greeting.

"No, Monsieur Casey," he replied, "they do not know me yet. I am from the country. I have not been in Zovgorod for long. You see," he added, his grim little face stretching into a grin, "I used to have a beard."

"How's Barstow?" I asked.

His eyes lighted up. I listened to a long panegyric on the "Professor's" virtues, his organising ability, his tactical brilliance and his ingenuity. Toumachin, Beker said without a hint of jealousy, had taken the Professor to his heart. Suddenly Beker seemed to become embarrassed and hesitated a little. I waited. Then he went on, choosing his words carefully.

"The Professor, your friend, Monsieur, he is inclined, perhaps, to the macabre in his tastes?"

I would have believed anything of Carruthers, but I asked him what he meant. He became more self-conscious than ever and went on yet more hesitantly.

"He carries a picture postcard of the Countess Schverzinski in his pocket. Now that, Monsieur, is *drôle*, for he cannot but hate her as do we all."

I remembered Carruthers' sentimental outburst on the night of the robbery.

"It may be," I suggested, "to remind him of his hatred."

He shook his head solemnly and explained. I cannot remember the exact words he used, but the picture they conjured up was vivid. Carruthers, it seemed, would spend hours at a time gazing at the postcard in an unmistakably sentimental fashion. In Beker's philosophy only one conceivable construction could be placed upon this phenomenon. Carruthers, according to him, was perversely attracted to the Countess. He discoursed at length on the implications of such an affair. "Macabre," I decided, was a mild word for him to have used when I had heard in detail the conclusions that he and Toumachin had reached. He inquired anxiously if I thought he was right. I said that it was a likely solution and he seemed relieved. The curious sense of unreality that I had experienced in my contacts with Carruthers had evidently been felt by Beker and Toumachin. It had worried them and they had immediately rationalised it in their own characteristic fashion. But I thought then, and for that matter do so still, that Carruthers had in him a curious streak of pure adolescence. He was like a schoolboy not yet quite grown out of his Red Indian games and suffering his first attack of calf-love; though, even as I write it, the description seems entirely inadequate and even disloyal to a man who was many things by turns, none of them measurable against ordinary standards of adult male behavior, all of them intensely human. In Beker's eyes he is a great man. In my eyes he remains—Carruthers.

Beker had news for me. The peasants in the outlying towns were ready to put the great plan into operation, though what exactly this plan now involved he would not say. I knew the bare outlines of it but, according to Beker, Carruthers had revised many of his ideas and it was now quite a complicated though, I was assured, infallible piece of mechanism. Zero hour, he said, would be very, very soon now. He left me soon after with vehement assurances that I would be called in the moment the ball opened. I went so far as to send a cable to New York:

BIRDS STARTING TO HOP. STAND BY. CASEY.

I felt slightly foolish then. If the whole thing fell flat I would be a joke.

I have written elsewhere and at length on the subject of the Ixanian revolution, of the political situation that led up to it and of the dramatic twenty-four hours in which the peasants' coup d'état was effected. But of the curious atmosphere which preceded the storm I have said nothing. Such tenuous abstractions are frowned upon, unwisely I think, by the students and politicians. These persons seem to think that revolutions can be foisted upon unsuspecting publics like new armament programmes or secret alliances. I do not believe that there was a man or woman in Zovgorod, with the exception of the members of the Government, during the week preceding the Young Peasants' bid for power who did not feel that there was something in the wind. Few actually knew anything—which was just as well, for the Countess's intelligence people were not stupid—but those hot sunny days brooded over a city in suspense, a city in which cafés emptied early and shutters were closed. If the Countess and her friends had not held themselves so aloof from the people, they could not have failed to sense the popular uneasiness.

On May the third I went for my usual morning walk along the Kudbek. As soon as I had left the hotel I had sensed that something was happening. By the time I reached the Kudbek I knew it for a fact. Groups of people were standing about in breathless and, I thought, somewhat furtive conversation. Anxious glances were being cast. The ordinary babble of conversation in the cafés had changed to a low hum. Clearly there was something to talk about. The police, of whom there was an unusual number in the streets, seemed nervous. I saw a man arrested for bumping into a policeman as he hurried along the sidewalk. I bought a paper. It told me nothing. I asked the waiter at the café what it was all about and he pretended not to understand. Half an hour later a troop of cavalry clattered past heading for the Chamber of Deputies. There were one or two faint *Bravas*, but that was all.

That day Beker was not due to telephone me until after

lunch, but I soon beat it back to the hotel in the hope that he would get through before. There was no message for me and I sat down to wait. Then I thought of Petar and rang the bell. Another waiter answered it and informed me under pressure that Petar was away sick. I drew my own conclusions as to the truth of this and cursed Beker for not calling in.

His call was due at half-past two, but I hung about frantically smoking cigarettes and trying to make up my mind not to ignore Toumachin's instructions by going to the Sa' Maria prospek, until close on nightfall. By the time he finally got through I was in a fury of impatience and leapt to the telephone with a long and corrosive speech trembling on my lips. I did not have time to deliver it.

"Apologies," said Beker's voice quickly. "The tobacco."

He hung up.

I grabbed my hat and coat and rushed out. "Tobacco" was the code word we had arranged to mean "come at once." I needed no urging. Avoiding the main thoroughfares as much as possible I sprinted most of the way. As I neared the quarter, however, I slowed down to a sharp walk. The streets were strangely silent. A huddle of men on a corner broke up as I approached. In the Sa' Maria prospek not a soul was to be seen.

At number eleven there was the same door-slamming performance as when Carruthers and I had first gone there. When Beker came, however, he drew me in quickly and led the way upstairs.

Toumachin's room was like an army corps headquarters during a battle. He and Carruthers were standing by the table with bent heads poring over large-scale maps. Disposed about the room were half a dozen Ixanians whom I did not recognise. There was a woman amongst them.

They were talking together in low tones. Toumachin greeted me effusively, Carruthers with a preoccupied air, and they returned to their maps. The others had raised their heads at my coming and Beker introduced me to each in turn as the American press representative in Zovgorod. The woman proved to be a "leader from the west." All their names were impossible to memorise. Then Toumachin waved me over to the table and gave me a chair.

"Mr. Casey," he said with a business-like air, "we fulfil our promise. Here is the situation. You know the broad outline of our plan. One object is to concentrate the army far away from Zovgorod while we carry out our plans here. For that purpose we have commenced our campaign by instigating two local peasant risings, one in Grad in the North, one in Kutsk in the South. The Kutsk rising began last night. Under our instructions the Party leaders there took possession of the municipal buildings and proclaimed an independent government. The Government here has ordered a force of four thousand troops to the district to suppress the rising. A battalion from the barracks entrained this morning. They and the forces from other parts will have arrived at their destination by tomorrow morning at the latest. The Grad rising was timed for dawn this morning. The Party there are working under identical instructions to the men of Kutsk. A further five thousand troops from other districts were ordered to Grad this afternoon. They will arrive by midday tomorrow. There will then be only a battalion left in Zovgorod. The nearest troops apart from that will be twenty hours away from this city. As I told you before, we have many sympathisers in the ranks and the proportion of Government loyalists in that battalion need not worry us unduly. Kutsk was chosen first because it is the smaller town and the Government, believing the rising there to be a local disturbance, have devoted more troops to the suppression of it than if the Grad rising had alarmed them first."

"Ingenious enough, Toumachin," I said, "but what about the people in those towns?"

"They will retire to the hills as the troops approach. They will be safe enough for the moment. It would take weeks to round them up. But things will not be allowed to get as far as that. From the east and west, small parties of men from other towns are converging on Zovgorod. Small parties will not attract attention. They have been at it for the past week. By tomorrow there will be two forces of our friends outside the city ready to enter at the appointed time. The moment the soldiers have passed a certain point their lines of communications will be cut by parties told off for the purpose. One o'clock tomorrow morning is the provisional time. Telegraph wires will be broken and the railway will be blocked. We have made arrangements to occupy the radio station and the aerodrome. Zovgorod will be isolated for twelve hours. During that time we shall occupy the city and proclaim martial law. Communications will then be restored and the troops will be withdrawn from Grad and Kutsk and their officers arrested pending their declarations of loyalty to the new Government. The Chamber of Deputies will then be summoned, dissolved and a new election proclaimed. It is then, Monsieur Casey, that we shall avail ourselves of your valued services. The telegraphs will be thrown open to you. Our first anxiety will be to secure the approval and recognition of Bucharest, then comes Paris, London and New York. Your influence will make it possible."

"But . . ." I started in bewilderment.

"My friend Casey will be more than equal to the task," interrupted Carruthers smoothly.

I could have killed him. God knows what he'd been telling Toumachin. People have the most fantastic notions of the power of individual newspaper men. But I had no time to protest. Toumachin was thanking me regally and a chorus of excited approval and self-congratulation arose from the others. I resolved to make my position as an impartial reporter clear to Carruthers at the first available opportunity and leave him to make the explanations.

I drew Beker aside and asked him for news of Groom. He was vague and, I suspected, intentionally so. The Professor had that affair in his personal charge; all would doubtless be revealed in time. I sought out Carruthers. He was more informative.

"Frankly," he said, "I don't know what he's up to or what he's staying on for. However, he can't move without my knowing and if he doesn't move tonight he won't get another chance."

"You see, Monsieur," put in Toumachin who was standing by, "the Professor has gained his point. That affair is out of the hands of Toumachin."

"Well," I said with a venomous glance at Carruthers, "the Young Peasants seem to have thought of everything." Carruthers preened himself, Toumachin looked not ill-pleased. A thought struck me. "By the way, what about those gentry who wanted to assassinate the President and blow up the dam?"

I could have sworn that the two exchanged meaning glances.

"Oh, those," said Carruthers airily, "we have directed their energies into other channels," and he grinned smugly at Toumachin.

This absurd air of over-confidence both irritated and alarmed me. They did not seem to realise that they were no longer playing at hole-in-the-corner politics and that they were trying to overthrow a Government in power. Andrassin, I felt, would have disapproved. But as I looked round at them again my irritation left me. Toumachin had returned to his table, the others to their conversation. Their faces were grave and their eyes were steady. I examined them one by one. There was not a stupid or crooked face amongst them. The broad, strong, coarsely chiselled peasant face of the woman was beautiful. It was then that I realised the reason for my ill-temper. It was the thought that I might fail these worthy people, that I was unequal to the part for which Carruthers and Toumachin had cast me. They must know now that they asked too much, more than I possessed. I had turned to tell Toumachin so, to tell him that other, better arrangements must be made, when there came the sudden purr of a buzzer in the room.

There was dead silence. Beker walked calmly to the window and looked out for a second, then he dashed to the door and was gone. I glanced at the scene in the room. The men had, instinctively it seemed, grouped themselves in a semicircle round Toumachin. The woman had not moved. Carruthers, I found, was at my side by the door. Then came the sound of Beker's feet on the stairs. When he came in he looked at Toumachin, but it was to Carruthers that he spoke.

"It's Plek," he said breathlessly, "he has been shot, but he managed to get here. Half an hour ago Groom and his men left by automobile for Kassen's laboratory."

14

MAY 21st AND 22nd

Nobody spoke for a moment. Then Carruthers glanced at Toumachin who nodded.

"Take Beker," he said. "I cannot well spare him, but he is worth two or three others."

"The automobile?" asked Beker.

Toumachin nodded again. "They shall be ready."

"Casey ought to come," said Carruthers, and I blessed him.

Toumachin pursed his lips. He looked at me. He must have seen the way the land lay, for he smiled faintly and shrugged. "Be careful, Monsieur," he said, "we cannot afford to lose our American champion."

There was no time for explanations now. With a curt "Come on" to Beker and me, Carruthers was already out of the room and halfway down the stairs. We followed at speed. When we reached the passage to the door we had to edge by the body of a man on the floor. The woman who opened the doorway was propping up his head and trying to give him some water. The right side of the torso was soaked with blood. His mouth was open and the whites of his eyes showed through half-closed lids.

"Plek," whispered Beker. "He's dead. A martyr of the revolution."

Outside the door we turned down the street towards the river. Carruthers broke into a run, but Beker said that we might attract attention and we walked quickly. The quarter was like a rabbit warren and pitch dark. Led by Beker we dived in and out of countless narrow alleys and passages. Lights glowed faintly here and there behind windows at ground level; once or twice I heard the sound of scuffling footsteps and a quick shutting of doors; but we met no one until we came to a small courtyard. I felt cobbles under my feet as we crossed it. Then I heard Beker give a peculiar whistle. The next moment a blinding light shone in our faces as a door facing us swung open, disclosing a large black Buick sedan. The light came from a lamp suspended from the roof of the garage. I heard the engine of the car start, then it shot out of the garage and pulled up with a jerk beside us. A man got out of the driving-seat and went back into the garage, followed by Beker. Motioning to me to stay where I was, Carruthers followed. I saw them talking excitedly; then Beker went to a telephone in the corner of the garage and the light was put out. I could hear him speaking, but the hum of the engine drowned whatever he was saying. Carruthers returned.

"Get in," he said.

He followed me.

"What's happening?" I asked.

"We're going to put a spoke in Mister Groom's wheel once and for all." I heard him chuckle to himself.

"What's this place?"

"Belongs to the Young Peasants. It's connected by telephone with that other place. Toumachin phoned them to have the car ready for us."

"What are we waiting for, then?"

"Beker's attending to some very necessary business. As a matter of fact I'm rather glad Groom decided to have his go at the laboratory tonight. If he'd left it until tomorrow he'd have been deported before he could do anything. We shouldn't have had this chance."

To my other questions he would make no reply, merely grinning and telling me to wait and see, as though I were a child asking for candy. A minute or so later Beker and the driver got in, Beker with a curt "*Bien,*" and we started.

For a few minutes the Buick wound in and out of courtyards similar to the one from which we had started. Carruthers said that they were remains of an early Ottoman occupation and that they had been practically uninhabited since the cholera epidemic of 1907. At last, however, we turned on to a better road and the car leapt forward. We were soon clear of the city and the black heights of the valley closed in upon us.

It had started to rain heavily and I could see lightning flickering over the hills in the distance. The road was badly holed and the rain whipped the loose dust among the stone rubble into a treacherous slime. The Buick bucked and slithered along at about forty kilometres an hour. It seemed like a hundred and forty. We could not possibly have gone faster and, as it was, we left the road twice. It was an appropriate start to a night during which my heart rarely left my mouth except to sink to my boots.

"Ifs" are as enthralling as they are unprofitable and I have often speculated as to the way in which events would have turned that night if chance had felt differently about us. In the end I always arrive at the same conclusion, namely: that if chance had been a jot less benign, I at least would now be as dead as Plek, Marassin and the pink-eyed officer, for we moved in a margin of safety the width of a hair. Time, however, has brought one thing into true perspective. That thing is Kassen's death. Whatever the actual facts of that brilliant man's end, I believe that Carruthers had always intended that he should die. To me he had said that he had "other plans" for Kassen; but that, I believe now, was a tactful deceit. He wanted my help and could not afford to let my squeamishness stand in the way of his getting it. In his declaration to Toumachin he said, in effect, that the Kassen secret must be placed beyond the reach of all men. He certainly realised that Kassen's death was an essential ingredient in the creation of that state of affairs. Perhaps the manner of this man's dying was the subject of the thoughts revolving in Carruthers' queer agglomeration of a mind as the Buick lurched along the Kuder Valley to the laboratory. I saw his face but once in the light of the match he held to his pipe. It was calm and thoughtful. Thus might the real Professor Barstow have looked as he contemplated a mathematical abstraction. Carruthers' personality always seemed several sizes too large for his body.

We had been travelling along the valley road for some twenty minutes before Carruthers leant forward and told the driver to extinguish his lights and stop. Beker got out with us and, telling the driver to go on for half a kilometer and wait, the three of us went forward on foot.

The rain had lifted slightly, but the lightning still flickered on the horizon and the road was already a quagmire. It was impossible to avoid the potholes in the dark and I was soon up to the ankles in liquid mud. For five minutes we squelched along on the level, then Carruthers bore to the right and the ground began to rise. We were now, I guessed, on the road leading to the stone quarry. The surface here was firmer as the road was drained by streamlets which I could hear running alongside. The gradient was about one in ten and we climbed for perhaps half a mile before Carruthers cautioned us against noise and ordered us into single file. We proceeded gingerly until I saw the sides of the quarry right above us. Then Carruthers stopped. Whispering to Beker and me to stay where we were, he disappeared into the darkness ahead. I could just see that the road degenerated at this point into a rough track. Carruthers returned a moment later with the news that there was a car fifteen yards ahead and that there was a man in it.

We held a council of war; that is to say, Carruthers told us what to do. A minute later I found myself following Beker off the road to the left, down a sharp incline, across a bog and through a clump of trees perched on ground rising almost perpendicularly. I slipped twice and Beker tore the skin of his leg against a knife-edge of rock, but once among the trees we had something by which to steady ourselves. We made the top at last and found ourselves standing on the track slightly above the level of the quarry bottom. Making no attempt to silence our footsteps we started to walk down the track towards the car. We had gone about fifty metres before we saw it, a big sedan without lights. I saw the door by the driving-seat open slowly; then, raising his voice slightly, Beker said something reassuring in Ixanian and the man got out. He stood peering uncertainly at us as we covered the last three or four yards. We were about two metres from him before he saw us at all clearly. Then he gave an exclamatory grunt and went for his gun. His hand did not reach it. A shadow moved suddenly behind him, there was a faint "snick" and he dropped to the ground.

Carruthers stepped round him and nodded to us. We bound the man with rope from the tool-box, gagged him with two handkerchiefs—one in his mouth and one to keep it in—and dumped him down among the trees. Murmuring that there was no harm in cutting off Groom's retreat, Carruthers removed the arm from the car's distributor and slipped it in his pocket. We resumed our march up to the laboratory. We were nearer than I had supposed. The track became a path. We halted before a small wicket-gate. Carruthers examined it and reported in a swift undertone that it was part of an electrified fence which surrounded the laboratory. The gate, however, was swinging on its hinges in the breeze and we passed through it.

We moved forward cautiously up the path. The familiar shape of the laboratory was visible now. It was in darkness except for a dull glow from one of the long windows in the High-Tension laboratory at the far end. Carruthers motioned to us to listen to him.

"There's one entrance to the end laboratory from the low buildings. I shall take that way. There'll be another door in the far side wall of the High-Tension building. Beker and Casey, you try that way. I want to get them boxed in, but don't do anything until I give the signal. Then shoot."

He moved off and Beker and I had turned to go when we came to a sudden standstill. A dreadful cry had come from the direction of the laboratory. It started as a long-drawn "Ah" and rose to a blood-curdling shriek. Then it was cut off as though a hand had been clapped over the mouth that uttered it. Beker and I stood still. My heart was pounding and my legs shook. The skin on my spine tingled. I heard Beker mutter an oath and felt his hand quivering on my arm. Then we heard Carruthers' voice hissing "Go on" and blundered through the dripping bushes toward our objective. We reached the wall eventually and paused a moment to get our breaths before we started to work our way along towards the High-Tension building.

There were loose stones underfoot and our progress was slow, for they crunched at every step. My stomach was turning with fear, not so much of the situation as of hearing that scream repeated. It had upset my nerve badly. To make matters worse, there were overhanging trees that shut out every vestige of light so that I kept running into Beker in the darkness. We managed it at last, however, and on rounding the corner of the building, came upon a small door leading into it. Beker stepped past me and, taking the handle in both hands, turned it slowly. Slowly it yielded and a thin blade of light split the blackness. Beker leant forward and the blade broadened until we could see inside.

I had never before seen the interior of a high-voltage laboratory. To my unscientific eye it looked very like a shot from an early German film about "the future." Suspended from the roof on a ganglion of long corrugated-glass insulators were two large copper globes. There appeared to be an arrangement for raising and lowering them. Two gleaming copper tubes descended vertically from the globes to another pair of insulators embedded in the concrete floor and thence passed to where row upon row of tall metal containers paraded against one wall. From the top of each container projected two smaller insulators like horns. I could also see part of an elaborate switchboard. A single powerful lamp hanging from the roof in an enamel reflector illuminated the place.

The general effect was highly decorative. Far from decorative, however, was the scene for which it provided so dramatic a setting.

Five men stood in a semicircle in the centre of the laboratory. I recognised Groom and Nikolai, with his arm still in a sling, amongst them; but it was the man in the centre of them who held my gaze. Lashed to the chair in which he sat, he appeared to be a mechanic for he was wearing brown dungarees. His head was lolling on his chest and he looked as if he were unconscious. This, I guessed, was the one who had screamed. I was soon to know why. One of the group advanced threateningly towards the seated figure weighing what looked like a short stick in his hand. Then I saw the stick whip as the man brandished it and realised that it was a rubber truncheon, the *totschläger* or "beater-to-death" of Nazi Germany and the persuasive element in many a Third Degree. The man with the truncheon made a show of hitting the mechanic across the knee with it. The man's head rolled back and he let out a hoarse shout of terror. I understood. A blow on the knee-cap is bad enough at the best of times. When that blow is dealt with a rubber truncheon the pain is unbearable. Moreover, the knee-cap does not numb as easily as other parts of the body, so that repetitions of the blow will intensify the agony. The device, a New York detective has told me, is far more demoralising to the victim than many of the more elaborate tortures.

The man with the truncheon twice repeated the feint of hitting, but the man in the chair had fainted and did not respond again. Another man rained blows on the mechanic's face with his fist. They jarred him back into consciousness and he raised his head in a pitiful effort to evade the blows. Nikolai stepped forward and spoke to him in Ixanian. I saw him point threateningly to the man with the truncheon. Groom stood by smoking placidly during the questioning. The mechanic evidently could not or would not tell what they wanted to know, for Nikolai struck him with his free hand and motioned to the truncheon expert and stepped back. The latter advanced again and, glaring at the mechanic, raised his arm slowly. The man in the chair flinched and shouted huskily. I heard Beker beside me draw breath sharply. Then my hand fastened on the gun in my pocket. I did not think or even care whether what I was about to do was against Carruthers' orders or not. I just knew that I could not stand by and hear the man in the chair shriek again. With a sweep of my arm I flung the door open and charged into the laboratory.

I have often wondered how much of the pyrotechnic display that followed this highly absurd action of mine can be attributed to blind fury and how much to the fact that I had never fired an automatic pistol in my life before. A little of both I think. In my excitement I must have pressed the trigger several times, for I signalled my entry with a fusillade of shots. The first two hit the opposite wall, the third and fourth sent up spurts of concrete from the floor. The next instant I felt a paralysing blow on my wrist and my gun clattered to the floor. I saw the man who had fired the shot levelling his gun again as the others sprang towards me, when there came a deafening explosion from behind me and the man went down on his face. If Beker had not decided to support my futile effort I should have been shot dead instantly. Before he could fire again, however, another player took a hand in the game. From the door on the far side of the laboratory came the thud of a silenced gun, there was a crash of glass and the light went out.

I felt Beker catch my arm. My next clear memory is stubbing my foot against a stone as we made for cover. "*Vite,*" gasped Beker breathlessly as we stumbled on. There were shouts behind us. "What about the Professor?" I panted in between breaths as we got back on to the path.

"The Professor is more than able to take care of himself," rejoined Beker.

Suddenly there came the thud-thud of Carruthers' automatic from the direction of the laboratory, followed by a yell of pain, then a spatter of intermittent firing. There was no pursuit now. We halted and listened. There was another shout and more firing. "*Sacré chien,* what a madness!" Beker was muttering. Then, telling me to stay and look to my wound, he started back to the laboratory.

I stayed and not ungratefully for I felt slightly dizzy and my wrist was beginning to ache. I put my hand to it and a spasm of pain shot up my arm. My hand came away wet and I saw by the faint light that the sky yielded that I was bleeding badly. I improvised a tourniquet with my handkerchief and a pencil to tighten it and applied it on my forearm above the wound. I tightened it savagely. I was bitterly ashamed of my rash behavior. It was not improbable that I had completely wrecked Carruthers' careful plans. I listened dismally for sounds of life from the laboratory and heard nothing but the drip of the bushes. I had no precise idea of my position. I was on the path, but at what point on it I did not know. I moved slowly back the way Beker had brought me. A few metres and I was at the fence. I paused. Then, quite distinctly, I heard someone moving in the bushes ahead. I withdrew from the path, crouched down in the undergrowth and waited. Without a gun and with a wounded wrist that was becoming more painful every minute, I could do nothing else. The rustling continued. It sounded as though someone was working his way towards the gate. Suddenly the beam of a searchlight from the roof of the High-Tension building stabbed the darkness. Carruthers or Groom must have found the way to operate it. Whoever it was, the area inside the fence was going to be an uncomfortable place for the other party.

The beam swung down like a huge finger and started to traverse the bushes. It was an eerie sight. There was a ground mist rising and in the searchlight it swirled like white smoke above the gleaming wet leaves. Huge moths flitted and whirled in the beam and once a small owl started up flapping wildly. The light came on slowly. Suddenly, from the blackness towards which it was moving, came the flash and crack of a revolver shot. The light jumped a few yards and stopped. There, picked out as though he were on a stage, stood Nikolai.

As the light caught him he crouched and dodged sideways. The beam followed him. He double backwards and forwards, but though he kept disappearing from my view, the man at the searchlight did not lose him. Nikolai must have realised that he was hopelessly trapped, for although he still kept zig-zagging among the bushes—presumably to make himself a difficult target for a gun—he was steadily working his way towards the fence near where I crouched. He was three metres from the fence when he hesitated, then, turning suddenly, he made a dash straight for it. He was in the full glare of the searchlight when I saw him grasp the top wire preparatory to squeezing through it. He got no farther. The moment his hand touched the wire he seemed to stiffen, his body twisted, his heels left the ground and his knees bent slowly as though he were bearing an insupportable burden. Then, fixed in that posture, he lolled gently against the fence. He did not move again. From the laboratory came the faint clangour of an electric bell.

The light moved on with a quick sweep round the laboratory and then went out. The filament was still glowing dully when I heard feet scrunching on the path and Beker's voice calling my name. I stood up and he saw me.

"It is well, Monsieur. The power is now off. Come in."

I opened the gate and we were nearing the laboratory when I heard the starter of a car grinding away on the track below.

"Groom," explained Beker. "He got away with another man before the power was switched on to the fence. It is as well. We are not anxious to have his death to account for to the British Consul. But the automobile will not start. They will have a long walk."

"What about the others?"

"Nikolai is where you saw him. The man I shot is dead. The Professor killed the other when he tried to climb up the ladder to the searchlight. He lies with a broken neck." He stopped, then added: "The Professor is a great fighter."

"What's happened to that poor guy in the chair?"

"He is, I think, dead. A weak heart probably. That treatment would have killed stronger men."

We found Carruthers in the small laboratory surrounded by papers. He was rummaging through the drawers in a small desk in the corner. He straightened himself as we came in.

"No use," he said briefly. "I can't find anything. I've tried the living quarters, every likely place. We shall have to adhere to our original plan." He turned to Beker. "Are the men there?"

Beker nodded.

"Look here," I burst out, "I'm darn sorry for what's happened, Professor. I guess I'm not cut out for this sort of job."

He grinned. "I wouldn't worry, Casey," he said. "I was just about to butt in myself when your fireworks started. You certainly stirred them up."

"If it hadn't been for Beker, they'd have stirred me up."

Beker's grim face relaxed into a smile.

"Anyway," said Carruthers, "how's the wrist?"

I showed him and he examined my tourniquet with a professional eye.

"It'll be all right," was his verdict. "But you'll have to have it dressed. See if you can find some lint."

He resumed his search. Beker disappeared outside. I went through a door and found myself in a bedroom with a smaller compartment fitted up as a bathroom adjoining it. I found a thick roll of lint bandage in a small enamelled iron cabinet fixed on the wall and took it back to the laboratory. Carruthers was crouching on the floor making a bonfire of the reams of notes and calculations that he had unearthed.

"Have you got the lint?" he asked as I came in.

I nodded.

"Good. I'll bandage it for you." He nodded towards the pile of papers. "The papers we want are not there, but I'm taking no chances. There may be stuff here that would give the right person the dope he needed." He paused. "You know," he went on, "I feel like a criminal, destroying all this brilliant work." He toed the charred remains thoughtfully.

"What are you going to do now?" I asked.

"You remember telling me about those hotheads who wanted to blow up the dam?"

"Yes—what about them?"

"Well, I'm giving them their opportunity to do some blowing up. There are six full-blooded nihilists with a hundred-weight or so of nitro-glycerine and shot firing equipment one hundred yards up the valley, and they're itching to get to work. I was keeping that picnic for tomorrow, but as soon as I knew that Groom was getting desperate I decided that I couldn't leave it any longer. This crew has been just over the other side of the hill in a village for three days now. Beker telephoned to them before we left to take up their posts immediately. They're getting the stuff into position now."

"You mean you're going to blow up this dump?"

He nodded solemnly. "Yes. I'm taking no chances. There mustn't be the remotest possibility of the Kassen secret surviving. Kassen's copy of the process may go elsewhere, but this place must go."

I found that I could hear footsteps crunching on the stones and the sound of low voices. "We'd better get out, hadn't we?"

"There's no immediate hurry. I want to delay it until the morning if possible. I don't wish to prejudice Toumachin's show by alarming them before he's well on the move."

"What about Kassen? The Countess still has her copy, too."

"Neither of them will be allowed to get away with it. Toumachin is seeing to that."

He started to bandage my wrist and for a time I

concentrated on that. It was very painful. Running through my mind, however, was the thought that, whatever Carruthers proposed to do, the Kassen secret was still as much alive as it had been on the day we had come to Zovgorod. Blowing up laboratories wasn't going to help and was, I thought, a trifle childish. But I was beginning to know my Carruthers and kept quiet about my misgivings. In any case, I did not feel up to arguing.

Carruthers quickly completed the bandage and gave me the roll of lint to hold while he cut it. My left hand is never very useful. I fumbled and dropped the roll. It fell to the floor. Suddenly Carruthers gave a yelp of excitement. The next instant he was on his knees unrolling the lint. I soon saw what he was after. As the lint unrolled itself, strips of paper were falling out. Each was covered with masses of minute writing.

Carruthers collected the last of them and stood up, his eyes gleaming.

"We've got it," he crowed, excitedly waving the papers in my face. "The second copy of the Kassen conditioning process."

I grabbed the papers and glanced through them quickly. He was right. There was no mistaking the similarity between the writings on them and those in the Countess's safe. The next moment Carruthers had grabbed my shoulders and was waltzing me round the laboratory. The festivities did not last long. Someone coughed and a dry voice said in perfect English:

"Highly diverting, but I am afraid I shall have to ask you to put your hands up."

A small, narrow-shouldered little man with a large head stood at the door regarding us with a thin, twisted smile on his lips. Behind him, with big German pistols in their hands, stood Marassin, the pink-eyed officer and another uniformed man. Over their heads I could see others.

We stood still and said nothing. I, at any rate, was beyond uttering words. The little man advanced into the centre of the room and bowed to Carruthers.

"Professor Barstow, I believe. My name is Kassen. You may have heard of me."

"Who," said Carruthers fulsomely, "has not?"

Kassen acknowledged the compliment with a gesture. He ignored me and glanced round the room. I watched his face apprehensively, but it was expressionless as his eyes stopped at the pile of charred papers.

"I hope," he said evenly without turning his head, "that you have found your visit instructive, Professor." His eyes alighted on the unrolled bandage. "Ah, yes, of course, I see you have." He carefully gathered up the papers that Carruthers had dropped, put them in his pocket and went through the door leading to the High-Tension building and we were left staring into the inhuman eyes of Marassin. The man had not spoken a word, but a wave of sick fear swept over me as I looked at him. Only a ceaseless twitching of his jaw muscles proclaimed the fact that he was alive. He had a necrophilitic quality that I found unutterably repellent. Suddenly, Kassen called out something and the third man of the trio who carried a hand-lamp followed Kassen into the other building. A moment later Kassen returned. His eyes were blazing. He snapped something at Marassin, then went up to Carruthers and struck him on the mouth. Carruthers did not flinch.

"So," said Kassen, his voice trembling with rage, "you have seen fit to torture my assistant to death as well as destroy my records."

"No, Monsieur," said Carruthers calmly, "that is the work of someone else."

Kassen drew back with a sneer of disbelief.

He looked ugly and I hoped that Beker would not delay his return too long. My eyes went involuntarily to the window. The sounds had ceased and I guessed that the nihilists had decamped. He must have read my thoughts, for he laughed shortly.

"You need not expect any help from the other member of your little expedition," he said; "we were fortunate enough to meet him on the road." He turned to Marassin. "Have him brought in."

Marassin called an order over his shoulder and there was the sound of a scuffle outside. I gave up hope. With Beker taken, we were as good as lost. Two soldiers entered. Supported between them was the owner of the rubber truncheon. It was the man who had escaped with Groom.

"Search him," directed Kassen.

The first thing to come to light was the truncheon. Kassen weighed it in his hand thoughtfully for a moment, then turned to Carruthers.

"An excellent weapon, Professor. You will be desolated to learn, however, that I have a powerful sense of poetic justice. If poor Vasa were alive, I should probably allow him to be the instrument of it." He shrugged. "As it is, perhaps Colonel Marassin will oblige me."

He turned to Marassin, who stepped forward. His jaw muscles still twitched, but now his eyes were glowing strangely. He passed his gun to his pink-eyed companion and took the truncheon from Kassen.

"They must be bound," he said.

We were in an unpleasant predicament. If we disclaimed

all knowledge of the man with the truncheon, they would start looking for Beker. If we said nothing we were in for a bad time. There was this deciding factor; we were probably going to be killed in any case, but with Beker at large we at least stood a remote chance.

We were seized, seated in chairs and bound. The ropes on my wrist were agonising, but I managed to keep silent. There was no point in inviting torture. The truncheon wielder, who seemed to guess what was coming and who wept and pleaded unceasingly, was trussed in the same way. Marassin flourished the truncheon menacingly.

"The owner of the truncheon first, I think," said Kassen.

Marassin advanced towards the whimpering occupant of the chair beside me, raised the truncheon and brought it down heavily on the man's shoulders. I heard his collar-bone crack and he screamed. There was a pause, then Marassin lifted the truncheon again. Kassen held up his hand.

"Please, Colonel," he said apologetically in French, "I have not the stomach of you military men. Also, I have thought of a better way of disposing of these men. I take it that they are to be disposed of? The Countess wishes it?"

Marassin spoke an unintelligible sentence or two in his high monotone.

Kassen nodded his head understandingly. "There will be no mistake, Colonel," he said. He broke into Ixanian for a moment or two and we were then carried into the High-Tension building preceded by the man with the hand-lamp.

Seen from the interior it presented an even more bizarre appearance than before. Kassen went straight to the switchboard and a dozen resistance lamps glowed. The assistant, Vasa, had been released from the chair, evidently by Carruthers and Beker, and lay on the floor. The cloth by his knee had been cut away, exposing a red mess.

We were set down under Kassen's directions against the one vacant wall. Then he left us to get a large wheel in motion at the other end of the laboratory. I heard an exclamation from Carruthers and, glancing up, saw that the two copper globes suspended from the roof were slowly descending. Except for the creaking of the winding gear there was silence until the globes were within a metre of the floor. Then Kassen rejoined us.

"Familiar surroundings for you, Professor," he said smoothly. "Not, of course, as grand as those in which you have worked, but the best brains in science have always been able to make do with mediocre equipment. I do not need million-dollar laboratories to supplement my abilities."

"Admirably put," said Carruthers calmly.

Kassen smiled. "I am glad, Professor, that you are taking this so philosophically. In fact, I deeply regret that there is no time for us to discuss my latest work. I have been able, let me tell you, to effect changes of state, polymerisations, you will understand, in the atomic structure of certain substances. I should like to tell you more about it, of how I succeeded in establishing what, for want of a better phrase, I may call colloidal suspension of a proportion of the atoms in these substances; but I must forgo that pleasure for a different one. I am going to kill you. You have had the impertinence to meddle with matters which do not concern you. You were warned. You took no heed. So you and your stupid friends must die. Your death will be sudden, but there will be a certain period of anticipation preceding it. In point of fact I propose to discharge a million volts across your bodies. You, Professor, will understand how I am going to do it; but for the benefit of Mr. Casey here," he bowed to me, "I shall demonstrate first in order that he may enjoy the same stimulating sensations."

A dozen retorts rose to my lips, but Carruthers said nothing and I thought it best to follow his lead. I comforted myself with the thought that Beker could not be far away now.

Kassen went to the switchboard and operated two large circuit breakers. Then he returned.

"The condensers are being charged," he informed us; "in a moment you will hear the eddy current vibrations commence."

We listened in silence. Marassin stood immobile beside us. The other men looked interested. Then, faintly at first, we heard a humming sound coming from the rows of horned containers. About two minutes went by. In that time the humming had risen to a loud and angry buzz. Then I noticed a blue glow surrounding each of the copper globes.

"Ionisation of the air," explained Kassen.

The blue glows intensified and became larger. I felt a curious sensation on the top of my head. It was as though my hair were lifting. I noticed then that the hair on Kassen's head was moving as though a stiff breeze were blowing. Suddenly the buzz went up a semi-tone in pitch. The next moment there was an ear-splitting crack like the sound of a giant stock-whip and a huge blue-white flame played for a second or two between the two globes. Simultaneously there was a crash from the switchboard as the circuit breakers flew out. A curious acrid smell filled the air.

"The smell, Mr. Casey," said Kassen, "is due principally

to ozone. There is also a little nitric acid created by the arc. A splendid entertainment is it not?" He paused. "Having aroused the interest of our audience," he added ominously, "we will now proceed to the second act."

We were lifted again and, this time, placed between the two globes. By this time, the man in the third chair was only partly conscious and his head lolled from side to side as they carried him. There was little room between the globes and our chairs were touching. I could hear him moaning softly to himself.

"What about it, Carruthers?" I whispered.

"We must hope for Beker," he returned, but I noticed that his mouth was set in a curious way.

There came an excited burst of speech from Marassin, to which Kassen replied briefly.

"Our friend the Colonel is becoming impatient," he said, "we must not disappoint him."

He went to the switchboard again and was about to press the breakers home when respite came from an unexpected quarter. There was a sudden commotion outside and the Countess swept into the laboratory.

She glanced round, saw us, then turned imperiously to Kassen. "I heard that Kortner had telephoned from the power station to say that the searchlight here was being used. What is the explanation?"

"These gentlemen here are the explanation, my dear Magda," he answered in a conciliatory tone. "Marassin and I found them rifling the laboratory. They had also been torturing Vasa for information that he did not possess. He is dead. In deference to Mr. Casey's American citizenship, I was about to electrocute them. They are, so Colonel Marassin tells me, under sentence of death."

She swept a quick glance over us. I saw Carruthers smile

faintly. She seemed to hesitate. Then she nodded. She was about to go when suddenly she turned on us in a cold fury.

"I warned you, Professor. I warned you, Mr. Casey. You chose to disregard my instructions and you will have to take the consequences."

She was trembling with rage. In that moment I saw that she was probably not quite sane. She controlled herself with a tremendous effort and turned to Kassen.

"Was there anything missing?"

He seemed cowed. "No, dear lady," he muttered, "nothing but some records which they burnt."

"Then get on with your execution."

She turned again to go. Kassen went to the switchboard. Marassin was drawing himself up and was saluting stiffly, either in honour of her going or in deference to our prospective decease, when the outer door of the laboratory on our right flew open and a volley of shots rang out. I saw Kassen and three of the other men, among them the pink-eyed officer, fall.

Thrusting the Countess through the door behind him, Marassin retreated, returning the fire from the outer door as he went. Another volley followed and the remaining two men, who had been firing wildly at their invisible target, pitched forward. Marassin was unhit, however, and disappeared. Then Beker rushed in at the head of five scrawny and wild-looking peasants holding rifles. Three of them dashed after Marassin and the Countess. The other two took up a defensive position by the door.

Beker cut us free. I think I must have been a little light-headed for I remember becoming hysterical about the oil that was oozing over the floor from a bullet-hole in one of the High-Tension condensers. Neither of them took any notice of me. Carruthers was bending over

Kassen. He was apparently quite dead, as was the man in the chair who had been hit in the head by a ricochet.

Beker's three henchmen returned crestfallen and reported that Marassin and the Countess had got away by car. They commenced to loot the bodies.

Carruthers turned to Beker.

"Have you a match?" he said.

Beker produced a box.

"Light one, Beker."

Beker did so and held it out.

Solemnly Carruthers drew a sheaf of papers from his pocket and put them to the match. The flames licked round them. He held the papers by the corners until they were burnt, then he ground them underfoot.

"There remains now your work," he said to Beker.

The other nodded.

A few moments later, Carruthers and I were walking down the hill towards Groom's disabled car. The man we had bound had evidently been freed by Groom, for he was nowhere to be seen. Carruthers replaced the distributor arm and the car started easily. We climbed in.

"We'll wait a minute," said Carruthers.

We waited in silence.

The rain had stopped and the sky was clear. The air smelt fresh and good. I felt drowsy and there was only the pain throbbing in my wrist to remind me that I had not just woken from a dream. Mechanically I noted the time by the luminous dial of Carruthers' watch. It was a quarter to one. In fifteen minutes the Ixanian revolution would begin. It seemed a very remote affair under the calm derision of the stars.

Suddenly there was a quick rumble and the roar of a big

explosion shook the car. In the direction of the laboratory there was a glare in the sky.

Carruthers put the car in gear, backed it into the quarry and then shot forward down to the valley road.

"Kassen, his laboratory and one copy of his secret," he murmured. "Now for the second copy."

15

MAY 22nd

On the outskirts of Zovgorod we received the first intimation that a revolution was in progress.

A barrier had been erected across the road. It was manned by a dozen or more armed peasants, grim, grizzly men, two of whom jumped on the running-board as we approached. Carruthers produced from his pocket a small card and displayed it. The sight of it was hailed with excited shouts and *Bravas*. A way was promptly cleared for us and we drove on.

In the city itself, all was silent, but as we approached the centre of it I began to notice groups of men standing at street corners in the shadows. Behind one such group I saw the shadow of a machine-gun.

"The outpost pickets," Carruthers explained. "They're there to deal with the police if they get troublesome."

We avoided the Kudbek and drove through back streets in the direction of the Countess's house. About half a kilometre from the square in which it was situated we were stopped by one of the pickets. The leader of the group came to the window of the car and saluted.

"The Countess Schverzinski has gone to her home?" Carruthers asked in French.

"Half an hour ago, Monsieur," was the reply.

"The servants and guards have been dealt with?"

"Two hours since, Monsieur."

"Good. From now on no one is to enter or leave the area without a pass."

"*Bien, Monsieur.*"

We drove on.

"Good staff work," I commented.

"I've been at it for a week," he answered, "preparing for just such an emergency as this. I'm taking no chances, Casey," he went on in the ringing tones he invariably reserved for the utterance of his more banal pronouncements. "There's too much at stake."

He stopped the car at the end of the square and we walked the rest of the way. The house was dark except for a single lighted room on the second floor.

"Are we going in the same way as before?" I said as we approached.

"With the guards and servants removed we can afford to be a little less informal," he answered.

"How did you know that you'd want them removed?"

"Put yourself in the Countess's place. If you were taken unawares by a revolution, what would you do? Take your most valuable possessions and fly the country, I should think."

I was unconvinced by this specious explanation but let it go. Carruthers, I had noticed, always liked to regard his incredible guesswork as masterly foresight. Guesswork or no, however, his arrangements had been made well, for careful reconnoitring showed that the house was unguarded.

We advanced up the front drive. A large Mercédès limousine with the radiator still hot was standing in front of the portico. We continued round to the side of the house. Then I remembered that, with my right arm partially out of action, I could not climb up over as I had done before. I told Carruthers.

"You needn't worry," was his reply, "we're not doing any climbing tonight."

He led the way to the servants' entrance and tried the door. It was open. We walked in and found ourselves in the kitchen. Carruthers struck a match.

On all sides there was evidence of the hasty departure of the servants. A dishcloth and an apron were lying on the floor. On the table was a half-finished meal set for four persons. We passed through the kitchen along a narrow passage with doors leading off it until we came to a stairway leading upwards. Here we stopped and listened. I thought I heard faint movements above.

"They're getting ready to go," whispered Carruthers.

I said nothing. The house was getting on my nerves. I once travelled on a giant liner on her way to the breaker's yard because someone had had the notion that there was a sob story in the trip. There was, but it was never printed. There was a pitiful loneliness about the deserted rooms and corridors that exercised a profoundly depressing effect on even the seamen. The stuff I turned out as a result might have been the outcome of a collaboration between Edgar Allan Poe and George Eliot. For me there is a curious air of tragedy in inanimate objects divorced from the warm proximity of the humanity for whose use they were designed. I have sensed it in an empty theatre and as I stood with Carruthers in the darkness of that old house I sensed it again. I pictured the scene that had been enacted there that night; the men on guard surprised at their posts by the sudden pressure of gun-barrels and whispered threats; the owner of the apron flinging it aside as he hastened to obey the curt commands to leave the goulash now glutinous on four cold plates; the rapidly methodical search of the house and then the sharp order to abandon. As I discarded these fancies impatiently, a question arose in my mind.

"Where's Prince Ladislaus?" I whispered.

"Left for Belgrade six hours ago. Very wise of him."

That surprised me. The Prince had not impressed me as a man with an ear to the ground. I said so.

Carruthers laughed softly.

"He was warned. We couldn't risk having him in the country. As leader of the aristocratic party he would have had to have been shot. That would have embarrassed the new Government. He has powerful relatives abroad."

"He might have told the Countess."

"He wasn't given time."

He pressed my arm enjoining silence and started up the stairs. I could see nothing ahead and counted nine steps before we came to a door set at a curious angle in the wall. Carruthers took my left hand and raised it above my head. My fingers encountered wood. I felt a wedge shape and moved my hand backwards and forwards. Then I understood. We were beneath the main staircase leading from the hall to the floors above, and behind the door used by the servants. Carruthers leaned forward and I saw the shape of it as it opened slightly.

We waited there for about five minutes. The darkest hours had passed and through the opening in the door objects had begun to take shape. I felt cold, my wrist ached and I was hungry. I longed, above all, for a drink.

For a time we heard no further movements from upstairs; then a door slammed suddenly and we heard footsteps over our heads as someone began to descend the stairs. The footsteps reached the hall and clicked across the parquet. A door opened and there was silence. Then I saw the door in front of us opening slowly and Carruthers' figure filling the gap.

We stepped out into the hall. From a room at the end of the hall, a shaft of light came through a half-opened door. Carruthers led the way slowly towards it. Outside the door we paused. There was a faint rustling of papers from within. Then I saw Carruthers raise his gun, lean forward and gently push the door open.

The room was the Countess's study and the occupant of it was the lady herself. She stood by the safe still in her fur travelling-coat. In her hand was a bundle of documents. A pile of charred and burning papers in the hearth explained what she was doing. As she came into view another bunch of torn scraps fluttered from her hand into the bonfire. She did not turn her head.

"Come in," she said abstractedly.

We went in, Carruthers with his gun levelled.

"I was expecting you, Professor," she remarked, as she dropped the remainder of the papers into the hearth.

I started, but Carruthers was unmoved.

"Madame's perspicacity does her credit," he said cordially. "I trust," he added quietly, "that you understand what I am here for."

She turned to face us with a smile. She might have been according an audience to the ambassador of a friendly power.

"I do, Professor, I do indeed," she answered. "I very

much regret, however, that we cannot accede to your request."

Carruthers raised his eyebrows. "We?"

"Colonel Marassin is just behind you," she observed.

I experienced a bitter thrill of fear. We had walked straight into a trap. We were to be defeated at the last by one man and one woman in a house surrounded by allies. We had been fools to suppose that we were a match for these people.

"If you will lower your pistol and step forward one pace very slowly, Colonel Marassin may defer his intention to kill you for a moment or two," said the Countess in French.

Carruthers' arm dropped to his side and the gun was snatched from his hand. Marassin advanced into the room until he was beside the Countess.

"My brother," she went on smoothly, "left a message for me before his enforced departure. The city, I believe, is in the hands of a rebel force."

"Someone must have been careless," murmured Carruthers, "but your information is correct, Madame."

She sighed. "Small things sometimes decide the fates of nations," she said. "If I had not been called to the laboratory, I should have received the message in time to recall troops from Grad and Kutsk to deal with the situation. It is, I presume, impossible now?"

"Zovgorod was isolated from the outside world an hour ago, Madame."

She accepted the statement without question.

"I thought as much. I have one great consolation. The peasant Government seems to have better brains to lead it than the foolish democrats who overthrew the monarchy. The Grad and Kutsk affairs were good ideas."

Carruthers bowed. "Madame is too kind."

Her eyebrows went up.

"So?" She looked at him keenly. "I should not have thought it. You have qualities unusual in a professor. I can see that we underrated you. I thought so once before, but Colonel Marassin assured me that you were as foolish as you looked. I will confess, however, that I still feel a trifle mystified. Armament manufacturers do not usually gain their ends by supporting radical movements. They encourage the more aggressive forms of dictatorship."

"That I can well believe," answered he. "I am afraid, Madame, that I am a very misunderstood man. Mr. Groom, too, had the misfortune to assume that I was the man I seemed."

"For whom do you work then, Professor?"

I saw a blank look come into Carruthers' face. He seemed to have lost his self-possession. The Countess waited in vain for his answer. She shrugged at last.

"It does not matter," she said. "Tell me, however, where is this man Groom at the moment?"

Carruthers recovered some of his assurance. "Mr. Groom," he said, "is at this moment wandering in the darkness towards Zovgorod. Mr. Casey and I are using his automobile."

"Then," she said thoughtfully, "you have taken nothing from the laboratory?"

"Nothing, Madame. The laboratory is, however, no longer standing. A few hot-heads were anxious to retaliate for Colonel Marassin's disgusting action in murdering Andrassin so foully, by blowing up the electricity dam. A more responsible section of the Young Peasants' party was able fortunately to divert their enterprise into more harmless channels. The laboratory is now a hole in the ground."

He spoke in French, doubtless for Marassin's benefit. A

slight movement of the man's lips showed that the remark had got home. The Countess had gone pale, but she betrayed no emotions.

"Was there anyone killed?" she asked quietly.

"In the actual explosion, Madame, I believe no. But in the fracas that followed the Colonel's attempt to stage an execution, a civilian named Kassen was shot dead."

I heard her draw in her breath sharply. She glanced at Marassin. His face was expressionless; the hand holding his heavy gun was rock steady, his eyes were fixed unblinkingly on us.

"I see," said the Countess at last. She walked to the window, and stood for a moment or two looking into the darkness. Then she turned to us again.

"What exactly have you been attempting to do?" she said.

"To prevent the use of Kassen's discovery and to destroy all evidence of its existence," he answered promptly.

"Why?"

"To preserve civilisation, Madame," said Carruthers; rather pompously, I thought.

She gave an exclamation of irritation.

"You talk like a politician. This so-called civilisation of yours, what does it amount to? A conspiracy of mediocrity. In what have you progressed from the barbarian? You have made life a little more comfortable for your unlovely bodies and a thousand times more uncomfortable for your minds. You have made virtues of humility and mercy because the majority of you are humble and weak and fear the few who are stronger. The slave desired weakness in his master and created moral superstitions to bind him. 'All men are equal in the sight of God'—the tyrant insanity of impotence that animates the small men who crawl about the earth calling upon those who live on the heights to descend and share the stinking air of democracy lest they imperil their immortal souls."

She curled the last words round her tongue and almost spat them out.

"Are we to understand," said Carruthers, "that Ixania's place in your scheme of things was on the summit of the heights?"

"Ixania," she answered him, "is a small nation. You do not belong to a small nation, Professor, nor you, Mr. Casey," she added, acknowledging my presence for the first time; "therefore you do not know what that means. Without colonies, without natural resources, without money to buy more than a bare livelihood, we struggle for existence. It is many years since a great house was built in Ixania, the peasants starve, the population is decreasing, our export trade is failing. We need capital and we have none. The very fact of our independence is proof of our innate poverty. If we had possessed one valuable asset, our territory would long ago have been annexed by one of the powers. The time has come when Ixania must take what she wants by force or starve. A miracle gave us the means. You, the member of a state that has always taken what it wanted by force, have, out of your absurd notions of the sanctity of human life, destroyed those means. You have much to answer for."

"If your peasants were lusty and well-fed; if your population were increasing; if your trade were overwhelming and your streets flowed with capital, you would still possess the craving for conquest," answered Carruthers. "Ixania is unproductive because you make it so. Your business men suck the country's life blood so that there is none to feed the body. Your soil is for the most part uncultivated because the wealth that should fertilise it maintains an army that is as unnecessary as it would be inadequate as a means of defence. I believe that the peasant Government will alter these things. They will make mistakes, it is true, but they will never make the mistake of believing that war can accomplish anything but destruction and misery. A man for whom I have no respect once told me that you were a patriot. Patriotism in high places is another name for personal ambition, intellectual dishonesty and avarice."

The Countess did not seem to have been listening. She waved a vague and impatient hand.

"Under other circumstances," she said, "I might find this discussion diverting. At the moment we shall, I regret, have to leave you. Colonel Marassin is anxious to kill you. I am indifferent to your fates."

She spoke rapidly to Marassin. He answered with two high-pitched monosyllables and raised his gun suggestively. She turned to us.

"The Colonel is insistent. You will excuse me."

She was about to sweep past us when Carruthers intercepted her.

"If we are to be shot in cold blood, Madame," he said calmly, "custom, I think, entitles us to make one request."

"What is that, Monsieur?" She was clearly in a hurry.

"That you produce the copy of the Kassen conditioning process which is in your possession and burn it in our presence."

My heart sank. The fatuity of this attempt to obtain a respite was pitifully obvious. I tried to realise that in less than two minutes' time a bullet would crash into my skull. Marassin was probably a dead shot. It would, I comforted myself, be painless. I wondered how the news would be received in the *Tribune* office in New York.

"Your request, as you must realise, is absurd," said the Countess.

"Consider, Madame," said Carruthers urgently, "you do not, I think, appreciate the position. This house is surrounded by armed parties. If you succeed in getting through their cordon you would be in no better case. No one will be allowed to leave Zovgorod for the next twelve hours without a special pass signed by Toumachin."

"I am grateful for the information, Monsieur," she answered quietly, "but I am afraid that I cannot alter my plans for a mob of thick-skulled peasants. As for the Kassen secret, Professor, I shall take that with me and nothing will stop me. The stupid have always preyed enviously upon great men, but those men's work has gone on. You have killed Jacob Kassen, the most brilliant man the age has produced, but his work, too, shall live. That I promise you."

With a thrill of hope, I noticed that, as she had been speaking, Carruthers had been edging ever so slightly to his left, so that now she was almost between him and Marassin. The latter could not fire without taking careful aim for fear of hitting the Countess. I saw him move hesitantly to cover us from a different angle. Carruthers caught him in the fraction of a second in which he was off his guard. Opening his mouth as if he were about to reply to the Countess, Carruthers suddenly bent double and launched himself in a flying tackle at Marassin's legs.

Marassin fired once and a shower of plaster fell from the ceiling above my head as the two crashed to the floor, struggling fiercely. I, I regret to say, lost my head completely for a moment and stood stock-still, unable even to think. Then I heard a rustle beside me and remembered the Countess. Before I could do anything, however, she had switched the lights out and was through the door. As I grasped the handle I heard the key turn. There were sounds of a desperate struggle from the opposite corner of the room and I fumbled desperately for the switch. In the inky light which came through the window, I caught a momentary glimpse of the two men locked together, saw them sway and then fall again. There was the faint sound of a car starting in front of the house. At that moment, my fingers found the switch and I pressed it. As the light went up, Carruthers was staggering to his feet again, and I saw Marassin's automatic in his hand. A second later I saw Marassin himself, his face ludicrously distorted with rage, grasp a small bronze that stood on the desk and draw back his arm to throw it. I shouted to Carruthers, but almost before the sound was out of my throat he had fired twice.

For a moment Marassin seemed turned to stone. His arm was at the summit of the uncompleted movement and stayed there for a second or two. Then he started coughing gently and the arm fell loosely. The bronze tumbled heavily to the floor. The man crumpled, still coughing, beside it.

Carruthers looked at Marassin for a moment, then at me. He was panting and licked his lips feverishly.

"Are you all right?" I said.

He nodded. "Where's she gone?"

"She locked the door. While you were on the floor I heard the car start. She can't get far, though, so we needn't worry."

He dropped the automatic into his pocket and went to the window.

"This way for us," he said. "You can jump down without

using your arm. That woman might get past anything and I shan't be satisfied until I've seen that last copy burnt with my own eyes."

He flung the window open and, with a glance at the now silent Marassin, stepped on to the balcony. I followed and a minute later we were sprinting as if the entire Society of the Red Gauntlet were behind us.

* * * * *

By the time we had reached the place where we had parked Groom's car I was glad to slump into the seat beside Carruthers who had the motor running by the time I caught up with him.

We stopped for an instant when we reached the picket. No explanations were needed. One man was nursing a broken arm, another lay on the pavement with a bad head injury. The Countess had driven the Mercédès straight through the cordon drawn across the road. They had had no time to scatter. The leader reported that she had taken the road leading to the western exit from the city.

We reached the barricade on the west road five minutes later. Nothing had been seen there of either the Countess or her car.

"She must have doubled back," said Carruthers as he turned the car round. "The nearest road to the frontier goes south-east and I think she'd make for the frontier rather than try to reach Grad or Kutsk. That south-east road, as they call it, is little better than an oxen track, I believe, and covers some rough hill country. The rain will have cut it up badly in places, but she might decide to risk it. At all events she's got a good start of us and we can't afford to do anything but hope for a lucky guess. We'll make for the south-east road."

We started off again at a tremendous pace. Groom's car was a fast one and Carruthers drove like a dirt track racer. Our tyres screamed almost continuously as we wound through the narrow streets on the fringe of the city. It took twelve minutes by the clock on the instrument board for us to reach the barricade on the south-east road.

Our headlights showed us that our guess had been correct. The trestles that had composed it were still being dragged back into position across the road. Several of them were smashed. Carruthers slowed and flashed the headlights five times as we approached.

The men on the barricade dropped the trestle they were holding and crowded by the side of the road. As we drew level a chorus of shouts hailed us and hands pointed excitedly in the direction we were heading. We crept through the gap in the barricade and then accelerated again.

"She must have doubled twice," said Carruthers as we got into top gear once more. "It can't have been more than ten minutes since she rammed that barricade."

We flew on. The road was passable for a time, but as soon as we started to climb the foothills our troubles began. The road rose in a series of steps—short, sharp hills, then stretches of level. It is difficult to say which were the worst, hills or levels. On the former we had bad wheel-spin and skidded wildly. On the levels we ploughed through miniature lakes of mud that frequently threatened to bog us down. At times it was difficult to follow the road at all, but the sky was lightening ahead of us, and after a while we were able to do without the headlights which, with the shadows they created, were more of a hindrance than a help. The only human habitations we saw were a cluster of stone hovels at the base of one of the steps. Then, for some time, we ran across a rolling plain, surprising on the way some scraggy mountain sheep.

There was still no sign of our quarry, but as the contour of the land probably hid the road more than a hundred metres ahead, we could hardly expect to see any. Our headlights blazing again, we continued across the plain for about twenty minutes. The road then took another sharp turn upwards and changed appreciably in character. Mud gave place to stones. Regardless of springs, Carruthers put on speed and the car leapt about madly as we climbed all-out in low gear. Jamming my back against the seat and my feet against the sloping floor-boards I hung on for dear life as we ground upwards. There were terrifying bends where the camber ran the wrong way towards sheer drops of anything from ten to twenty metres. Carruthers drove amazingly well and beyond having to reverse once to get round a particularly suicidal corner we did not pause. The radiator was boiling long before we reached the highest point of the road, but we made it at last. We were about halfway down a long descent and had been going for just over an hour by the clock when we first saw the Mercédès.

Ahead, the dark mass of hill dimly outlined against the blue-black beginnings of the dawn was broken by a pin-point of light. It was moving slowly in a diagonal path across the hill and I guessed that the Mercédès was ascending a corkscrew road similar to the one we had just climbed. Carruthers nodded when I suggested it.

"We can't estimate how far she is away," he said. "It may be the distance that makes it look slow, but it's far more likely that the road's too bad for speed. In any case, the frontier's only an hour and a half away now if she travels fast. Don't forget we're going across Ixania at the narrowest point. We've got to catch up soon."

By this time we were again climbing and the light disappeared from view. If Carruthers had driven fast before, now he drove like a maniac. I shut my eyes and held on. Then I felt as if we were falling sideways as we took a corner and decided that it was better to keep my eyes open.

I could see as we neared the hillside two or three minutes later that the view we had had of it when we had spotted the Mercédès had been illusory. For one thing, it was not nearly so high as it had appeared then and the road ran to the side of it. The slow transverse movement of the lights of the Mercédès that we had observed was due neither to the distance nor to a steep corkscrew gradient but to a long encircling curve. The Mercédès had been moving round it and we had seen the reflection of its headlights from the rear.

Carruthers had obviously arrived at the same conclusion. "We can't be more than three minutes behind now," I heard him mutter.

The going was better here, although Carruthers had to exercise a certain amount of care in avoiding the small boulders which littered the road in places, from the slopes above.

The sky had paled noticeably by the time we had rounded the hill. Before us lay a deep pass running between two enormous peaks on which the snow was just visible by the light of a small pale moon that had oozed from behind a bank of cloud. The road to the pass zigzagged down the precipice below us. About halfway down was the Mercédès, nosing slowly round a bend, its headlamps swinging like searchlights into space. We commenced the descent.

Going up a mountain, whether you travel on foot or by car, is always easier than going down. For the next quarter of an hour I lived in constant expectation of death. Standing in front of the wrong end of a gun was, I told myself, an infinitely preferable situation to that in which I now found myself. Carruthers let the car run down the slopes, braked violently as we approached the bends and slid round them almost broadside on. Once our near-side rear wheel seemed to hang right over the precipice at the side of the road and we swayed horribly. Carruthers, however, jerked us back on to the road somehow and we dashed on. As we approached the bottom I could see that we were now only two bends behind the Countess who was taking fewer risks than Carruthers. After another sickening two minutes the lead was reduced to one bend and I could plainly hear the snarl of the Mercédès' exhaust. Then we began to close in.

The noise of her sports motor probably prevented her hearing our approach, but she must have seen our car for she put on speed. I understood the reason for Carruthers' haste. If she got on to the straight dry road to the pass we would never catch her. Groom's car, fast though it was, would be no match for the Mercédès on a clear run. There were only two bends to go before the bottom. At the first of these we were not more than twenty metres behind her. She took the corner beautifully, but Carruthers with his brake-and-slither tactics gained a few more metres. As we tore down the straight towards the last bend, Carruthers produced Marassin's gun.

"As soon as she's round the bend," he said grimly, "I'm going to burst the rear tyres."

The two cars shot down towards the last bend. It was a sharp right turn and a shelf of rock overhung the road. I heard the squeal of the Mercédès' brakes and felt Carruthers bracing himself against the cushions as he braked in his turn. I saw the Mercédès slide out and get halfway round the hairpin, then the Countess seemed to lose control. She was going too fast and instead of completing the turn the Mercédès swerved suddenly and shot straight out over the edge of the road. A moment or two after there was a crash as it hit the ground below.

We pulled up with locked wheels just beyond the bend, jumped out and ran to the side of the road.

For several seconds we could see nothing, then a flame shot up from about eighteen metres below us. By the time we had scrambled down to the bottom of the slope the Mercédès was a blazing mass. It lay on its side, wedged between two rocks. The heat was intense, but we got near enough to see that the Countess was not inside. We found her a short distance away.

Carruthers dropped on his knees beside her and raised her head. The light from the burning car shed a terrible light on the scene. She had, I thought, been killed instantly. Slowly, Carruthers drew a wad of papers from the pocket of her travelling-coat and held them up to me.

"Burn them, Casey," he said in a curious voice.

I took them and started towards the car. Something made me look back when I was halfway. Still on his knees, Carruthers was raising Marassin's gun to his head. A few strides brought me back to him. Snatching the gun from his hand, I flung it away into the shadows.

"Coming back?" I said.

He raised a face stained with tears and contorted with misery. He looked at me for a moment. Then he climbed painfully to his feet. I handed him the papers. He looked at them in a dazed fashion.

"Better burn them yourself," I said.

His shoulders hunched, he stumbled towards the blaze and threw them into the heart of the flames. He did not stay to see them burn, but started to climb back towards the road. As I saw his face again in the flickering light I realised for the first time that he was a middle-aged man.

* * * * *

The sun had not yet risen when I was awakened by the car stopping at the barricade outside Zovgorod. Carruthers looked ill and drawn in the morning light as he talked to the guard while a way was cleared for us. From the city came a rattle of machine-gun fire. The guard went away and returned with some meal cakes which we munched as we drove.

"How long have I been asleep?" I asked.

He grinned faintly. "Ever since the car started."

"Do they know what's happened in the city?"

"Toumachin's people have installed themselves in the Palace and the Chamber. All the outside forces of peasants have entered the city and are patrolling the streets. Everything has gone well. The only place where they're having trouble is at the barracks. Most of the troops left there and many officers went over to the peasants when the Minister of the Interior ordered them to shoot the rebels down. A few, led by some of the Red Gauntlet officers, are being besieged in the barracks. You'll want to send a cable. Better let me have it."

I did as he suggested. After that I remember walking into my room at the Bucharesti and sitting on my bed. Then, for the next eight hours, I slept.

16

MAY 22nd AND AFTER

The events that constituted the *coup d'état* of the Ixanian Peasants' Party and of their formation of a Government are too well known to need more than a brief recapitulation here.

To make the situation clear, it is necessary to go back to the time when Carruthers and I were floundering through the mud of the south-east road from Zovgorod in the wake of the Countess Magda Schverzinski. Many things took place in Zovgorod during the early hours of that morning—most of them in silence. The majority of the citizens of Zovgorod went uneasily to sleep under one Government and woke up no less apprehensively under a new one.

The entire *coup* was carried out with great aplomb and efficiency and the only shots were fired in the region of the barracks before the surrender of the republican officers and their few adherents, and in a street near the Cathedral where a body of police came into conflict with an armed picket.

Communications were severed promptly at 1 A.M.

An hour later, Toumachin and his council occupied the

Chamber of Deputies. This manoeuvre met with no resistance. Toumachin had taken the precaution of commandeering a number of official automobiles for the occasion, and the company that had been posted to guard the place presented arms punctiliously as the invaders swept into the courtyard. These troops remained aggressively on guard for five hours before their commanders discovered the facts of the situation. By that time a company of pro-peasant infantry had been ordered from the barracks to relieve them. Their officers, a sergeant and four men were the only members of the cavalry to refuse their allegiance to the new Government.

By 3 a.m. the Presidential Palace, the railroad yards, the airfield, the radio station, the telegraph offices, the telephone exchanges and the newspaper offices and printing works were held by the peasants from the east and west provinces who had poured silently into the city on the stroke of two. Machine-guns were mounted at all strategic points by the outpost picket and a "protective" cordon was thrown round the presidential residence. That was at three-thirty.

At this point the situation became critical. The police who, so far as their sympathies were concerned, were an unknown quantity, had massed near the Cathedral under the leadership of the Minister of the Interior, hastily summoned from his bed. They had already had a brush with a picket and things looked ugly. What happened subsequently is not very clear, but it appears that, thoroughly unnerved and unable to communicate with the barracks by telephone, the Minister had hurried off personally to call out the military. It seems, however, that on presenting his request for military support to the commandant, that worthy had refused to take orders from anyone except the Minister of War. Meanwhile, Toumachin and his henchmen had visited the houses of the Cabinet Ministers, roused them and, while the dazed politicians were still rubbing the sleep from their eyes, announced the fall of the Government and demanded their resignation under pain of property confiscation. All except the Prime Minister and the Chancellor of the Exchequer, whose fortunes were for the most part safely invested in foreign stocks and bonds, complied when the situation was explained to them. The two who refused were placed under close arrest. Among the compliants was the Minister of War, whose interest in shares, fair and unfair, had been confined, more tenuously, but no less profitably, to the perquisites of his office. Three minutes after he had signed his resignation, a messenger arrived from the commandant of the barracks asking for instructions. The ex-minister was about to climb back into bed at the time. He sent the only possible reply: that, as he was no longer Minister of War, he could give no instructions.

By this time, Toumachin had left with his retinue to interview the Minister of Agriculture, and the guard that remained foolishly allowed the commandant's messenger to return to the barracks with the Minister's message. The result was that the commandant decided to risk acting on the advice of the Minister of the Interior and ordered his subordinates to clear the streets of the insurgent peasants. The consequences might have been disastrous for Toumachin's party if the commandant had not been unwise enough to attempt to fire the hearts of his soldiers by parading them and delivering a speech. Most of the troops were recruited from peasant families, and when the commandant exhorted them to shoot down the peasant rabble without mercy there were murmurs. When, in the full flood of his peroration, the commandant referred to the rebels as "camels of peasants," a highly uncomplimentary mode of address in Ixanian, the murmur became a roar. Led by their non-commissioned officers, the troops refused to obey orders and, after beating the commandant and two other officers to death, marched with enthusiastic cries out of the barracks in the direction of the Chamber of Deputies.

By this time, Beker was back in the city in charge of the street forces. Fortunately, for a few of the troops had decided by some curious logical process that the occasion was one for looting, he was able to intercept them before they reached the Kudbek, parley with their leaders and persuade them to split their force up into companies. Two of these companies were sent back to surround the barracks, one was dispatched to the Palace, and the remaining one to the Chamber of Deputies. It was a wise decision in an awkward situation, for the soldiers, free from the restraint of discipline, might have become a source of embarrassment to the Government.

No time was lost in conveying the news of the troops' decision to the assembled police who, on hearing it, announced their intention of remaining neutral but vigilant. This suited Toumachin's purpose admirably, and at four-forty-five he received the Chief of Police. This was a sensible man, and after assuring Toumachin that his sole anxiety was for the maintenance of order, he confessed that he, personally, was not unsympathetic towards the aims of the Young Peasants' Party. With great tact Toumachin volunteered to withdraw some of the pickets from the streets and intimated that he would welcome their replacement by official police. The Chief departed an ally and the pickets were duly withdrawn from the main thoroughfare. This move probably saved a good deal of bloody conflict between the police, soldiery and peasants, and certainly contributed largely to the early consolidation of the peasants' position.

Soon after five, Toumachin and the new Council waited upon the President with the resignations of the cabinet, excluding those of the Prime Minister, the Chancellor of the Exchequer and the Minister of the Interior, who was now a member of the beleaguered garrison in the barracks. They were received in the Presidential bedroom. The old man was in pitiable fear of his life and readily agreed to accept the tendered resignations and to request the missing ones. Toumachin then presented two documents for his signature. The first declared Toumachin commander-in-chief of the army. The second was a proclamation of martial law. The President signed them both. Toumachin thus became constitutional head of a provisional government and *de facto* ruler of the country pending free elections and the subsequent repeal of martial law.

By 8:30 A.M., a special edition of the Zovgorod *Noviny* was on the streets. It proclaimed the change of government and probable date of the elections.

The populace was nervous and excited. As the morning wore on, there were one or two "incidents" and about thirty persons were arrested, but by noon things had quietened down. This process was hastened by the publication of a second edition of the *Noviny* in which a long list of the immediate reforms proposed by the provisional Government were announced, together with an assurance that there would be no persecution of political opponents.

All this was ancient history by the time I was awakened soon after one o'clock.

I was very angry with Carruthers, who had been sent by Toumachin to rouse me, and furious with myself. If there's one thing worse than falling down on a story, that thing is sleeping on it. I had done both. The news that my cable, authorized by Toumachin personally, was the only press report that been allowed out did not wholly satisfy me. I should, I told myself, have been on the spot getting an eye-witness story. As it was, I had to rely on hearsay. The fact that there had actually been nothing remarkable to witness since our return to the city soon after 6 A.M. did not strike me at the time.

Carruthers, who had treated himself to a bath and a shave at my hotel, looked clean but ghostly. He had not slept. He declared that my exhaustion was a natural reaction after the nervous stresses and strains of the previous night. He was probably right. I have stayed on a story for three days and nights without sleep; but on that occasion I was not labouring under the hourly expectation of sudden death.

My wrist, I found, had been properly dressed, the throbbing had ceased and, beyond a certain amount of stiffness, was in working order. I suddenly discovered that all I needed was something to eat. In answer to my ring, Petar appeared, wreathed in smiles and accompanied by an enormous meal. Not even Carruthers' pipe, which he smoked heavily while he talked and I ate, could spoil my appetite.

At two, Petar announced that a car had arrived from Toumachin to convey me to the Chamber. I finished my bath hurriedly and a quarter of an hour later was sitting beside Carruthers with an armed policeman and a military chauffeur in front. It was not until then that I realised that

I had made no attempt to deny the responsibility to which Carruthers had committed me.

"Look here, Carruthers," I began, "I've been meaning to speak to you about . . ."

"I know," he interrupted with a grin. "But let it wait until we've seen Toumachin."

"OK. It's your responsibility, not mine," I retorted.

He smiled.

A minute or two later we passed between machine-guns at the entrance to the Chamber of Deputies. We got out at the steps and were led through a maze of corridors to a first-floor room guarded by two soldiers with fixed bayonets.

It appeared to be an ante-room, for a pair of double doors, from behind which came a hum of voices, was set in one wall. An orderly stood at ease before the door. Our arrival was evidently awaited, for, as we were ushered in, the orderly clicked his heels and went to a telephone on the table. We heard him utter an Ixanian version of our surnames. Then he put down the receiver, clicked his heels again and, going to the double doors, flung them open. We walked through.

The scene was impressive. Sitting at a huge glass-topped desk sat Toumachin. Facing him in large leather armchairs sat three men, one unmistakably a countryman of mine. All looked solemn. Disposed about the room were one or two men and the woman whom I recognised as having been of the company in Toumachin's lodging the night before.

As we entered, Toumachin rose to his feet and extended his hand with a welcoming beam.

"I have been given an account of your adventures of last night," he said; "the Council and I are most grateful for your efforts." He bowed slightly towards the three armchaired men. "Permit me to present you to their Excellencies the United States Minister, Monsieur Englebert, the French Minister, Monsieur Chappey, and the Roumanian *chargé d'affaires*, Monsieur Vitchescu." He flourished a hand towards us. "Professor Barstow and Mr. Casey of the New York *Tribune*."

We shook hands all round. Englebert looked at me curiously.

"I had a message about you from Washington last night, Mr. Casey," he said grimly. "I was requested to keep you out of mischief. It appears that I was a little too late."

"Sorry, Minister," I said. "It's a pity I didn't get in touch with you sooner, but the circumstances were a little unusual."

He smiled. "I have already been hearing about your experiences from Monsieur Beker. I understand from Monsieur Toumachin that you have undertaken the job of official press officer for the new Government."

It was a question rather than a comment. I hesitated, then made up my mind. I turned to Toumachin, who had been watching us steadily.

"Monsieur Toumachin," I said, "will you permit me a few moments' conversation with Minister Englebert?"

"I understand perfectly, Monsieur," he answered courteously.

The minister and I withdrew to the ante-room.

"Look here, sir," I began when we were alone, "I'm in a bit of a jam."

He nodded. "I guessed as much. It's not for nothing, you know, that newspapers instruct their correspondents to keep themselves out of foreign party politics."

"That's all very well," I went on, "but I've got a story out of this, sir. Unluckily they've got the idea that I'm some sort of international whiz-kid; but, even if they do have to shed some of their illusions, they do need someone to look after their PR campaign and, personally, I'd like to help them. The only thing is: if there's going to be any trouble, if I'm going to embarrass you or the state department or the Roumanian *chargé d'affaires* or anyone else, then it's off."

He shrugged. "I think you need have no fears on that score. Technically there has been no revolution. Toumachin has acted shrewdly in fixing the affair within the limits of the constitution. I anticipate no complications. We had the *chargés d'affaires* of one or two neighbouring states here before you came. Unfortunately the Britisher is away hunting in the North, but the Frenchman, for one, doesn't care much what happens here and, as long as these people don't start any wars, neither will any of the others. I'm inclined to think, however, that you've completely missed the point so far as your possible usefulness to Toumachin is concerned."

"How?"

He contemplated my neck-tie thoughtfully. "Well, I don't know how Toumachin put the proposition to you. I should imagine he would convey the impression that you were to act as a sort of extraordinary foreign minister with the fate of Ixania quivering at your finger-tips."

"Something like that," I admitted.

He nodded. "I thought so. That's the Ixanian way. If you'd been in this country as long as I have you'd know that an Ixanian always says half what he means or—double. In any event he never says exactly what he means. All the same, I think you underrate your importance to Toumachin's Government. I should imagine that his chief worry at the moment is financial. Ten to one he'll want to raise some short-term loans. The only way he can get them is by creating a favourable impression on the money markets as quickly as possible—plans to reorganise, establish new industries and so on. That's what he wants you for, Mr. Casey."

"I see."

"Speaking unofficially," he went on with a faraway look, "I should advise you to give the matter your consideration. What this country needs . . ." He stopped himself. "You must dine at the Legation as soon as you can spare the time," he said; "you might bring Professor Barstow with you. My wife and I will be interested to hear an account of your adventures." He hesitated. "By the way, who is that highly unprofessorial gentleman?"

"Certainly not Professor Barstow," I said with a grin.

"Ah—just so," he said, and I realised for the first time what the word "diplomacy" means.

Ten minutes later I had become an Ixanian Civil Servant.

* * * * *

For the next few days I saw little of the outside world. Installed in an office in the Chamber of Deputies with a French-speaking male stenographer and a telegraphist, I bombarded the international news agencies with pro-peasant stories that sometimes brought blushes to the cheeks of even the enthusiastic Beker. I had also to handle the delicate business of reporting the death of the Countess Schverzinski without making it look as if the accident to her car were a frame-up engineered by the new Government. As a precautionary measure it had been arranged that her funeral should take place in Belgrade. Prince Ladislaus had demanded a princely price for his co-operation, but the situation had been too serious for haggling and the money had been hastily credited to him through an Italian Bank.

After accepting Toumachin's offer, I had felt guilty about my desertion of the *Tribune*, and the moment communications were restored, I placated my conscience by sending Nash a full exclusive story of the whole affair, omitting nothing but the business of the Kassen secret. Toumachin and Carruthers had both been insistent upon the point and even threatened to censor my reports unless I agreed to their proposal. I was quite ready to do so as, now that the episode was finished, I realised more than ever the futility of trying to tell the story convincingly. To my special cable report to the *Tribune*, I added a postscript explaining the circumstances and resigning my appointment. This postscript produced a characteristic reply:

> STORY FINE. REGRET CANNOT ACCEPT RESIGNATION. DON'T BE A DOPE. ADVISING IXANIAN GOVERNMENT VIA WASHINGTON THAT YOU ARE LOANED THEM FOR SIX MONTHS. HANSEN TAKING OVER PARIS JOB TEMPORARILY. LET US HAVE YOUR HANDOUTS FIRST. NASH.

I sent off a long and heartfelt letter of thanks, wired Hansen in Paris and settled down to enlightening the financial world on the subject of Ixanian potentialities.

About two days later I was in the midst of dictating a vehement affirmation of the solidarity of public opinion in Ixania and the certainty of an overwhelming mandate for the Peasant Party at the elections, when Carruthers wandered into the room. I had not seen him for two days, and as I was glad of any excuse for stopping work, I asked him to have a drink.

He did not answer but perched himself on the edge of my desk and sucked absently at an empty pipe. I noticed that he was looking desperately thin and ill, and said so. He muttered that he was "all right." He seemed to have something on his mind.

"Everything OK?" he said at last.

I assured him that it was. He nodded vaguely and started fiddling with the stem of his pipe. He did not look at me as he went on:

"I'm leaving for Paris tonight."

This was a surprise to me. I had heard from Beker that big inducements were to be offered to the "Professor" to stay in Ixania; but I said nothing, and waited for him to go on.

"You see," he said carefully, "my work is finished here now. There's nothing more for me to do." He got to his feet as though they were weighted with lead. "I'm going by the night train."

"That's the train they're sending the Countess to Belgrade on, isn't it?"

He nodded and turned to go. I put a hand on his arm.

"Look here, Carruthers," I said. "You're a sick man. Why not stick around a bit, get fit again and see what happens. You're sitting pretty with the Government, they'd give you their back teeth if you asked them."

"You forget," he answered wearily, "that I'm not Professor Barstow. They're bound to find that out sooner or later."

"You needn't worry," I assured him. "Beker was asking me yesterday who you really were. They're not quite dumb, you know. As a matter of fact, their hunch is that you're a Soviet agent. For all I know they may be right. Englishmen have been more unexpected things. I suppose you don't feel like telling me all about it? Frankly, I'm curious."

I did not tell him that the British Consul had that very morning endeavoured to pump me on the subject, but I found out later that Carruthers had been playing hide-and-seek with his country's representative for the past twenty-four hours.

Now he seemed about to answer me; then he stopped. There was a hunted look in his eyes. They avoided mine.

"It's no use," he mumbled, "my work is done."

Before I could stop him he had gone.

* * * * *

At nine o'clock that night I stood on the departure platform at Zovgorod station. With me was the British Consul. The horn sounded for the train to start.

"Doesn't look as though he'll catch it," said the consul gloomily.

The train began to move and soon rumbled slowly into the darkness beyond the swinging arc-lamps. The consul said politely that "it couldn't be helped" and invited me to broach a case of whisky he had received that day from England.

When I arrived back at my hotel a note was waiting for me. It was from Carruthers.

> DEAR CASEY (it ran),—
>
> I'm sorry I can't stop to say good-bye. I have an idea that your curiosity may get the better of

you—once a reporter, always a reporter. I'm leaving by the afternoon train. Don't worry about me: I expect that I shall stay with my friend the *Chef de la Sûreté* in Paris. He is a good fellow. Good-bye, my friend. I don't think we shall meet again but—who knows? Think kindly of me—

CONWAY CARRUTHERS.

That was the last I heard of the man who called himself Carruthers. Two days later, the Havas Agency reported that Professor Barstow, noted English savant, had been the victim of an attack on the Bâle-Paris express.

17

October

It was some months before I was free to devote myself to the problem over which I had spent so many fruitless hours of conjecture; that of Carruthers' identity. By September, however, Toumachin and his Government had established themselves politically and financially in the graces of London, Paris and New York, and my term of usefulness came to an end. Early in October I returned to Paris to resume the work that Hansen had been doing so capably in my absence.

One of the first things I did on my arrival was to turn up the French newspaper reports on the subject of the Bâle-Paris express incident.

They were surprisingly uninformative. Professor Barstow had been discovered between Mulheim and Belfort apparently suffering from severe concussion. A large bruise on the head suggested that he had been sandbagged by a train thief. The occupants of the neighbouring compartments had been unable to throw light on the occurrence. The thief had obviously been disturbed at his work, for there was money in the Professor's pocket when he was found. Of Professor Barstow's mysterious disappearance from England five weeks previously nothing was said. Even more curious was the omission of all reference to the incident in the many newspapers controlled directly and indirectly by the French armament combine. The only comment on the affair appeared in a left-wing sheet which declared bitterly that here was yet another outrage for which the Freemasons must accept responsibility.

A day or two later I called at the offices of the Chemin de Fer de l'Est and asked if and when I could interview the *chef de train* of the express concerned. I was told that Monsieur Abadis would arrive in Paris from Bâle the following day.

I duly ran M. Abadis to earth at the Gare de l'Est and, after some necessary preliminaries, induced him to give me his recollections of May 26th of that year.

He was inclined, at first, to be reticent, but when he found that I was more interested in the other passengers in the coach in which the wounded man had been found than in Professor Barstow himself, he opened up a little. I was anxious to test a theory I had formed. Had there, I asked him, been another person with an English passport in the coach? There had been. He himself had interviewed the other occupants of the coach in the hope that someone had seen the scoundrel. Could M. Abadis describe the Englishman? He smiled tolerantly. One saw so many with English passports and so many months ago . . . he shrugged. I described Groom and his eyes lighted up. *Si, si,* he remembered the gentleman now. The name? Ah, that was to ask too much. Groom? He shook his head slowly. Grindley-Jones? No, it was lost. Coltington? *Si, si, si!* . . . Mr. Coltington, that was he; now he remembered. The gentleman had left the train at Belfort when the police came on. Denis, the *wagon-lit* attendant, had remarked that it was strange to leave a fellow-countryman when he was in distress.

I asked one more question.

"What did Monsieur Barstow say when he recovered consciousness?"

The lips of M. Abadis tightened. Clearly, he had his instructions.

I did not pursue the matter. I had discovered what I wished to know. Groom, obviously under the impression that Carruthers had kept the Kassen secret for himself, had made a last desperate effort to gain possession of it. I left the discreet *chef* richer by a further hundred francs.

A fortnight later I had the occasion to go to London for a day or two and seized the opportunity to make inquiries about Professor Barstow. I learned at his house in London that he was in a sanatarium in Brighton. I went to Brighton by the next train.

The matron of the sanatarium was polite but firm. Professor Barstow was not allowed to receive visitors. I asked to see the doctor in charge. He was out but would return in two hours' time. I waited for three.

The doctor looked at me suspiciously when he heard what I wanted. It was obvious that he did not like Americans.

"Why are you so particularly anxious to see Professor Barstow?" he asked. "Are you a relative?"

I had prepared my story.

"No, but I read the story of the Professor's curious disappearance and seeing a photograph of him in a newspaper a few days ago I thought I recognised him as a man I knew in an hotel in Zürich last May. I wished to see if I was correct."

He looked more intelligent.

"That is a little different. We are particularly anxious to establish Professor Barstow's whereabouts during his recent unfortunate—er—illness. Particularly anxious, I may say, in view of certain . . ." He dissolved into an elaborate silence and pressed a button on his desk; he looked out of the window until the Matron appeared.

"Is Professor Barstow awake?" he said.

"No, doctor, asleep."

He turned to me. "If we are quiet, Mr. Casey, we shall not disturb him."

"Let me get this clear, doctor," I said. "Do you mean that Professor Barstow has been suffering from loss of memory?"

"That is—er—within limits—correct."

"And he doesn't remember anything of what happened to him in May?"

"Er—no. But perhaps . . ." He stood up.

Followed by the matron he led the way to a room at the rear of the building. There was linoleum on the floors of the passages. Everything was very clean. He opened the door softly.

It was late afternoon and the autumn sunset was glowing across the room through the slats of an open venetian blind. We tiptoed inside.

The man on the bed lay on his back, his fingers lightly clasping the sheets across his chest. I looked at his head turned slightly to one side, at the grey-streaked hair disordered by the pressure of the pillow. Then I looked at the long fingers I had so often seen forcing tobacco into a battered pipe with nervous dexterity and my mind went back to a moment in which those same fingers, grasping a heavy German automatic, were being raised towards the head that now lay peacefully on a clean, white pillow.

The man in the bed coughed once in his sleep and turned on to his side. The fingers disappeared beneath the sheets. The doctor motioned me to the door.

"Well?" he said when we were outside.

I shook my head. "No, it's not the same man."

He sighed. "A curious case," he commented as we went downstairs again.

I agreed.

The sea front was almost deserted as I made my way back towards the bus-stop. Out at sea a light was beginning to wink in the misty region beyond the last red reflections of the sun. The surf hissed lazily through the pebbles. A breeze had begun to blow off the sea and I turned up the collar of my overcoat as I walked on. It was cold for the time of year.

EPILOGUE

Such cases of dual personality do occur. C. G. Jung in his *Collected Papers on Analytical Psychology* describes the case of a young German girl who was subject to periods of amnesia, or loss of memory, during which she exhibited a completely different personality.

Ordinarily, the girl was only partly literate and of a low standard of intelligence. The second personality, however, spoke fluent and cultured English and broken German. The girl's normal personality had never been taught English and was, indeed, ignorant of even the rudiments of the language. The explanation was curious.

For some time previous to the first manifestations of amnesia the girl had stayed with some relatives in whose house an English student lodged. She had heard a considerable amount of English spoken. At the time it had meant nothing to her conscious mind. Her subconscious mind, however, had recorded it faithfully. When the second personality emerged, it had simply drawn on this record for its own purposes.

* * * * *

Statement by George Alfred Rispoli,
Waiter at the
Imperial Hotel, Plymouth

My name is George Rispoli and I am a waiter at the Imperial Hotel, Plymouth. On the 19th of April last I served a gentleman named Carruthers in room 356 with breakfast. I remember the gentleman clearly because the chambermaid told me that the pillow in his room had a patch of blood on it when she went to clear up, also because I had to go out to the travel agency in the town and get him a ticket to Paris. Also, he gave me a good tip. About ten o'clock he phoned for breakfast. When I took it in he was standing looking out of the window with his back to me. He had on a dressing-gown over his pyjamas. He told me to leave the tray and get him an ABC, which I did. When I came back with the ABC he was still looking out of the window.

I reminded him that his coffee was getting cold and without turning round he told me to pour it out. "No milk and three lumps of sugar," he said.

I did so and left him. He had a sharp sort of voice, but not disagreeable. I did not see his face at all.

About an hour later he rang down for a ticket to Paris, first class via Cunard liner from Southampton to Havre. I was sent out to get it and did so. Soon after that he left the hotel giving me ten shillings for myself. That is all I know.

(sgd.) G. RISPOLI.

Note. According to Professor Barstow's housekeeper, he always took milk in his coffee. On page 32 of *Conway Carruthers, Dept. Y,* however, there occurs the following: "Carruthers sipped at his coffee appreciatively. He liked it thick and black and sweet; it stimulated that keen, incisive brain of his. Whenever a problem confronted him, he sought refuge in his coffee and his pipe."

*　　*　　*　　*　　*

From the New York Tribune, *May 24th, 193–*

COUNTESS'S DEATH DIVE

Reports from Zovgorod (Ixania) state that the Countess Magda Schverzinski was killed two days ago when her car left a mountain road in the Kuder province and plunged down an 80-ft. precipice.

General Toumachin, head of the new Peasant Government in Ixania, has sent a message of condolence to Prince Ladislaus, brother of the Countess, who is at the moment in Belgrade. At the request of the Prince, the body will be taken to Belgrade for the funeral. (Obituary, page 8.)

*　　*　　*　　*　　*

From the Giornale d'Italia, *July 10th 193–*

DISTINGUISHED ARRIVAL

Prince Ladislaus of Ixania has purchased the Palazzo dei Fiori at Viareggio. He expects to take up residence there during September.

*　　*　　*　　*　　*

From a London trade journal for the week ending September 10th, 193–

IXANIAN TRADE DEVELOPMENTS

The decision of the Ixanian Peasant Government to disband their armed forces which caused such a stir in political circles last month has now been followed by the announcement that Ixania has concluded a number of commercial treaties with neighbouring states. Among the subjects of these treaties are bristles, timber and beet sugar.

Production of the latter commodity is being heavily subsidised by the Government, as also is a new confectionery-manufacturing plant, the machinery for which was recently supplied by Dunwiddy and Helpman Ltd., a subsidiary of Cator & Bliss Ltd.

Further developments in this big reorganisation process may be expected. It is reported in some quarters that electrification of the Ixanian railways is contemplated as part of a comprehensive transport reconstruction scheme to include the building of roads and a new airport near Zovgorod to be used as a re-fuelling station for trans-European air mails.

EPILOGUE

Under our "Tenders Invited" column this week appear notices from the Ixanian Government regarding the supply of fertilisers and Diesel-engined tractors.

* * * * *

Extract from an article entitled "The Danger Spots of Europe" which appeared in a London daily newspaper on October 20, 193–. Investigation revealed that the author of the article is prominently represented in the list of shareholders of Messrs. Cator & Bliss Ltd.

. . . but one thing is clear; the Cause of Peace cannot but be endangered by unilateral acts of disarmament of this kind. In announcing the policy of absolute disarmament to which he has committed his unfortunate countrymen, the head of the Ixanian Cabinet said:

"*If an aggressor or group of aggressors were to advance into Ixanian territory, our present army and air force would be unable to stop them. It has been estimated that armed forces numerous enough and adequately equipped to defend Ixania in such an emergency would cost a minimum of fifty million pounds in modern equipment and another ten million pounds a year to maintain; that is without taking into account the indirect losses which the withdrawal of tens of thousands of able-bodied men from productive activity would entail. We cannot afford that fantastic minimum and we will not squander our substance on defences that fall absurdly short of the minimum!*"

"This is idealistic folly run mad. An unarmed Ixania is a potential cause of war. Every possible pressure should be brought to bear on this Government of untutored peasants to restrain them in their policy of "pacifist" aggression.

The fools' Paradise that the League of Nations . . .

* * * * *

From the New York Tribune, *February 4th, 193–*

TRIBUNE CORRESPONDENT HONOURED

The Order of the Red Star of Ixania has been conferred on William L. Casey, foreign correspondent of the *Tribune*, by the President of Ixania. The award follows the publication of Mr. Casey's book, *Ixania Today and Tomorrow*, to which M. Toumachin, Ixanian Government leader, contributed an introduction.

* * * * *

From a South American paper, August, 193–

SOCIAL NOTES

At the Hotel Paradiso last night, His Excellency the Minister of War, Señor Patiago, was to be seen entertaining a party of friends. Among his guests were His Excellency the Minister of Finance,

Señor Guadalez, Señora Guadalez and Señor Harcourt–Groom, the famous English sportsman.

*   *   *   *   *

From the "Proceedings of the Society of Physicists" for the July quarter 193–

Professor Henry Barstow received a warm welcome on the occasion of his reading a paper entitled "Some Comments on Kalmen's Observations concerning Planck's Quantum Theory." This was Professor Barstow's first appearance at the Society's gathering this year following his recent long and serious illness, on his complete recovery from which we offer him our sincere congratulations. The speaker's remarks were followed closely by the large audience that attended. At the outset, Professor Barstow caused no little amusement by declaring that his convalescence had provided him with an unprecedented opportunity for calm consideration of what he described as "Professor Kalmen's incautious adventures into space-time." The Lorentz transformations could not, he contended, be taken as a starting-point for . . .